DRAGON'S DILEMMA

The peace that Mayland Long has sought for centuries has once again been shattered. His beloved Martha's only granddaughter has disappeared. A wild psychic force is loose on the wind. And one of Martha's motley band of Celtic musicians has just been found dead, hanged with a rope of twisted grass.

Now it's up to the Black Dragon to find the killer among them. Even if it turns out to be himself. . . .

Bantam Spectra Books by R.A. MacAvoy
Ask your bookseller for the titles you have missed

TWISTING
THE ROPE
Casadh an t'Súgáin

R. A. MacAVOY

BANTAM BOOKS
TORONTO · NEW YORK · LONDON · SYDNEY · AUCKLAND

TWISTING THE ROPE

A Bantam Spectra Book / October 1986

Grateful acknowledgment is made for permission to
reprint the following:

Lines from "There Was a Lady," by Triona
NíDhomhnaill from the album Relativity.
Copyright © 1985 by Triona NíDhomhnaill.
All rights reserved. Courtesy of Green
Linnet Records.

Titles from "Irish Dance Tunes for All Harps:
50 Jigs, Reels, Hornpipes, Airs" by Sylvia Woods.
Copyright © 1984 by Sylvia Woods, Woods Music,
and Books Publishing (Los Angeles, CA).

Excerpt from The Maha Prajna Paramita Hridaya Sutra.
Translation as used by The Zen Center, San Francisco.

ISBN 0-553-26026-X

Published simultaneously in the United States and Canada

Bantam Books are published by Bantam Books, Inc. Its trademark, consisting of the words "Bantam Books" and the por-
trayal of a rooster, is Registered in U.S. Patent and Trademark
Office and in other countries. Marca Registrada. Bantam
Books, Inc., 666 Fifth Avenue, New York, New York 10103.

PRINTED IN THE UNITED STATES OF AMERICA

KR   0 9 8 7 6 5 4 3 2 1

This Is for Dorcas

All chapter headings in this book are either titles of traditional dance pieces or quotations from traditional songs. The headings from Chapters 5 and 6 are taken from "There was a Lady" as sung by Tríona NíDhomhnaill; "Da Mihi Manum" I learned from *The Penny Whistle Book* by Robin Williamson; "An Caoineadh na d'Tri Muire" I heard from Jim Duran; and most of the others I took from the book *Irish Dance Tunes for All Harps: 50 Jigs, Reels, Hornpipes, Airs* by Sylvia Woods. I have no idea who first sang "The Foggy, Foggy Dew" for me. I learned "The Bear Went Over the Mountain" from my mother.

The Santa Cruz, California, of the story has been geographically twisted (like a rope), to fit the needs of my plot. It is possible that Trondur Patursson never gave a medallion to Pádraig ÓSúilleabháin, as I have it, because Pádraig is an imaginary character, while Patursson is not.

Thanks to Ngiao Marsh

. . . Form does not differ from emptiness:
Emptiness does not differ from form.
That which is form is emptiness:
That which is emptiness, form . . .

. . . all dharmas are marked with emptiness:
They do not appear nor disappear,
Are not tainted nor pure,
Do not increase nor decrease.

Therefore, in emptiness, no form
No feelings, perceptions, impulses, consciousness;
No eyes, no ears, no nose, no tongue, no body, no mind;
No color, no sound, no smell, no taste, no touch, no
object of mind;

No realm of eyes and . . . no realm of mind-consciousness;
No ignorance and also no extinction of it.
No old age and death
And also no extinction of them.
No suffering, no origination, no stopping, no path,
No cognition and also no attainment
With nothing to attain . . .

Gate—gate—paragate—parasamgate! Bodhi!
Svaha!*

*"Gone, gone, gone beyond, gone altogether beyond.
O what an awakening. All hail!"

Taken from *The Maha Prajna
Paramita Hridaya Sutra*,
as used by
San Francisco Zen Center.

Off to California

The blow rang through the motel room, freezing six of the seven people within it in midmotion. Theodore Poznan had a brush wet with nail polish in his left hand, while the index finger of his right was stiffly pointing at the ceiling. His hair, bleached in layers from straw to medium brown, slid forward off his shoulder and hung by his face. His beard jutted forward. His eyes were vaguely reproachful.

Elen Evans had a face of great delicacy and short hair cut with wisps around the ears and down the neck. She lofted a two-foot-long iron piano-tuning wrench with a wooden handle, which she had been using on her triple harp. Her expression was ironical.

Martha Macnamara, exactly thirty years older than Elen, was caught with a paper cup in her hand. She looked flustered and slightly apelike, with her round eyes and open mouth. She thought the words "oh, dear" and she wondered if there was going to be a brawl. She was also a bit glad (glad in spite of herself) that Pádraig had pounded the table in that way: hard, loud, and just at the moment he had wanted to.

Seated in the corner by the Formica table was a slight middle-aged man with black skin and Chinese eyes. The light of the wicker-shaded lamp put a shine on his black hair. His name was Long, and he held a three-year-old girl on his lap. This child's blue eyes were open very wide as she stared at Pádraig Ó Súilleabháin.

Pádraig himself was the sixth person frozen by the violence of his action. He was a young man who looked still younger, and a shade of purple spread from his ears to his face and down both sides of his neck. His fist, rough-chapped and very clean, slowly relaxed on the tabletop and then clenched again.

The little girl broke the silence. "Why did Poe-rik hit the table? Did he want to hit—" The remarkably long fingers of the dark man's hand curled over her mouth. Leaning down, he whispered something into her ear and then bounced her twice, forcefully.

The seventh person in the room—the one who was not shocked by Pádraig's outburst—was holding him up, with the neckband of the boy's sweater turned inside out, and was examining the tag with a show of interest. He raised his eyes now as Pádraig craned about and glared at him.

"No need to lose control, boy," said George St. Ives. "I was just curious why a traditional musician, or at least what passes for traditional these days, and what passes for a . . . Well, anyway, haven't we got enough plastic in the world around us already without wearing the stuff in front of people?"

Pádraig opened his mouth, but there was a brief pause before he replied: a pause of uncertainty. "I thought . . . I thought that I would do better to try to look nice in front of people. Instead of looking like I was after digging a hole somewhere."

George St. Ives had gray eyes surrounded by wrinkles, and his forehead wrinkled as he held the overstretched fabric up to his face. "'One hundred percent acrylic. Machine wash cold. Cool dryer. No bleach.' Red plastic with five-pointed stars in some sort of metallic thread. Wouldn't be very suited for digging a hole, would it? Nor for any other manly activity." His voice was gravelly but expressionless. His heavy face was a bit yellow.

"I can wash it." Pádraig wrested his sweater out of the older man's grip and started to stand up. "If it were *báinín*, how could I, in all these hotels?" His chair fell over. The pulling had left a sag in the back of his sweater. He looked foolish and knew it.

St. Ives watched Pádraig's distraction dispassionately and he smiled. "Did some girl buy it for you, Sully?"

Pádraig, who had retreated the length of the bed, turned back again. His sweater was now off center on his shoulders and he shrugged into it, saying: "My mother bought it for me. She said it would go in the bag well, without wrinkles." Then he rubbed his face with both hands. "Oh, this is stupid! Talking about my jumper! You are only looking for another way to rag me. To hell with it."

"There's the ticket," said Ted Poznan, who was sitting on one of the beds. He shook the bottle of nail polish and prepared to coat his second finger. All the fingernails of his right hand were long and thick with old, yellowed polish. "One's mind is her own mastery."

Elen, seated below him, made a weary gesture with all fingers spread. "Why 'her' own mastery, Ted? Is the mind a female?"

Teddy gave her one of his very many earnest gazes. "Why shouldn't I say 'her' instead of 'his'? I used to use 'tey' for either, but so few understood, and I try very hard not to use sexist language."

"Oh, you succeed, Teddy. How you succeed!" She ran her hand absently along the pegs of her tall harp as she spoke to Ted Poznan, but she did not look away from Pádraig. "There is no one more politically correct than you. Not in all California."

Long stood up, letting Marty Frisch-Macnamara slide off his lap like a cat. He retrieved a tissue from his jacket pocket and blew his nose, which was red. His amber-brown eyes, too, were bloodshot and he was breathing with his mouth open. It was a miserable cold.

"Eight weeks," stated Martha Macnamara, in tones of great conviction. "It's eight weeks today since any one of us has seen home. Remember that, everyone, and be charitable."

It looked as though the bad moment had frayed and dissipated in the general weariness, but George St. Ives was not reconciled. He glanced at Martha, whose band this was, and then away. His gnarled, nervous fingers played patterns against his hip. "I don't think there's anything out of line in objecting to things that destroy our . . . direction, here. After all, we have gone through a lot of sacrifice. The bitterness of being ignored by critics. The full houses that still don't pay. . . ."

"This is not an original tune, George," said Elen. "We've done all variations, in the past eight weeks."

Martha broke in. "So George thinks I made a mistake in not trying for any really big halls. Well, maybe I did. But it was a decision I had to make a lot of months ago. *And* may I say it's better to sell out a little hall than sit like little toads in a big empty pond. And this tour will make all I predicted."

"Even if we don't find the missing cash from last night?" asked Teddy.

Long cleared a phlegmy throat. "That is my responsibility."

Martha pointed a monishing finger at him. "You will not make that up out of your own pocket! It's fortunes of the road."

"And I am the road manager."

"But I am the high mucky-muck herself, and I say—"

St. Ives raised his voice. "Enough! I was not talking about money. If I wanted money, I'd be in a very different line of work. I want my music to be heard. This year. Tonight. Life is uncertain and all the old arts are breathing their last at once. Here we are, a few who know what's being lost. I had hoped . . . We might have . . ."

Almost everyone looked away from St. Ives. Many sighed. Marty wiggled.

If he noticed this lack of enthusiasm, it only made him more determined to speak. "Not that the music we play is in any sense correct by Celtic traditional standards: how could it be, with Pozzy on a Spanish guitar, Sully with his nineteenth-century German transverse flute, and then of course the squeeze-box: a factory-made sealed package of Victorian origin, which one can neither tune nor repair. . . ." St. Ives paused in sorrowful consideration of the weaknesses of the button accordion. "But hey! We don't have to court the modern audience with bizarre clothing."

Martha scratched her scalp with both hands until her gray hair bobbled up and down. She looked very bothered. "George, if we followed your ideas of what was traditional, there would be no one up there but you on the pipes."

He appeared to consider that. "No. I'm willing to grant that the harp is traditional to Celtic music."

"Thanks, George, but I doubt I have the strength to endure your approval," drawled Elen. She put the instrument in question protectively onto her shoulder and continued tuning.

"Then be at ease, Miss Evans. I said the harp, not the harp player. There is nothing more traditional in your musicianship than in, say, Ravel." He rubbed one heavy-knuckled hand over his eyes and winced at some private ache.

With an unnaturally innocent expression, Elen Evans looked around her. "La! Ah believe Ah have been insulted!" She met Pádraig's eye.

Perhaps her glance was merely languid, and it was Pádraig's own hurt he read into it. But Ó Súilleabháin, who had stood miserably silent in his twisted sweater, now went from red to white and lunged for the piper, hands balled into fists. He did not touch him, however, for he came up against the afflicted Mr. Long. That gentleman had somehow wandered between the two in search of fresh Kleenex. Pádraig's arm was softly circled by a dark hand, which he could not remove. "*Bí cúramach, a Phádraig,*" said Long very quietly, and then he turned away.

The tissue box was on the table beside St. Ives. Long brushed the stocky piper as he reached around him, and St. Ives staggered.

With the first signs of real temper, St. Ives pushed back, succeeding only in pushing himself backward onto the mattress, which swayed beneath his weight.

"Take a walk, George. Cool off." Martha spoke quietly, but all in the room turned to her in surprise, even

George. He pursed the mouth that was hidden in his curly, bisonlike beard. He swelled beneath his layers of sweaters. He rose to his feet, but appeared to reject the soft suggestion that had really been a command.

Long was beside him, shoulders almost touching. He blew his nose again, discreetly. "Lovely afternoon for a walk in Santa Cruz, St. Ives," he said, with a genteel enthusiasm. "Blue sky, ocean breezes. A good way to regain a flagging inspiration. To reflect, perhaps, on the death of old arts. If one doesn't fancy a nap, of course.

"I myself"—and he tossed the tissue into the bedside basket—"am going to nap." He looked significantly from the bed to St. Ives.

Much to the surprise of most in the room, the piper walked out without another word. They heard his feet echoing down the hall and out the back door of the motel, for St. Ives stayed in a place apart from the rest of them.

Elen glanced at Long with exaggerated respect. "The big lady's muscleman?"

He blinked sore eyes at her. "Well, it is my bedroom, Elen. He could scarcely stage a sit-down in it."

Her gaze grew even more disbelieving. "Sure he couldn't! George would never be so rude. I think he must believe you're carrying a gun."

At the reminder that this nicest room in the mediocre motel belonged to Long, all the musicians rose also. But Mr. Long had walked from the space between the beds back to the breakfast table, where he smiled graciously and sat down again, showing no more signs of going dormant.

"I don't, Daddo," said Marty, edging away from him. "I don't fancy a nap at all. I more fancy a walk, I think."

No one answered her. Relief was audible through the room as they realized the awkward scene was over. "Ravel," said Elen Evans contemplatively, as she began to strike octaves on the left row of strings. "I really prefer Debussy." She plucked a great, rolling, unsettled chord along the length of the harp, top to bottom.

Teddy spoke to the unhappy chord, rather than to

Elen's dispassionate words. "Don't be put off your center by that, Elen. I don't think George feels very well. Inside himself. I see him as off balance. Harried from within, you know. He needs some sort of adjustment."

Her face looked rather like Stan Laurel's, so blankly she gazed at him. "Spiritual in nature, Teddy? Or chiropractic?"

"Either or both. Or nutritional. I wonder about his amino acids. . . ."

"I prefer past-life regression, myself."

"You have a marvelous gift of acceptance, Ted," said Martha appreciatively. "I admit he pisses me off wonderfully, when he gets going like that. And he doesn't even nip at my ego, as he does to yours."

"George doesn't *really* twist the screws in Teddy." Elen smiled like a madonna, plucked an octave and winced at the sound. She uttered a quiet and very nasty curse and twisted the big turning wrench once more. "Not as he does to Pat."

Ted blew on his ugly nail. "He isn't exactly wild over my guitar. I can hear his teeth grinding every time I add a chord progression. But that's *his* problem, not mine.

"And he really does care, you know. About the accuracy of what he's doing. There's few enough who do."

Pádraig Ó Súilleabháin glanced worriedly at Ted. "Do you think . . . Did I do wrong in getting angry at him? Maybe I didn't understand enough. . . ."

"Getting angry doesn't help, that's for sure, Pádraig," said Ted, putting his hand on the Irishman's shoulder and shaking him in warm fraternal fashion. "But I really feel with you in your reaction. It's really a gut-wrencher to keep your balance when someone around has lost his. What's important now, though, is to keep your channels open with the guy."

Pádraig blinked. "To . . . ?"

Martha, who had been combing her hair in the mirror, stopped long enough to laugh at his expression. "That's Californian, Pádraig."

"Mellowtalk," added Long helpfully. "I believe he

means you are to continue to encourage conversation with St. Ives—or possibly to dredge the mouth of his harbor."

"Now *there* I'm willing to help," said Elen, with a wicked giggle.

Ted nodded left and right. "Okay, okay, you have my full permission to make fun of me. Any time. Otherwise I'll start taking myself seriously."

He cracked his neck with the heel of his hand and gave a satisfied yawn. "It's all part of the cycle, friends and neighbors. What goes around, comes around." He rose, examined his ugly, guitar player's fingernails, stretched his lean body left and right, and left the room. "Oh, the wavelengths of rapture! Sweet-home California!" he called back from the doorway and then he was gone.

"He does that on purpose," muttered Martha. "He can talk perfectly good English when he wants to. I think it's important to him to have some strong ethnic identity."

Elen Evans giggled. "I asked him why the hell he wanted to play Celtoid traditional, when his heart is so purely new age, and you know what he said? Jigs and hornpipes ground him. Me, they knock flat on my keister!"

Martha sighed. "And yet Teddy plays his part very well. He has an ear for the traditional sound and he makes no ruckus. Doesn't seem to go into turmoil like . . . some."

She grunted and drummed her fingers on her knee. "What grounds him is grinding me down, I think."

Long spoke with some asperity. "That is not the music, Martha, but the musicians. You should take some privilege as well as responsibility from your position. Forbid George to bother you."

"Forbid . . ." Martha uttered a one-syllable laugh that was more than half a choke. "My dear, to stop George from 'bothering' would be simply to stop him from existing!"

"I agree," added Elen. "St. Ives's basic essence . . ."

"His interest is to convince you all of that, but really he is as capable as the next fellow of coming to terms with . . ."

"Dock his wage," suggested Pádraig, with a shade of malice.

Martha put her back to the wall and tucked her skirt neatly around her legs. "I forbid you all to bother me further about this," she said.

"Oops," said Elen, and they all relapsed into silence.

The walls of the motel room were white, brightened by the light of sky, sea, and pavement. Occupied as it was by slumped figures and dull faces, it might have been a dentist's waiting room. Marty Frisch-Macnamara hopped over and pulled the Levolor blind awry to look out at the beach and the Santa Cruz pier. The others, deprived of their wrangle, hadn't as much energy. They looked at each other.

"I'm sorry," said Pádraig, speaking to Elen. "To be at hitting people in front of you. I'm not a brute."

Her small dark face went round through astonishment. "A brute? You, Pat? Perish forfend!"

Pádraig shifted uncomfortably, because he wasn't quite sure what she had said. His blue jeans gapped a bit at the waist, for Pádraig Ó Súilleabháin had lost weight on this tour.

Martha, leaning against the headboard of the other bed, slapped both hands on her knees. "Eight weeks," she repeated. "This tour has lasted for eight weeks and taken in nineteen American states plus B.C. I think no one is responsible for anything he or she has said or done in a long while. Except me, for making you all go through this."

Mayland Long turned toward her. Such was the peculiarity of his attenuated frame that it seemed not only his head and neck that twisted about, but his whole torso. Sunlight glowed against his suit of raw silk and made his pale eyes almost yellow, but the brightness could not touch the skin of his face and hands.

"Are you regretting it, Martha?" The question was wondering, and Long folded his hands together (the fingers extending past the opposite wrists), waiting for her reply.

Martha frowned, eyes unfocused. A moment later she snorted in most unladylike manner. "Regretting it? I am not. Not a bit of it. I knew there would be moments—that there would be sparks—with a group of musicians as able and as different as we are. People don't do good work if they don't care about things—sometimes the silliest things—and there's no musician like a traditional musician for having untraditional opinions. What counts is the music we've made."

She rose from the bed. Her wraparound skirt with tiny sailboats on it was not straight. There was a flat spot at the side of her head where her newly bobbed and waved hair had touched the headboard. But her blue eyes caught the window light like circles of sky and everyone in the room listened when she spoke, even Marty, her granddaughter.

"And I got what I wanted there, all right. We've made our little bit of magic. In Chicago we caught fire, and then, last night, in San Francisco"—she scratched her head, a small smile softening her mouth—"we were up to... past our own limits."

An answering smile came from Elen Evans. She felt her shoulders sink down and realized just how tense she had been, until now. She met Long's eyes and wondered if he understood the overwhelming importance of the thing Martha had just said. To people like herself, and Elen, and even St. Ives, who simply had to play this music, whether people wanted to hear it or not. . . .

Long was different. He was not a musician. Certainly he had no Celtic background, to spark his interest in the history of it. One never knew why, with Long, for his face showed nothing. That was an advantage, she guessed, in a road manager. Maybe it was easier for a Chinese, or Indonesian or . . . What was he, anyway?

Besides dotty over Martha. Elen Evans put her face against the box of her triple harp to hide her grin.

"For some of us the limits are easy to find!" It was Pádraig again, and the words were bitter. Before Elen could move from behind her harp to answer him, he was out of the room and gone.

She followed, scooping up her big net bag and dropping the piano-tuning wrench into it. The bag swung and struck against the dresser with a sound of cracking wood. She cursed the thing with a calm and placid curse as the door closed behind her.

"Oh, dear," said Martha, sitting down hard in the other wicker chair. Long met her eye. "We haven't heard the last of this," she said. "From St. Ives, I mean."

"I'm not having any fun yet," Marty announced, coming back to Mayland Long's lap. "I just thought I'd tell you, Daddo. In case."

Martha gave a rather brittle laugh and threw the Kleenex box across the room.

The ocean was divided; as far as a hundred yards out from the Santa Cruz pier it was a warm jade color, while from an abrupt line at that distance it ran a cold, uncompromising blue. The tide came in in great soft rolls, with no white showing. Mayland Long and Martha Macnamara sat together on a bench at the end of the pier. Small breezes blew around them, some scented with flowers and some with fish. Marty stood leaning over a fenced opening through the floor of the pier, whence came the barking of seals. She wore yellow trousers, a white T-shirt, and plastic sunglasses edged in white and yellow daisies. Long's index finger was locked in her belt loop to keep her from falling in. That black hand was glittering with scales, for he had been helping the little girl feed the seals. No one, not even Marty, had spoken for five minutes.

Martha let her attention drift with the tide from the blank western horizon to the bright Ferris wheel on the boardwalk, and on to the point lighthouse. She was thinking about Mendocino, where she had lived for the last four years, and wondering why one could get most achingly homesick in a place very like one's home. And why did a person go out on the road again, when she didn't need the money, and was old enough to know where she wanted to be? She turned to Long expectantly, as though she had asked the question aloud.

But he was not following her thoughts at all. Instead

the dark head was drooped forward, eyes closed. His nose was obviously very sore and his skin tight over the bones of his face: so little flesh.

Martha caught her lower lip in her teeth, for she suddenly noticed the gray hair at his temples. Had she known he was going gray? Dear God, to have him beside her every day and not to notice. No, surely she had noticed, on some level. It was just that she was so tired today. Things didn't look right.

And what if Mayland *was* looking older? So was she. She hadn't made him follow her from city to city and country to country like this. It was his idea. And she hadn't made him . . . what he was. Whatever ofttimes sad thing he was.

His eyes opened, focused directly at her. The virus had exaggerated the epicanthic folds at the outer corners of them, making him look more Chinese. "I have no idea why people do the things they do. None whatsoever."

She was taken aback. Had she been speaking aloud, after all? "Do you mean yourself—why you're here—or why I wanted to leave Mendocino at all?"

The eyes narrowed to slits and he laughed. "Neither one. I was talking about the altercation in the motel room. One would think I would understand human nature by now, considering how long I've been studying it."

Martha frowned in thought. She could look quite fierce that way, despite her round blue eyes and pink-petal complexion. "You can't see why Pádraig got angry . . . ?"

"Any creature will react to assault by fighting back, if it can't run away. No, I more wonder *why* St. Ives attacks, and why he chooses Pádraig as his victim so often. The boy is no threat."

The wind caught Martha's skirt as she stood up. She put one hand against her knee to hold it as she walked over to stand beside Marty. Down below, in the shadow, the smooth lumps of seal with their small-dog faces lay resting on the pier's cross braces, and floated staring up from the black, swirling water. "No more fishies," she called down to them, and when Marty let out a seallike sound of protest, she added, "No more money to buy fishies.

"Pádraig is not a competitor to George. He's his natural prey. You can see how George plays on the poor creature's emotions: all the scale from fury to discouragement to self-loathing. Pádraig is only twenty, while George is almost *my* age."

"Positively a museum piece."

"Well—old in his craft, anyway. But Pádraig's being hit with everything new at once: the geography, the people, this crazy lifestyle." She shrugged. "And I promised his mother I'd take care of him."

Long blew his nose. "Don't be silly, Martha. You cannot be a life-support system for the boy. At least he has his health. That is a great good fortune and a reasonable cause for envy." He came to stand beside her, and he looked down at the seals. One of them raised its head, barked, and then they were gone in a gleam of disturbed water. Marty let out a yelp of protest.

Martha nudged Long's side companionably. "Pádraig's father runs a fishing boat out of Dunquin, my dear, and Pádraig himself is one of the best sailors on Iv Ráth. Dinghy races. He's taken me out in a *naomhóg* under sail too. (I thought I would die.) But he's no good working with his father."

"They don't agree?" Long put one hand around Martha's shoulder and the other hand on Marty's flaxen head. The little girl shook it off.

"Seosebh doesn't explain things well. And he has a temper. He calls the boy an *asal* and—poof!—he *is* an ass. Long ears and all. Makes stupid mistakes with the net. Jibs where he should jab with the gaff—or whatever. It's no good.

"It's the same pattern here. I've seen him at home, or in the Óstán Dún an Óir, in complete mastery of his material, playing his accordion like six-handed Shiva. The tourists had no idea what they were getting with their Guinness! But . . ."

"Here he isn't doing that?"

Martha swayed against the white bar of the paling. "Mmph? Okay, I guess. But he's scared and miserable, and he plays like a boy that's scared and miserable. He hears himself and knows it's no good. Round the circle. What is it Teddy says?

"'What goes around...'"

"Oh, yes. 'Comes around.'" She touched his mouth with her fingers. "How could I have forgotten?"

Mayland Long sighed. He swiped his nose once more and dismissed the problems of Pádraig Ó Súilleabháin. Leaning gracefully over the rail, he looked for seals. Skin divers went out from the beach, walking like ducks and delighting Marty Frisch-Macnamara. She threw popcorn to them as they passed beside the pier. For an hour the only concern among the small party was the wind in Martha's skirt.

"Judy doesn't like old George." Marty made this announcement as they were halfway back to the motel room. Her grandmother sighed. "Why should Judy be any different than the vast majority of humanity?"

Long looked down at the little girl he was carrying. "Who is... Martha Rachel Frisch-Macnamara, where are your sunglasses?"

She slapped her eyes with both palms and made an outsize grimace of astonishment. "I have no idea, Daddo. No idea in the slightest!"

Martha took her and set her on her feet. "Sometimes she sounds so like Elizabeth I get the chills!" She saw Long looking intently back the way they had come and said, "Don't bother. We went the whole length of the pier and across the beach and a busy street. Probably by now they're at the bottom..."

But he had already turned back and was halfway across the street against the light, moving between the cars smoothly, with an odd dignity. Martha watched him slide through the beach crowds, avoiding all touch, yet with his gaze fixed on the far end of the pier. Could he see the ground that far in front of him? Could anyone?

Martha shook her head. There was no telling what he could do. Here he was, so fine, learned, and wealthy: a live-in babysitter for a three-year-old. Taking beginning keyboard lessons. A millionaire road manager for a group that toured in a dilapidated van.

It was all so splendid that she laughed aloud.

Marty looked up resentfully. Like most people, she disapproved of private jokes. "Judy gets scared a lot. Not like me."

Marty had been with the group for four days, long enough for Martha to learn something of her grandchild's outgoing nature. "Is Judy a hotel maid or is she a waitress?"

Marty snorted, sounding just like her grandmother. "*Ní h'ea.*"

Martha translated this negative in her mind. "So Pádraig has been teaching you Irish. That's nice."

Marty grimaced again at the extent of adult stupidity. "Not Pádraig, Martha. Daddo. Only, it's Chinese."

Martha didn't think so, but she didn't want to belabor the point.

"And did he tell you to call him 'daddo'? Did he tell you what it means?"

The little girl nodded strenuously. "It means 'grandfather.'"

Then Martha set her lips and stared after Long, whom she could no longer see.

"Worshipping at the source of all earthly energy?"

Martha gave a little jump. It was Ted standing behind them, the wind blowing through the layers of his hair. He was smiling, and though his face was young, the skin around the corners of his eyes crinkled. He wore shorts and rubber thongs on his feet and nothing else. He looked rather like a young sun god himself, and his exposed skin was the color of fresh cherrywood.

Californians, she said to herself. "Actually, Marty and I are keeping off His Worship with para-aminobenzoic acid. We burn."

"The skin comes off my nose," said Marty in corroboration.

He nodded and then sat down on the pavement next to Marty, forcing passersby to step out into the street. Martha was about to say something about this when she noticed that none of the people inconvenienced looked in the slightest put out.

Californians.

"That's a bummer. But, you know, it gets better. Just you lard that stuff on every time you go out, and the sun will get in so slowly that you'll turn without ever burning."

"To turn is *casadh*," said the girl. "In Irish, it is."

Martha stifled an impulse to contradict Marty and say the word was Chinese.

Ted's dark innocent eyes went even more innocent. "Is it? Like to turn brown, you mean?"

"To turn anything. To turn a tune, fr'insanse."

It occurred to Martha that Teddy was sailing very near the wind, discussing things with Marty. She was very demanding of grown-ups. If he had shown the least hint of condescension . . . If he had let her tell him things he already knew. But he never did that; Ted Poznan was a great favorite of Marty's. Martha was encouraged to add her bit of education to Marty's little store. "That's our theme song, Marty. 'Casadh an t'Súgáin': 'Twisting the Rope.' We play it twice every night: fast and slow."

"I know that."

Martha wondered if the dismissive quality in Marty's reply came because she hadn't sat down on the pavement, like Teddy.

"I talked to George." Ted looked up at Martha. "I think we can get our friend straightened out."

Martha would never have called George St. Ives her friend, much as she respected his music. But neither would she have dared to talk about straightening him out. She said nothing.

"I think he's blocked inside, and then lashes out in pain. Anyone would. Once he opens up, the great, good things can come in: like the sunlight."

Ted spoke with real enthusiasm. Martha felt a sudden question in her mind whether he was very intelligent. He was an accomplished guitarist, but she well knew that musical ability was a thing apart. She tried to imagine George St. Ives's bulky and usually unwashed body naked under sunlight. Her mind's eye, forced in this manner, wanted the image to go away.

"Did you tell *him* this?"

"Yeah, I did. And, you know, we really communicated."

Martha blinked. She stooped and began to sit down on the pavement next to him when she remembered her troublesome skirt. "He didn't curse you out or tell you to mind your own business?"

Ted beamed up at her. He seemed quite comfortable with their difference in stations. "No, Roshi. George doesn't—"

"Don't call me that." Martha's voice was quite sharp.

"Sure thing, Martha. No. George doesn't pull that on me. Or if he does, I don't notice. Flow-through, you know? Flow-through.

"And I really think I can help him."

Martha stared out at the sea, which, from this angle, was bright as aluminum foil. "In the five days left on this tour?"

"Sure. Enlightenment is instantaneous, you know."

Martha bit back her angry retort. She managed to say with reasonable calm, "Why? Why bother with him? You never met him before last month."

Ted turned his face up to the sun and closed his eyes. A fly landed on his forehead. He ignored it. "George St. Ives is a great musician and an old soul: a repository of the real tradition. I want to do what I can."

What "real tradition," Martha wanted to know. It was her understanding that St. Ives had learned from sessions and assorted recordings, just as she had, and as had most living "traditional musicians." In fact, she could name at least six pieces he did where his sources were in her own extensive disk library. And, she had known his aunt, in Ottawa, and was in some position to separate the man from his image.

She decided to keep this question to herself. After all,

George *was* a very good piper, and perhaps her own resentment stemmed from nothing more than that George had a habit of fighting his way into her solos.

"Here comes the Dragon," said Ted.

Martha started and spun around, to see Long coming toward them, making his bullfighter's progress through traffic.

"Why do you call him that?" she asked very tightly.

Ted rocked with amusement. "That's what his name—Long—means in Chinese. Isn't that great? Don't you think it really fits him too? You know, like when he's looking over a new arrangement or an instrument he hasn't seen before and his eyes positively glow with passion to have it?"

"Passion?" Martha echoed weakly.

"Yeah. Real passion. Age doesn't matter a bit, Martha."

Then Long was with them, and the missing sunglasses were in his hand. He greeted Ted, who bestowed upon the group one last slosh of sleepy affection and then was gone. "One of the earpieces has suffered a little, but no irreparable damage."

Martha took them without looking. "Do you know what Ted just said to me, Mayland? He said age doesn't matter."

Long shot a burning glance at the young man's back. "Impudent puppy. It certainly *does* matter!"

"Oh, well, don't be upset by it," said Martha. "How could he know? He's only in his twenties. Scarcely older than Pádraig. But doesn't Ted have an appealing smile, my dear?"

Then, in the same tone, she added, "I wonder if he's *on* something?"

"Casadh an t'Súgáin"

I feel that I have to... to make up for twenty years of practice that I haven't had." Pádraig put his flute down on the dressing room table. The old rosewood tube had but one key and a worn silver mouthpiece. The Paolo Santori button accordion which lay next to it was brand-new and bright red.

"Well, you can't," stated Elen Evans, sitting herself beside him. "So don't bang your head against walls." She gazed at nothing-at-all in the corner of the dressing room. "Besides, Pat, you don't need to."

Pádraig Ó Súilleabháin had a baby face. He set his smallish mouth stubbornly. "I missed the bridge last night that Martha wrote out for me and everything. Nobody else has to get music written out for them. You do it all yourself."

Elen had to giggle. "You got it a bit different, that's all, ducks. Seriously, how could anyone but me arrange things for this one-of-a-kind dinosaur I play? Martha gave you that bridge because you *asked* her to, and though it was pretty nice of her, it was no better than the kind of thing you fuss around with, and probably lots harder to finger. After all, it's not her instrument.

"And believe me, Pat—no one but ourselves *dreamed* there was anything amiss last night, and we only knew because you practiced the thing so much. Too much, I think."

"George knew, and that was what counts."

Hearing St. Ives's name, Elen sat quite still for a moment. Then she propped an ankle over the opposite

19

knee and played with the flounce of her skirt. "Diddle St. Ives, Pat. He's a cancer to all concerned. In fact, let me be nice and catty for a moment: he's not who Martha wanted for the tour. I myself might have thought twice about coming, had I known he'd be in the group."

Pádraig looked up from his sulk. "You say he's not who Martha wanted? There was someone else?"

Since Pádraig Ó Súilleabháin ended all his questions on a fall of the voice, it took Elen a fraction of a second to realize they were questions. "Folsom," she replied. "Seán Folsom. We were set up until a month before the tour and bang! He's got a cracked spine. Fell off a roof. St. Ives was what she could get."

A smile touched Pádraig's face, like a glimpse of sun on a dark day. He hit her on the upper arm, rather too hard. "She only asked him then? She asked me six months before. She asked me first." But he was immediately sober again.

"You say you wouldn't have come. But you came after all."

She shrugged. "I couldn't let Martha Macnamara down: not for any reason. I *wouldn't*, for one thing. She's too decent a lady. And then professionally, it'd be the kiss of death, wouldn't it? Everyone knows she's good, and she fulfills her promises. Both to the houses and to the people she works with. So I gave a great sigh and said 'La!' And here I am."

"I'm glad," said Pádraig, and then he looked away. "But I think it isn't Martha herself who keeps everything right but her boyfriend."

Elen grinned, and this encouragement was enough to induce Pádraig to add, "And they aren't married, are they?"

Elen Evans sat up straight on the hard bench. "I'm sure I never asked. They don't project that image, as Ted might say, but I never thought it my business . . ."

Pádraig shot her a glance almost gleeful in its mischief. "But isn't it funny? They are not young kids, to be getting in trouble. Why are they at it?"

Elen opened her mouth but no sound came out for some seconds. Pádraig laughed aloud at the expression on her face. At last she clapped both long-nailed hands on her knees and said, "My dear infant, how long have you been out?"

The baby face went bleak again and he turned half away. "Not long enough to play with Macnamara's Band. Martha knew I blew it too."

Evans hit her knees again, much harder. "You moron! More of that, Sullivan, and I'll haul back and hit you one."

Pádraig had pulled back one sleeve of his dazzling sweater and was scratching a red spot on his forearm. "Go ahead. I'm not worth anything anyway."

With complete spontaneity Elen did so, slamming him in the center of the chest with her right fist. Pádraig fell backward, landing on his rear on the concrete floor. Elen hopped, cursed, and licked her palm, where her sharp harper's nails had bit into her hand. Then she saw Pádraig flat out on the concrete staring up at her.

"Pat! What have I done? I've hurt you!" She got down on her knees and put her wounded hand behind his head.

"Not at all. I fell over from the surprise of it," he said, disentangling his legs from the bench. He grinned and blushed simultaneously. "It was a rotten hit. No strength in it."

"I'm not in practice. My aggressions are more subtle." Elen got up and dusted off the lavender cotton of her skirt. With a moment's alarm she made sure the fall had not done harm to any of the instruments that had been left in the room for the afternoon. She pushed back her little curls of hair and sighed. "Let's take a walk."

Landaman Hall was as much a theater as a concert hall, and as in many theaters, the back of the stage opened directly onto a loading dock, which was usually closed by roll-up steel doors. These were on the east side, and barely visible along the alley that ran between the Hall and the supermarket which adjoined.

As Martha and company passed in front of the building on their way back to the motel from the beach, Long happened to look in and see a square of darkness where the doors hung. "That's odd," he said and strolled down the alley, still carrying Marty.

Martha had been a few steps in front, and his sudden diversion took her aback. "What's odd?" She followed him into the cool shadow of the alley. It was chilly, after the sun, and pleasant to the skin.

The right-hand door was open, and she could look up into the ceiling of the backstage. No lower, though, because she was not a tall woman and the dock was high. "Don't they know we left our sound equipment in there? Or is Santa Cruz so faultlessly honest . . . ?"

Long chuckled and expressed disbelief. Setting Marty on her feet, he grabbed the lip of the dock in his hands and heaved up.

There was the disheartening hiss and pull of silk unraveling. He dropped again and stared at the rusty bolt which had caught his jacket front. "Oh, damn," he said very primly, and sought about in his pocket.

"It can be mended," said Martha, but Long was too involved to pay attention. He drew out a pigskin box about half the size of a cigarette case. It had some very pretty little nail trimmers in it, and a small pair of scissors, and also stainless-steel tweezers, which he took out and held at the very tips of his long fingers. With surgical care he reached into the tangle of hanging threads and puckered fabric and pulled.

Fascinated, both Marty and her grandmother watched one thread after another sucked back into its place in the weave. Long's face was hard with concentration. At last he let out a sigh and snapped the pigskin case closed. "It will never be the same," he said, and gave one more rueful glance at the dock.

"I'll use the door after the approved manner."

Martha thought that was just as well, considering not only the dirt but also the possibility that thieves had opened the door up there. If one had to walk in on thieves, one could at least avoid doing so head first, clawing at the concrete. Besides, there was a large stone or cement pediment of some kind, tilted at a nasty angle over the edge of the dock. Being theatrical in nature, it was probably papier-mâché, and it did have a cable wrapped around its middle, holding it in, but still...

It piqued Mr. Long that he had not been given the key to the Hall. Most managements along the tour had been more trusting. Or more realistic. It was mere luck, now, that he found a man vacuuming the lobby, and it was sheer persistence that made him continue his rapping on the glass door until the fellow heard him over the racket of his machine. He was a colorless man dressed in janitorial drab.

Infuriating. The fellow refused to admit the dock gate was open. No one had been in the theater all day except himself and the musicians, and the big steel gates were never opened except for deliveries. He did give Long the key from the front stage to backstage.

The carpet and seats of Landaman Hall were dark blue plush, which exuded odors musty and a feeling of chill restraint. The woodwork, in the orchestra pit and up the sides of the stage, was gray. The walls were white, but of course in the dim light they appeared gray also, and Mr. Long felt a moment's doubt that Macnamara's Band would be able to infuse warmth into such a sepulchral chamber. Especially with the lack of warmth existing within the group itself.

But one would never know that, he reflected as he went through the doorway that led to the stage-left stairs. On stage, they gave the impression that they were one mind and one heart, and even the creaky little digs and puns with which they filled the time between numbers seemed imbued with family feeling.

Six weeks ago it had seemed that Pádraig Ó Súilleabháin's rough antics and awkwardness around Elen Evans would prevent any lasting peace—not that they showed it on stage. Eight weeks ago St. Ives had spent his days gazing at Weird Teddy Poznan with clear and steady loathing. That had been before Pádraig's Celtic cachet had worn off. And Elen, too, had exchanged some muted hisses with Teddy over sound levels. Who would have thought the great antagonism of the tour (and Martha said at least one was inevitable) would have been St. Ives versus Pádraig?

Long crossed the waxed, white-wood stage, stepping neatly around the swags of rope and the black cables of their own equipment. Perhaps, he thought, it was more accurately stated St. Ives versus Everybody. He yawned. Coughed.

The wall which divided the front stage from the back was jointed and ran in tracks in the floor and ceiling. It was padlocked shut, but set into one of its sections was a door of normal size and shape, with a Yale lock in it. A stiff double loop of black cable peeked from beneath the door, and Long wondered if it was part of the band's equipage. If so, then perhaps there *had* been thieves. He glanced over his shoulder at the bulky boxes on stage: the tuners, the amps, the complex gear that made it possible for Elen's triple harp to compete against the sound of the pipes. It appeared intact. He turned the key in the lock and touched the doorknob—

Which flew out of his hand. Long snapped face-front in time to see the entire wooden door flying away from him across the day-lit backstage, as though it had taken wing. It was a sight designed to engrave itself upon a man's memory: the upright rectangle, with empty brass hinges on one side and brass knob at the other, outlined starkly against the larger rectangle of the open dock gate, with an open trunk full of pipes at the right edge of the rectangle, looking like a sea trap overflowing with crustaceans, and the white wall of the supermarket beyond. Surreal. Dada. Perfect Magritte.

Then Long himself was picked up by the foot and slammed to the floor. He landed on his side, and his head was only saved from impact by his flailing right arm. The same incomprehensible force which had sucked away the door rushed him across the dirty floor of the backstage, past the trunk and toward the open dock.

He heard a crash which did not sound like wood and he heard Marty cry out. He saw that the thing which had him was the black cable that had been stretched under the door. He curled into a ball, and twisted the snag from his foot, but as he came free he went over the concrete dock and into space.

The lip of the dock was below Long, and by instinct he grabbed on to it. So large were his spindle-fingered hands, and so strong, that his grip held, and Mr. Long came to earth feet first, slamming his stomach and the side of his face only slightly against the side of the dock.

There was Martha, standing two feet to the right of him, holding Marty against her. Martha's mouth was wide open, showing her very nice teeth.

Marty wore a small replica of her grandmother's expression. "Daddo!" she cried, and hopped in place. "How wonderful! Do it again."

"Don't you dare," said Martha. "Whatever it was, Mayland, once was enough." She glanced from him to the door, which had come apart, to the pulverized pediment that had first gone over the edge.

Long released his grip on the dock. His hands were scraped and the left one was a touch bloody. He felt a sore spot over his left cheekbone. His clothing was very dusty.

He peered left and right. "At least," he said in a shaky voice, "at least this time I missed the bolt in the wall." Mr. Long stepped back from the dock.

At his feet lay the door, which had come unlaminated. He took it by the knob (somewhat gingerly) and lifted it to examine the other side.

There was more of that black cable, snarled—no, tied—to the other side of the knob. A foot away from that knot was another which seemed to do nothing but tie off a fifteen-foot loop of the stuff. The far end of the cable lay in a pile of shards, gravel, and stone dust. "That was a little pillar," offered Martha. "That toppled over the side here.

The black cord was tied around it." With both hands Martha prevented Marty from making her own investigations.

Long stood back and surveyed the whole mess. "No pins in the door," he said, and shook his head in wonder. "By all the auspices! A trap."

"It might have killed someone," said Martha.

"It most certainly might have killed someone," said Long, rubbing his face.

There was a howl of profanity from up on the loading dock, and they all glanced over to see the theater janitor, whose pale face was livid. "What the hell is going on here?" he roared, gesturing grandly over the wreckage.

No one had an answer for him.

"It would help if the janitor could remember exactly which of us had been going in and out this morning," said Martha, sitting on the toilet seat lid with an expression of worry on her face.

Mr. Long was in the bathtub, soaking his battered body. He stared at the shower head with his eyes unfocused. Occasionally he made small sounds of discomfort. "Of us, Martha? Does the deed proclaim itself the work of one of Macnamara's Band? That fellow doesn't strike me as the best watchdog to be had. Any demented soul—"

"Setting a trap for a perfect stranger? Possible, I guess. But"—Martha clapped her hands on her knees—"there is no crazy like a crazy musician."

Long let his gaze drift from Martha to the shower curtain and thence down to his toes, which were sticking out of the water: very dark. "Not for a perfect stranger. There was reason to expect someone in particular to be using that door."

"Huh?"

Long closed his eyes and recalled the tableau of the sailing door once more. "In the far corner of that back room was St. Ives's music trunk, filled with pipes. I noticed it on my trip through."

"Ouch," said Martha, in reference to Long's short flight, and then "Ouch!" in a different tone, as the implications struck her. "And yet you still think it wasn't one of the band?"

He stirred, making warm waves that sloshed over his scraped cheekbone. "I think rather that we can't know. Unless someone tells us. Or we call the police in."

Martha's face tightened. "Jesus! Do you think we should?"

Long, in contrast, closed his eyes. "I have been thinking about it. Had it not been myself who touched that door . . . Had it been George, he might have been killed. Had it been Marty . . ." Long scowled and nudged open the hot-water faucet with his left foot. "But I'm inclined to believe that the catching of the foot was not really part of the joke as planned. Perhaps the punch line was only to make a person—George, let's say—stand like a fool while a part of his usual reality suddenly behaved in very unusual fashion. The door, however, had a large gap at the bottom—a carpet had been there, possibly—and the finished setup turned out to be about ten feet too long to work. Hence the knot and the loop under the door."

Martha looked very dubious. "So no police?"

Long shook his head and sedately lowered his head under the waves.

Pádraig seemed to have a great deal of difficulty understanding. "To play a trick on Mayland?" Naw, he's the last person I'd rag. Now, Ellie here. She'd be great sport to tease." He poked the harper in the ribs. She did not look pleased.

Martha tried again to explain that the joke was probably not intended for Long, but for George, but that it was a badly thought out and dangerous joke anyway. Halfway through her explanation, she realized she was assuming Pádraig *was* the joker, and that it wasn't fair. Her explanation faded off.

Pádraig didn't look offended, however. He leaned against the south door of the theater with his hands in his pockets and he nodded all the while she spoke.

"Terrible. Was the old man much hurt? A shame, if it was supposed to be George."

"It would have been pretty shameful if it *had* been George!" said Martha, losing her temper. Pádraig took a startled step backward. "Don't twist my ear, Auntie Martha! It wasn't me that did it."

He spoke simply and looked her in the eyes, but Martha still wasn't certain she believed him. He was so much the obvious suspect. She glanced at Elen, who had been standing in the shade, pretending not to listen. "It wasn't her, either," added Pádraig. "I've hardly let the lass out of my sight all day. I'm trying to get her out of patience with me, you see, and I can't seem to do it."

Elen broke into a laugh more robust than her figure and face seemed to promise. "It's true. He's been a pest. So unless we did it together, this deadfall could not have been set up by Pat. Or me."

"And *did* you do it together?" asked Martha helplessly.

They answered, in perfect unison, "We did not."

"That's a good example of what I'm always saying," said Ted, when he in his turn was asked. "Snarls in thought, and in the emotions. Knots, holding back the flow of essence through our bodies and our minds. We are tripped and thrown down, sometimes maimed, sometimes destroyed, because of—"

Martha had had enough. "Goddammit, Teddy! This was not something Mayland could have avoided by taking an enema. He fell into a nasty trap: one probably set for George. Did you set it?"

Gently, sadly, Teddy shook his multicolored head. "Never, Martha. George sets enough traps for himself."

The back door of the theater was steel, and opened reluctantly onto a paved parking lot. Elen and Pádraig, once Martha had gone, sagged out the door and onto the pavement not looking at one another.

"Nice of you to give me an alibi," said Elen, her voice a bit unsteady. Pádraig squinted at her in the sunlight.

"No thanks necessary," he said, and followed this with a rude snort. He turned his head away uneasily, until his eye was caught by something beyond.

"Look at that!" Not touching Elen Evans, he led her to the wire fence that divided the theater yard from its neighbor.

"The empty field?"

"Ryegrass," he corrected her. "Or mostly ryegrass. All wasted. They could have had three sheep in there, or even a cow."

Elen eyed him with amusement. "Maybe nobody was clever enough to think of it till now."

"Well, now it is too late. The grass is too tall and dry to be of any use, except as straw. Ah! Wait, Elen, I have an idea. We can make a rope of it—*súgán*, like the tune we play."

"Twisting the rope? What kind of invitation is that, Pádraig? I've heard about . . ."

But in his enthusiasm he was already over the six-foot fence. "We will need first a big knife, so I can cut the hay close to the ground. Then a stick to twist it . . ."

Elen took the broom handle in both hands and gave it the first twist. "I didn't know anyone still did this sort of thing."

Pádraig Ó Súilleabháin was pounding his end of the rope with a broken brick, adding new grass, as Elen backed away, in the manner in which a spinner adds rough wool to the thread. His motions were rough with enthusiasm. "It's still done. For halters for horses and cows and sheep. They don't cost money, and it doesn't matter how soon the beast chews on them. They also used this kind of rope to hold the thatch down, but now mostly they use bought rope.

"But the visitors—the tourists—like thatched houses. You can get a lot of business if you have a thatched house."

"I'll remember that." The late-spring California sun beat down on Elen's head. She held her end of the rope taut and twisted as instructed. The beating and wringing of the tall grass bled juices which smelled very green. Pádraig's short hair was littered with dust and weeds and he looked happy in a bull-like way. She was now fifty feet away and had to step back again as he added more substance to the rope. "Is this the part where you slam the door on me? In some versions of the song, that is?"

He looked up, flushed with effort. "I would, of course. But we're in the car park and don't have a door, so you are safe." He smiled at her an instant longer than the joke required.

Elen replied, "Who is safe, you little bugger?" But she whispered it, and Pádraig was now fifty-five feet away.

The walls of the theater dressing room were an unfortunate green, and they deadened Long's complexion as he sat alone at the table, playing his electric keyboard. His positioning at the instrument was odd; the length of his fingers forced his hands to curl over like the talons of a bird as he worked the keys. This anatomical singularity was not entirely a disadvantage, however. He could hit almost any key on the little instrument without moving his wrists, and crossed thumb-under a sixth at a time. Long's supple back was carried rigidly straight, for once. It had been impressed upon him that he should keep his back straight. His music lay propped against the button accordion.

It was late afternoon when George St. Ives came in and found him there. Despite the heat of the afternoon, St. Ives was wearing his disreputable woolen sweater and corduroys. Heavily he stepped the width of the room and stood behind Long. Breathing.

"Gawd. That again. I thought we were done with that now that Sully's decided it's too much for him."

"This is hardly the same arrangement that Pádraig was learning. This is—as you might say—single-syllable music, suitable for beginners such as myself." As Long spoke, he continued the piece: slow, even, hard on the downbeats. Just a shade mechanical. Part A twice. Part B twice. Again.

St. Ives had a large, daunting presence. It hovered

over Long, who came down hard on the downbeats just the same.

"Simple isn't its problem," said St. Ives, deep in his throat. He stepped closer. The B part ended and began again.

"Damn music-box rhythm you got."

Long heard him shuffling in his thick-soled work shoes over to the cabinet where his assortment of bagpipes were stored. For another minute there was silence from that corner, and then the squeak of a reed. Finally, a blatt of the regulators announced that St. Ives was about to play the elbow pipes.

Long stopped his own playing to listen, as politeness seemed to require it. Besides, he could no longer hear himself. George St. Ives played "Kid on the Mountain," and he played it very well. There was a great deal of life in the tune as he played it, and a strong, free rhythm. It was much faster than Long's version and highly ornamented. When it was done the older man complimented him very sincerely and went back to his slow, metronomic lesson.

St. Ives gave a roar of laughter. "Goddamn. Nothing shakes the rich man!"

Long's smile showed a bit of tooth. "I think you're quite right, St. Ives. One becomes used to being in command."

St. Ives leaned against the table beside him and said, conversationally, "You'll never be a musician, though."

The piper was between the sheet music and the single, naked bulb in the middle of the room, but Mayland Long had days since memorized the tune, and only looked at the paper through habit. "Isn't it fortunate that I never aspired to such estate?"

"Then why this, then? An hour of this *dah*-dee-dah, every day?"

"It is my lesson." Their eyes met, and Long noticed that St. Ives's were squinting and his forehead was drawn, as though with a headache.

"From *her*, eh? You . . . get into that?"

Long's laugh was mild, almost uninterested. St. Ives

shifted in place two or three times and finally got up and wandered out of the room.

With a sigh and a yawn Long ceased playing. He turned off the machine and blew his nose. He was very glad the man had gone, for he himself had been getting sick of playing "Kid on the Mountain," but would rather have died than allow St. Ives to think his influence had stopped him.

He was considering whether to quit his hour with five minutes still to go or to start the next tune in the book, when Ted Poznan sailed in, naked save for a pair of running shorts. He collapsed on the sofa and folded his hands over his sun-darkened, concave stomach. He stared at the ceiling vaguely. "Hey, Dragon," he said, not bothering to turn his head to Long. "This place has really bad feng shui."

Long picked up the keyboard and put it back in its neat, flat carrying case. "You mean the door facing north?"

Ted's eyes widened. "I hadn't even thought of that. I was thinking of Sea Street—three lanes wide and straight as an arrow, pointing directly at this poor defenseless little building."

Martha walked in, freshly showered and wearing a cotton dress of more manageable design than the wraparound skirt. She was in time to catch Ted's last phrase. "What's pointing at the building?"

"The street outside, Martha," Long explained. "The auspices are very bad, you see, when a long street, or river for that matter, points straight at a dwelling or a tomb."

"Tomb?" she echoed.

Ted, without moving on the couch, called out, "Uncontrolled life-force, crashing destructively against our individual realms. Forced, unnatural chi, bombarding us like cosmic rays."

She threw a glance of mock dismay at Mayland Long, who replied with a grin. "The front gate facing north is also as bad an aspect as could possibly be."

George St. Ives had come in behind her and was

filling the doorway. He listened to this talk silently and then stepped through. Ted Poznan's eyes flickered. Long looked politely up and Martha turned, but St. Ives said nothing, walking past them all to his instruments, his hand on his forehead. Ted raised up on one arm and murmured a question to him. The piper only grimaced and shook his head.

Martha broke the tension. "Do remember, fellows, that we have to play here both tonight and tomorrow. Try to keep a good face on it, no matter how unnatural the chi."

There was a sound of laughter from outside the room, in the direction of the vacant parking lot. Everyone looked up, even St. Ives. "It's Elen and Pádraig," Long explained. "They have been out there most of the afternoon."

"Playing in the parking lot?" Martha asked.

Ted made an expansive gesture with both naked arms. "Why not? Parking lots are real too."

"Making something, I believe."

St. Ives lowered himself onto the padded arm of the couch, not far from Ted Poznan's head. "Making what? Bacon?" He showed his teeth. "All we need is for her to dance her little dance for the boy and he'll be worse than useless to us."

Ted Poznan's vague gaze sharpened. He looked up at St. Ives and it seemed there was a question on his mind. Martha's round blue eyes went pale with anger. "As we've only five days more of the tour, George, I won't worry about either Elen or Pádraig too much."

It was Long who said what all were thinking. "She could hardly do worse to him than you, St. Ives."

St. Ives had been rubbing his face. He put both hands down and his bloodshot eyes looked much older than did Long's. "Later for that, rich man. After we play."

But Long seemed not to have heard. He rose from the bench, brushed his light linen trousers, and went to the back door. He was just in time to open it for Elen, who looked surprised to see them all. She was smiling broadly.

So was Pádraig Ó Súilleabháin, but his smile froze

and faded as he found himself the center of attention. Elen took something from his arms. It was dry and tawny and fell in loose loops onto the floor. "Behold! Sixty-odd feet of hand-twisted rope."

There was a moment of pleasant confusion as Ted, Martha, and Mayland Long came forward to see it. Long, who seemed to know something of the craft, was both interested and approving. He suggested they try rice stalks next time, for a tighter twist. No one made jokes about courting, and St. Ives did nothing worse than to laugh.

Martha sat on the lid of the john again, for that was the only privacy she had, what with Marty everywhere, and she thought about what had happened to Mayland and the door. She felt it was her responsibility to do so, since no one else seemed to want to. Not even Mayland.

George, when delicately questioned, had admitted to leaving his pipes in the backstage room. He had been the first in, when unloading, and hadn't known where the dressing room was. He had since moved them downstairs. The inner door had not been locked, when he had gone in that morning. The rolling door, of course, had been.

Martha had found herself unable to say to St. Ives, in so many words, that it looked like someone had set a trap for him. Maybe intended as a harmless joke. Maybe not. He was so easy to set off.

And she was not sure. She almost wished she had called the police when the matter had first occurred. Now everything had been handled by people, and the whole setup taken apart. The door was right now being replaced (with recriminations from the management) and the black cable was coiled on the wall.

At least no one had suggested that they pay for the concrete pediment.

The band ate together that evening, as they had used to in the first two weeks of the tour, when there were still things to talk about.

Elen Evans, despite her name, face, and triple harp, was American: born and raised in Georgia and having lived for some years in California. One of her old friends had stopped by today and left an enormous bowl of mixed salad, and Mayland Long had placed beside it two quart-sized cardboard containers of curry.

Carefully Ted Poznan speared out tomatoes, sprouts, and asparagus from amid the meat and cheese. Ted was on a mucus-free diet. Pádraig Ó Súilleabháin followed him, regarding the array of foods distrustfully and taking only the meat. Elen, alternating moods of gaiety with five-minute broods, ate almost nothing.

George St. Ives did no better, though he had taken a large helping of curry. He sat in the corner by his pipes, as close to Ted as to anyone, and as always he drank down a quart of Miller beer with his meal.

Marty Frisch-Macnamara liked scallops and ate all those on Long's plate as well as her own. Another of her favorites was asparagus dipped in mayonnaise. She wandered over to Pádraig where he sat on the floor (not too near to Elen Evans) and stood before him eye-to-eye, sucking the woody end of a stalk as though it were candy.

Pádraig looked up from his plate of ham and buttery bread. "Do you like that . . . stuff, Máirtín?"

It seemed such a silly question to the girl that she did not bother answering it, but stood, and sucked, and stared.

Pádraig made a face. "It's nasty. Ugh! Put it away now before your face becomes green." He poked her in her round belly with his finger. "Go away with it or I'll hit you one."

Marty sensed the emptiness of the threat and did not bother to move.

"Marty knows what good is." Ted Poznan had alfalfa sprouts in his hair. His eyes were still sleepy as they beamed on the child. "Here, lady. Come take some of my wonderful sunchoke slices."

Marty went, uncertain but hopeful.

"We're teaching her to have no more manners than a

dog," Martha said to no one in particular. "Elizabeth won't like that."

She wiped her mouth with a paper towel. "Business for the day." There was attentive silence. "Just like last night. Unless someone has a sudden inspiration?"

Pádraig Ó Súilleabháin went rigid and he stared at Martha's feet. When no one else spoke, he said, "Do *you* want us to make any changes, Martha?"

"No." Her voice was flat and weary. "I think I'm too tired to make room for them."

"Well, that's it, then. Meeting adjourned," said Elen, who looked around in challenge, as though she feared something more *might* be said.

The light was still good at a quarter to eight, when Martha walked out for air. Though Santa Cruz was a city and filled with pavement, the evening heaviness came from the black-green hills to the north, and smelled of evergreens. The line of people waiting at the door should have gratified her: would have gratified her only a few weeks ago. But she was tired, and California had spoiled her, with its new-age society and passion for old-age music.

Thank all assorted gods for Mayland, and his altogether unexpected rapport with Marty. Without him, whatever would she do with the child? Of course, had he not been along, she would never have consented to take her granddaughter for the week, no matter what day-care centers folded or new houses got built. Elizabeth herself had been known to complain that following tours had blighted her young life. Well, Marty seemed to be suffering no blights. She was as easy-tempered as her father, Fred. Fred: the Californian.

Standing at the street corner, where buckets of cut flowers were being taken in for the night, Martha watched the restless movement of the gathering audience.

Odd, that the people who liked her music should dress so differently than she did. Egyptian shirts and skirts of Russian cotton. Drawstring trousers and necklaces of bone. Human bone, perhaps: reminder of mortality? Someone else's mortality, at least. These people looked very much alive. It was not that Martha disapproved of "tribal" dress, but she could not imagine herself carrying around so much anthropological meaning upon her person.

Most of them so concerned with authenticity too. Well, they'd be disappointed tonight, for Martha had four musicians with her and no historical anthropologists at all. Except maybe Ted, who was more well-meaning than accurate, and George, who was so picky about authenticity when it served his purposes to be so.

Too bad about the feng whatever. Sea Street *did* look like it was determined to pierce Landaman Hall through, and the slim trough of marguerites planted in front of the main door only emphasized the peril. Did they often find wrinkled cars in their lobby? That would be inauspicious site planning, all right.

George St. Ives came down the street from the other side with another brown bottle-bag swinging beside him. He was not alone. The young woman beside him had frizzy fair hair and a dazed sort of look.

George was a magnet, thought Martha, and she wondered why. Didn't appeal much to her.

He walked heavily up to the door, where it took him a while to convince the man in charge to let him in. He rolled as he walked, as though he had just come off a ship.

Martha tried to remember anything about his past that would explain this. He was always called a "Cape Breton piper," whatever that meant. It had nothing to do with his playing style, surely, for that was as flexible and many-rooted as Martha's own. Maybe it referred to his dirty woolen sweaters. He had two very good solo albums and had been around forever.

Pádraig Ó Súilleabháin didn't walk like that, nor did he look like a fisherman in any accepted way, except that his hands, she had noticed, were dotted with tiny scars from hooks.

Martha could see a movement of heads along the line, and heard a sudden drop in the chatter level. Chickens, with a hawk overhead, she thought. George must have had to say his name. Yes, that was it, for now the crowd swayed suddenly closer. He stood in front of the open door as though the man had nothing better to do with his evening but hold it open for him, and he spoke with the fair-haired woman. She went up on her toes and gestured a lot; she was excited.

Martha grinned with her mouth closed. She herself could parade up and down in front of the Hall and create no stir. Even if she were announced by megaphones (and that odd thing had happened to her once or twice) people would look past her, seeking the celebrity. Such was public life for a woman turning fifty-five. And just as well too. Put an adoring young boy in front of her right now and she'd be reduced to asking him his school, and what books he liked to read.

But wait. George stepped aside and let the young woman in ahead of him, giving Martha a chance to see her face more closely. It was Elen's friend Sandy, who had come all the way up from Santa Cruz to San Francisco last night to greet them, who had baby-sat for Marty this morning while they had settled in and unpacked, and who had made the overwhelming salad. For a moment Martha felt like an old fool, and what was worse, a jealous old fool. She found herself yawning.

It was time to get it all going. *That* would wake her up, surely. The night a performance couldn't at least open her eyes, it was time to quit for good.

Off She Goes

Elen glanced up from the tag of dirty paper taped to the back of the sound box of her harp. There at the left end of the stage was Pádraig, slouched on his stool, avoiding the lights. Beside him stood Ted, his bleached hair unearthly in the brightness. On Elen's other side she was aware of George St. Ives, though she wouldn't look at him, and on the far end was Martha Macnamara in a neat print dress, shining against the dark.

Elen had no illusions about her central position. It was not because of her importance to the group, but because the triple harp made such a pretty picture. She hoped the lights hadn't yet put it out of tune.

Martha asked an A from Pádraig. The accordion emitted a brief squeak: all that was necessary. She looked from one face to another, as though to ask whether anyone was going to contradict that sound. Ted touched a string so lightly she couldn't hear. Elen, on the harp, didn't bother, for she had spent the last twenty minutes doing nothing else. George St. Ives looked only bored.

Putting the fiddle under her chin, she turned to the audience, as though to ask permission. The house was full and the response came to her like the stirring of a single, large animal. She raised the bow and reminded herself, as she had every night for nearly thirty years, that she was fiddling and not playing a goddamn violin.

"Casadh an t'Súgáin" was the theme song of this tour and this band. It had been Martha's idea to call the group by the same name; the tune was capable of a great many changes of timing and mood. But within the first

39

week of rehearsals Elen Evans had made some joke about Macnamara's Band and it had stuck. A group brought together for so short a time needed no title more pretentious.

Martha began it by herself, very slowly and in the Connemara *seannós:* so intricate and heavy was the ornament that the tune seemed to lose itself in its own complexity. As she played she was counting to herself in little grunts inaudible to the microphone, for she had a horror of getting bogged down in this music and losing the drive forward. She did not bog down—she never did—but neither did she forget to count.

The lights shone down on her closed eyes. She slipped a turn and replaced it with a slide, smiling to share the humor of it with whoever might have noticed.

Elen came in, a bit sharp on her middle E but very good withal. Very close for a harp. Four bars later Pádraig entered and then Ted on guitar, almost unnoticeable except for the stability and feeling of confidence it gave the music. She felt a little spurt of fondness for Ted, who had never been known to miss a rehearsal or to throw a tantrum. His guitar played the role of "bridesmaid" to everyone else's instrument, and he never seemed to mind. Perhaps he was so bound up in his many esoteric studies he had no ego to spare for his work.

She felt a warmth for all of them. She found she was smiling at Elen, who replied in kind.

Once around they went, with the uillean pipes providing a keening high D above it all, and then the pipes tore away from them and doubled the time.

Martha, who was out for this bit, sat down on her stool very primly, legs crossed at the ankles. Her fiddle lay across her lap. "Well, that *does* work," she said to no one at all.

Long sat in the motel room, reading the *Green Fairy Book* to Marty. She had a great deal of affection for this book, and had covered the front binding with silver crayon. Her "Daddo's" taste in the stories, however, was not quite hers. He liked the moralistic French tales, such as "Prince

Vivian and Princess Placide," whereas she preferred the Grimm ones. Consequently, even though she was wearing her snuggies with bunny feet, she was a bit bored.

Mayland Long, though he was the picture of grandfatherly composure, leaning back in the motel tub chair, actually shared her sentiments. He would have liked to have heard the performance, though it was the same performance as last night's and much the same as those of a month past. He was not of the sort who got tired of things quickly. Besides, these days, performances were the only times the band was pleasant to *be* around.

And perhaps Prince Vivian and company were a bit musty, what with the fairies always interfering: tripping people up with their own vices. One grew to resent them.

He lost his place and raised his head to see whether Marty, wrapped up on the big hard motel bed, was still listening. Their eyes met in perfect understanding.

"Why won't they let us go along, Daddo? This isn't any fun."

Long sighed. "You were there last night, Marty, and then this afternoon you were tired and cranky because of it."

"I'm tired because I had to walk around with Sandy this morning, and I'm cranky 'cause I have to stay here!" She shook her yellow feet until the bunny ears flew around like whips. "But I wouldn't be cranky if I were at the music, with Martha."

These sentiments were so in line with Long's that he could not criticize them. He only said, "You mean 'Grandmother,' don't you?"

"Elizabeth said I'm to call her 'Martha,' so she won't feel old."

"There is nothing wrong with being old," answered Long with some acidity. He got up, losing his place in the *Green Fairy Book*, and went to seek another box of Kleenex. "As long as you have your health."

Martha's little travel clock was standing on the bathroom shelf, where it had been exiled for the crime of ticking. Long glanced at it. Eight twenty-five. By now they were through their opening and well into the set that began with "Fanny Póer." If not through that also and into the Breton pipe solo. He looked at his image in the mirror with a sort of drear satisfaction: red nose, watery eyes, and lips cracked painfully in the middle. He thought about George St. Ives, who always looked a bit like this, and wondered if that was what made the fellow so unpleasant.

There was a sound from behind him: high, thin, sustained. The wail of a car alarm, perhaps. That would be enough to set the cranky child into her own wailing. Along with it came a draft of cold air which reminded him the window in the bedroom was still open. Long stepped out to close it.

He stepped into darkness, thick and clinging. In surprise he clutched at the doorway. There was the large, ginger-jar table lamp, shining no brighter than a night-light by the bed. And there was the pudgy form of Marty just where he had left her, but half-coiled and with both hands covering her face. Over all was cold—bitter cold—and foul air. The wail rose in volume, accompanied by a meaningless grumble and chatter. It seemed to be coming from Marty.

Long let out a dry hiss, not knowing he was doing so. He dived across the beds for the baby. Her pajamas were damp and her skin cold. She was stiff. Was she even breathing? He flipped her over on her back and pulled the tiny, short-fingered hands away from her face.

He gave a start backward, for it was not Marty's face he saw in the circle of her downy flaxen hair. It was heavier, crude, with a sloppy mouth and a large forehead and staring, round eyes. A goblin's face.

"Marty!" He took her by the shoulders with his elongated hands and shook her. "Marty! What is this?"

"What is what?" she answered, irritably.

There was no wailing and no cold, and a sweet summer breeze blew the curtains against the window screen. "What is what, Daddo?"

Long made no answer.

*　　*　　*

What an audience this was; Martha knew they were extraordinary when she found that she had turned her back on them in her effort to keep in tune and time with the harp player. Rarely did she feel so secure in concert. With certain rowdy crowds in the Midwest she had hardly dared turn her eyes away. But these kids in their bright costumes sat like good children in church. Except that they clapped with great enthusiasm. Such manners.

The thought hit her that they probably all had either strong political beliefs or history doctorates and the group would be crucified in the papers tomorrow as bourgeois revisionists, but she resolutely pushed that from her mind. Tomorrow was tomorrow.

There was a moment when she was free to wipe the sweat from her face with the linen hanky she kept for just that purpose. (At least she didn't have to worry about Mayland walking off with it; afflicted or no, he thought handkerchiefs barbarous.)

Little thoughts like insects flitted over her concentration, harmlessly. How bright the lights were—like the afternoon sun on the pier. She hoped her dress wasn't visibly sweaty. George's reed sounded fuzzy. Hah, he noticed it, too, and dropped out for a couple bars. There he was again. All better.

Had someone tried to hurt old George? One of these other threads in her lovely fabric? Martha could not, at the moment, even entertain that possibility. To knock his obnoxious block off—yes, possibly. Metaphorically, of course.

Or was it George who engineered the whole elaborate setup? Why, then. For attention? To get Pádraig in trouble? Martha put the whole thing out of her mind.

Next, according to the schedule they had evolved, came "Kid on the Mountain." She shot a carefully neutral glance at Pádraig, to find him looking at her. She looked away again. George, who began the piece, filled the bagpipe.

But it wasn't the elbow pipes he had in his arms, but his goatskin Polish set. The reed must have been really bad on the others to make him switch. If he wasn't careful, he'd drown them all out.

With the first sound of the drone Martha knew something was wrong, but it took her a good two bars before her ears told her what it was. The Polish pipes were slightly sharp to the standard they were using. Sharp to the accordion, which could not be retuned. This was a real problem, as Pádraig was next to come in, with the solo that had broken his nerve only yesterday. Surely George himself could tell . . .

She looked over at Pádraig and mouthed the words "stay out" as she put the fiddle under her chin. But the young man wasn't looking anywhere near her now. His face bore a look of worried surprise and he was getting ready.

Dammit! Martha chewed her lip. She might have come in in Pádraig's place, fingering sharp and avoiding open strings until the pipes dropped out, when she could modulate down to the rest of them. But it was too late. Here was the accordion, on time and perfect, but sounding dull and dimwit, as though it, and not the pipes, were off-key. Pádraig's face was greasy.

Then the guitar uttered a series of unrehearsed and very brash major chords, perfectly in tune with the accordion. Martha glanced her approval at Ted. If they were going to be out of tune, at least let the boy be spared.

The harp added some very heavy bass fifths, and now it was the bagpipe that sounded strident and tinny over the rest of the music. Martha turned for the first time and gave George St. Ives a look of wonder and accusation. But his shaggy head was bent over the pipes and his eyes quite closed. Martha wondered if perhaps it was no plot against Pádraig at all, but only that the man was drunk.

But even if the audience was composed of Marxist traditionalists, as she had feared, they were not tonally demanding, for they were dancing in the aisles and had made a circle at the base of the stage.

The pipe dropped out of the music before scheduled. Had George finally realized? Both Elen and Ted looked to

Martha questioningly. "Whatever the hell," she said, perfectly audibly, and the band gave it hell enthusiastically, for fifteen minutes unbroken.

Somehow it was an hour later than they usually broke up. Martha was sailing with exhilaration and fatigue. Her fingers shook. She put her fiddle into its case and looked for Pádraig, who would run away if one didn't catch him.

He was at the foot of the stairs, and had already been caught. "What are you, Czech? Sound Czech, like my brother-in-law. He plays the accordion too." It was a motherly looking woman of middle age, wearing a velvet djellaba with enormous sleeves.

Pádraig grinned. "I am from Minnesota. Excuse me." He barged through, using his instrument as a ram. Martha tried to follow and came face-to-face with the motherly looking woman, who recognized her as someone who had been on stage.

"He isn't a Czech? Or something like it?"

Martha shook her head. "Not very like it. Sorry."

"Oh! You're not Irish!" The woman couldn't keep disappointment out of her voice. "No, not all of us," said Martha, trying to squeeze by before Pádraig disappeared.

As she made it into the clear aisle, she heard the same voice asking, "... but which one of them is Macnamara? I missed him."

Elen Evans pushed past Ted on the stairs of the stage, almost bowling him over. He watched her go toward the dressing room with only the mildest reproach in his spaniel-brown eyes, for Ted made endless allowances for other people.

It took him a good fifteen minutes to work his way through the people waiting to say a word to him, for Ted never cut anyone off. In fact, he enjoyed talking with people, and strangers interested him more than close friends. He was the best of the band members for explaining the provenance of the various pieces they played, for Ted was polite and cared about such things. When he closed the double door behind him and passed down the hall to the dressing room, he had a wide, unforced smile on his face and three new telephone numbers in his pocket. He stopped at the dressing room door to shift the heavy fiberglass guitar case from his right to his left hand, and then he paused with his hand on the knob.

It was George's voice, and he was saying, "You know, Elen, if I caught the plague, you'd probably think I did it on purpose, so you could catch it from me."

The answer, in Elen's voice, was too sharp and rapid to carry. Ted was left undecided, his hand on the doorknob and his guitar pulling his left shoulder down uncomfortably.

"Thanks for the vote of confidence, my dear. But sometimes my mistakes are just mistakes. You know? Like people make? I hadn't played those Polish..."

The unwilling eavesdropper caught almost none of Elen's reply, except something about a dog being able to tell the pipes were sharp. To that St. Ives replied, "Well, I'm in a position to contradict you on that, because I'm sick as a dog right now, and ought to know.

"Don't make me into your personal little devil, Elen. I don't do anything to hurt the group."

Her one-word reply came through the door perfectly.

"I *don't*, bitch! It means something to me. If you think about it for one solid minute with a clear head.... It wasn't exactly convenient for me to drop everything and join this tour. I wanted to play once with the old lady fiddler, while I had the chance. I may not be perfect, but I don't... don't walk out on my responsibilities."

There were steps approaching from down the hall. Ted had to open the door, or be caught standing there. He opened it. Elen turned to him, wide-eyed. He expected to find fury in her face, but instead she looked alarmed and frightened. St. Ives did not raise his buffalo-heavy head from his pipes.

Putting the guitar down on the deal table, Ted made an exaggerated grimace of pain and flexed his fingers. "Friends and neighbors, I have got to get a second case for my baby. This one is overkill for everything except dropping it out of an airplane."

Elen blinked as though she didn't understand what Ted was saying and wiped her forehead under the fringe of hair. Her vague glance drifted by him as the door opened once again to admit Mayland Long, carrying the triple harp under one arm.

He was dressed in sport jacket, white shirt, and flannel trousers, which made up his usual casual outfit. "Has anyone seen Donald Stoughie?" he asked.

Elen stared and St. Ives shook his head. "Don't know who the hell that is."

"The booking agent for the place. He was supposed to be here with our money after the show. The box office doesn't know where he went. I am concerned."

Three people blinked at him and looked helpless. Sighing, Long put the instrument down in the corner of the room and walked back out again. Elen followed.

She caught up with him halfway along the hall, where he stood leaning against the dirty wall, staring at nothing. His hands were balled in his jacket pockets, a position which Elen had noted was characteristic of the road manager. She thought it a shame, for long fingers was surely no deformity.

"Are you really upset about Stoughie, or did she tell you what happened out there?"

He looked up and his eyes were almost colorless against the dark face. "She told me nothing, except that she wanted the room to . . . talk with Ó Súilleabháin. I came to the Hall to meet the agent."

"Oh. I thought you looked angry about . . . something else." Elen felt a little foolish.

Long, who was exactly her height, looked across at her and broke into a smile. "No. It is *you* who look angry. I looked . . . I don't know how I looked, but I certainly wasn't angry. What will I be angry about, once I know about it?"

Elen shrugged and tossed her head. "Oh, shit. I don't

know. Nothing, I guess. Maybe *She'll* tell you. I've got to find Pat."

"*She* is the kitchen cat," said Long with a smile. "You'll find Pádraig with Martha Macnamara." He watched Elen stalk away down the hall and out the front door. Long went out the back door.

Despite his criticism, he found it gratifying when people called Martha by an italicized pronoun. But the smile quickly faded, and Long remained leaning against the wall for some minutes more, as the apparition in the motel room grew less and less real in his memory.

Ted Poznan and George St. Ives passed by, walking together. "I can help," Ted was saying. "I really can help." Long did not greet them and they did not stop.

He heard the sound of lights being flicked off. Really, he *would* have to locate that agent. Carefully he blew his sore nose and walked away by himself.

The Foggy, Foggy Dew

The connecting door was ajar between the motel bedrooms and all was still in the growing daylight. In one room Marty Frisch-Macnamara lay in the center of a bed so large for her that she had not managed to rumple the covers, while her grandmother sat cross-legged in the corner of the floor, her bottom on a stack of brick-hard motel pillows and her knees on the carpet.

In the other room was Long. He shared the characteristics of both the others, being as flat out as Marty and as wide-awake as Martha. One black arm lay outside the covers, glistening with sweat, while the rest of him was hidden under layers of sheet and blanket. He shivered occasionally, and occasionally closed a scratchy eye, experiencing the cold virus in its fullest manifestation.

Martha heard him sneeze. He sneezed again, and then again, until he was in such a fit of sneezing one could hardly tell when one stopped and the next began. The fit ended in a great wheeze. This entire pattern was so much like the roll of the wooden gong in a zendo that she bowed, swayed from side to side, and got up, yawning.

She found him sitting up, naked to the waist and glistening against the sheets. Crumpled tissues surrounded him like the floral offerings to a god.

"Bad night, dearie, wasn't it?"

His glance was apologetic. "I kept you awake, didn't I?"

Martha shook her head violently, sending her hair in all directions, and she sat down on the bed to gather up the offerings. "Nothing ever keeps me awake. Nothing. Probably because I'm selfish by nature. But how *are* you this morning? Any better?"

He rubbed swollen eyes with his fingertips. "Martha, the only way I can imagine I will get better will be if I split my skin and leave it behind."

She started slightly and dropped her collection of tissues into the great brown grocery bag by the bed, which was more than half full already. "Warn me if you are going to do that."

"I doubt I shall," he said, and with the depth and quality of his voice, these few words held an immensity of pathos. He lay back down again, closed his eyes, and pulled up the sheet.

Martha slid off the bed and went to the window, which opened after only a few brisk jerks. The sea breeze of morning came in, letting her know how stale the room had been. "Well, why don't you simply stay in bed, Mayland, and let me handle anything that might come up today." She forestalled any protest by adding, "I've been doing it for a long time, all by myself."

He gave a great sigh. "I'm in the middle of things, Martha. How can I explain them all? There is finding Stoughie, and the room confirmation in Los Angeles, and—"

As a thought occurred to Martha, she cut him off. "Say, did you ever find out why we came up short? The five hundred?"

There was silence from the bed. She turned to find Long staring at the ceiling. "I think I have," he answered at last.

"Well, what was it? Did you miscount?" Quickly she amended her words. "No, no, of course you didn't miscount. What, then?"

Two black hands appeared around the edges of the sheets and flexed and drummed together. "I . . . don't like to talk about things until I'm sure of them, Martha. It can do more harm than good, I think."

"Oh." She dismissed the matter easily and went to

the closet to see if the wrinkles had hung out of her favorite dress. "No luck. I'll have to steam it. But then we're not supposed to have luck while playing at Landaman Hall, are we? Because of the north entrance, or the street, or whatever."

The top of Martha's form had disappeared among Long's suits and her own dresses, and she did not make a very dignified picture from behind. Yet Long appreciated it, full of virus as he was.

She emerged flushed and victorious, brandishing a steam gun in one hand and the dress in the other. "I won't know what to do with myself when this tour is over. Unless I get roped into helping Elizabeth put up the drywall. I hate mudding drywall."

Without opening his eyes Long said, "You could try marrying me. That would take up a good afternoon."

Martha crowed like a cock. "Hah! If you want to be happy for an afternoon, get married. But if you want to be happy for a lifetime, slaughter pigs. Or something like that—my memory for proverbs is worse than for lyrics." Still giggling, she darted into the other room to look at Marty.

"Still sound. It's a wonder! Probably because she kept waking half up during the night, babbling about Judy."

"You said nothing woke you up at night," Long remarked slyly.

"Nothing does. Except babies. I cannot help having been a mother, and a traveling mother at that." Martha filled the steam gun from the bathroom sink, and called out, "Usually you propose with more enthusiasm, Mayland."

"Usually you reject me with more vigor." In a different tone he asked, "Who is Judy, that Marty should babble about her in her sleep?"

Martha's head appeared around the door. "I don't know. Some little friend, I suppose. Maybe it was the babysitter from yesterday morning. Why?"

He played his lesson scales over the covers without looking either at his hands or at Martha. "The babysitter's name was Sandy, remember. Judy is . . . frightened of George St. Ives, I am told."

Martha came out of the bathroom, the steam gun making patterns in the air like cigarette smoke. "Did you hear about the problem we had last night—with George."

"I gathered, from one look at Elen's face, that there had been a problem. I might have guessed it was with George, but, no. I didn't hear about it."

"Then what, sweetheart? Was Marty being difficult? Very difficult?"

Long made a small, unlikely sound, like the hissing of a kettle. "No. Marty did nothing wrong. It was . . .

"I don't really like to talk about things until I'm certain."

Martha's eyes opened very wide. "You think Marty took the five hundred dollars?"

Long laughed and then of course he started to cough.

Ted watched a white stripe on the ocean, almost at the limits of visibility. It was fog, he guessed, sailing in from the west, into Monterey Bay. He was glad he had gotten up early, for the sun made a great deal of difference to his day.

He took off his shirt, though it was only nine-thirty and still brisk on the beach, and placed it carefully on the flattened bag that had contained his juice and his companion's black coffee. After an energetic stretch (his movements had to be energetic, considering the temperature) he began to do prana yoga.

George St. Ives watched this demonstration from half-closed, sore-looking eyes. St. Ives wore two woolen sweaters under his denim vest and he had his hands stuffed into his armpits. "If you're about to blow your nose, do it into the sand, not at me."

Ted smiled beatifically. "You know very well what I'm

doing, George. There is nothing like the sea air to energize your spine. And what else are we, but long, serpentlike, flexible, and very sensitive . . . ?"

"I prefer to think of myself as a slimy tube with a mouth at one end and an asshole on the other." St. Ives settled back against the concrete wall and closed his eyes. With his flattish nose and great amounts of hair, he resembled a bison enduring a worse-than-average winter storm.

Ted Poznan chafed his arms and scooted a few inches forward, away from the pillar and into brighter sun. "Hey, I can resonate to that too. Eating and shitting, eating and shitting . . . it's a rhythm like any other. Like the seasons. Sacred in its way."

St. Ives groaned. Poznan scooted closer to him. "But you shouldn't have to feel *limited* by that. You can be a magical serpent and an asshole, too, if that's your karma."

A tinny little scream, not of fright but of anger, caused both men to look out toward the open water. There was a family group, well bundled, walking the line where wet sand meets dry. And there was a large dog galloping gracelessly away from its masters and toward the land, something hanging from its mouth. It saw the two men seated at the base of the little wall and was diverted by curiosity, or by the smell of their breakfast.

The dog was a mongrel with a good strain of mastiff in him. His face, with its loose eyelids and pouchy jawline, looked much like St. Ives's. The two creatures stared at each other intently. The dog mouthed the child's sweater he was carrying.

"Put it down, fella," said Ted. "Come on, boy. Baby needs his sweater. Be an old soul. Give it back."

The dog smiled at Ted and flaunted the little sweater teasingly. Ted reached out and missed. The dog gave a heavy little dance.

"Drop it." St. Ives's words were not loud, but they were imbued with threat. The dog dropped it, and St. Ives let the sweater lie in the sand until the owner of it scampered up. The boy, perhaps six years old, glanced uncertainly up at St. Ives, who gave him a look identical to the one he had given the dog. Without a word the boy took his sweater and ran off.

"So did you get me the drugs?" As St. Ives asked this question a very cold blast of air hit shore, spraying their faces with sand. Ted got into his shirt in a hurry. "Something better than drugs, George. Much better."

"Goddamn!" St. Ives beat his fist into sand. "No goddamn *trips* from you, Teddy! No more fucking Feldenkreis and soy-sauce religion! You know what I need."

Very soberly Ted replied, "Yes. You need to be comfortable in your body."

"I want to be free from pain for once!"

Ted was silent for five seconds, listening to the drum of the ocean. He took a breath and began. "You're undernourished, overfed, and alcoholic, George. You've abused that poor—poor slimy tube of yours for twenty years."

"Thirty-five!" George St. Ives corrected him, with some venom. "So what do you offer me—bean sprouts?"

Ted shook his head, causing the wind to lift the bleached layer. His skin was bronzed to a color between biscuit and peach. His every feature and movement, muscular and unconstrained, hurt St. Ives to see. From his shirt pocket the guitarist took a plastic bag with a single capsule in it.

"Drugs," stated St. Ives, relieved. He took the capsule and fingered it, as though there were virtue in the green and yellow coloring itself.

"Not a drug. Something different. MDM."

St. Ives's eyes narrowed. "I don't need hallucinations, Teddy. D.T.'s are bad enough."

"No hallucinations. Adam doesn't work that way. It . . . it's a little like the sun itself. Where things in you have gone rotten, or are blocked, it opens you up."

"Like Ex-lax?"

Ted's glance was half reproachful. "Why not? Like Ex-lax. Only no cramps! It promotes healing, George.

Believe me, I've done it, and sometimes I started out feeling so messed up and off center inside, and then... You'll feel so *good*, you won't believe it!"

St. Ives continued to play with the little bag, thoughtfully, until Ted asked him to put it away. The heavy head came up, then, and the sore eyes were sharp. "What is it, Teddy? Schedule one?"

Ted Poznan's body stiffened with anger for just a moment. "Till last year it was as legal as aspirin. Fascist narcs pushed it into the same class as heroin. No explanation, no excuse. Never a public referendum. And they did it just so they could make a haul. They watched what places and people were healing with it, and then 'bam!' Betting that at least one in three would continue trying to use it. Easy marks!"

"Schedule one," repeated St. Ives, letting the rest slip by him. The capsule went into his pocket. "With that risk, it better be worth it." He stood up, brushed the sand off, dropped something into Ted's lap, and shuffled off through the sand.

Ted stared at the little roll of bills. "Hey! Hey, George, I don't want this. Hey!" He took three steps after St. Ives, and then, being Californian, darted back to clean up his garbage.

"Hey. It's not that easy, George. There are things I ought to tell you. Dietary restrictions..."

The wind blew increasingly, carrying spray with it. By the time Ted had caught up with George St. Ives, the fog had touched the beach.

Mayland Long sat on the bench at the bus stop outside Mr. Stoughie's office, where his unshakable will had brought him. Unshakable but perhaps ill-advised, he reflected, as he watched the populace walking up and down the flowered street under the flowering trees of Pacific Mall. His sickness was making them all look very strange. But then perhaps they really did look strange. The man with the ill-fitting suit of tails and the orange Mohawk, for instance. Had he not been overweight he might have appeared quite threatening. Long peered out of the corner of his eye at an elderly woman in a loud print dress, trying to decide whether she appeared mad or only dowdy.

He was really feeling ill now, with every warm breeze hitting him with fever and every cool breeze with chills. His scraped cheek stung, along with the bruise over his ribs. And breathing was such an effort, with both nostrils plugged. Martha had been right. Of course.

But he had had no intention of allowing Martha this errand. It was the sort of thing he did best.

Don Stoughie, the booking agent of Landaman Hall, was a man of forty years and generally good appearance. His thinning hair was trimmed in a style that was neither old age nor new, and the Mexican wedding shirts which he wore over his stretch Levi's were washed and pressed professionally. He was a Santa Cruz businessman.

Stoughie paid no attention to the bent black man at the bus stop, for he was long past noticing the street people. He put his key into the lock of the door and opened it. Halfway up the stairs he heard a sound behind him and turned to see the old fellow coming behind him. He had a moment's attack of nerves. "What do you want?"

Long ascended three more stairs and stopped under the staircase skylight. Stoughie, seeing his apparent harmlessness, relaxed a little. But only a little, for the incongruity of Long's face and coloring did not reassure him. The suit of raw silk, however, turned the trick. "Sorry. I get nervous in dark places."

"Unfortunate. There are so many dark places."

Stoughie grunted recognition, hearing the voice. "Long, is it? I spoke to you on the phone last week. Macnamara's manager?"

"The manager of the tour business," Long corrected him. "No one manages the fiddler except herself." He continued up the stairs, thereby forcing Stoughie up, willy-nilly.

The office was small and swimming with dust. On the wall was a poster of Big Basin Redwoods State Park, framed in imperfect glass, and a topographical map of Santa Cruz. Long, without waiting to be invited, sank down into a wicker chair against one wall, next to a low table with a wide, flat book on it. It was difficult in the light from the single window to make out the title. He found that a single sweep of his fingers over the dust made it all much clearer. *Investment Property, Monterey Bay*. With a Monterey pine against the sunset. And the ocean, of course.

"Funny," said Stoughie, seating himself behind his desk. "From your voice I'd assumed you were a much bigger man."

Long's puffed eyes were without expression as he answered, "I have a cold, Mr. Stoughie. It has shrunk me considerably."

Stoughie grunted appreciatively. "I can buy that. Every time I get the flu I'm sure I go down from five eleven to five feet even. Lose ten pounds too." Stoughie slapped his sides in indulgent fashion, as though he wouldn't mind having the flu tomorrow.

"I am told that this is not influenza, but merely a cold virus." Long spoke a touch aggrievedly. "And I will do my best to keep you out of contagion's way.

"But as you couldn't manage to be at the theater last night, as per our agreement. . . ."

Stoughie's chin went out. "Did you really expect me to?"

"Pardon?"

"After the shambles that you people made of my theater yesterday?" Stoughie had an arctic blue eye, but the effect was marred by the twitching of the left corner of his mouth. "I haven't even been able to get an estimate of the damage yet, but when I do . . ."

Long heard a humming in his ears. He knew a moment's doubt as to whether he were hearing the man correctly. The virus was responsible for so much.

"If you are referring to the door which flew out of my hand . . ."

"A safety door valued at over a thousand dollars, and that's just—"

Long sat up in the position of a cobra ready to strike. "That was nothing but a standard, hollow interior door, as I am in a position to know, Mr. Stoughie. What is more, there is no evidence of any kind to connect that bizarre trick or trap with any of Macnamara's Band. Further—"

Stoughie gave a sideways, ironical look. "G'wan. Everyone knows about you guys. Musicians on tour. It isn't the first time."

Long's anger threatened to dissolve into perplexity. The buzzing in his ears grew louder. "I must assure you this *is* the first time we have been accused of any sort of rowdiness. The band has only been in existence for a few months, and after all, we're a folk band, not the Who. But if accusations are to be made, I think that I, who was both snagged and dragged in your theater—"

"I just represent it," said Stoughie unexpectedly.

"In *your* theater, while trying to see to the safety of our sound equipment, and by parties unknown." Long found himself lost amid the periods of his own sentence. His eyes were distracted from the agent's face by a small movement outside the window.

It was a hummingbird. A pretty little hummingbird with its nose stuck down the tube of a honeysuckle floret blooming in the window box. Was that what was humming in his ears? Long felt a desperate, lonely affinity with the hummingbird, and with tremendous effort he pulled his attention back to Stoughie.

The man sat up and his blue eyes opened wide. "Don't try it, buddy," he said, in the accents of a genre movie. "You couldn't stand the heat."

Long stared at him, bemused. "Oh, I've never had any problems enduring heat, Mr. Stoughie. It's this cold that has me down."

Both of the agent's feet pressed with belligerent strength against the back of his desk, underneath. Mr.

Long could see the panel before him bulging out, and he wondered what would happen if it broke. "Threatening a suit, eh? You know, musicians have tried that before, with me. You might ask them where it got them."

Long sighed, blew his nose, and watched the bulge move with the currents of Stoughie's anger. "We spoke with Sister Sue Frye before scheduling last winter. She advised us strongly against doing business with a man who is so reliably underhanded."

"How dare—" The bulge shone under the fluorescent lamps.

"But we—I—have a different hand dealt to me than Sister Sue did. I have an excellent and reputable lawyer, Mr. Stoughie, as well as the money to feed him indefinitely."

Long heard a crack, and watched a dark line appear along the walnut-toned plywood panels of the desk. Stoughie heard it, too, and his feet withdrew. He sat up. "Listen, Long. Landaman Hall is owned by a corporation. Do you think you can fight a corporation in court?"

Long chuckled. "Fight a corporation? Of course. Probably I could *buy* your corporation. Most certainly I could buy your theater. But I wouldn't want to—the feng shui is very bad."

"The what?"

Long ignored his question. He was looking again at the hummingbird. "I have a suggestion, Mr. Stoughie. If you would really like to joust with me in the arena of the law, why don't you pay the band its little bit of money? Both with suit and countersuit, it would strengthen your case tremendously." So pleasing was the form and coloration of the little nectar drinker that Long smiled as he spoke.

Stoughie was a picture of disbelief. "You're putting me on, brother. I know what kind of small bucks a man makes, hauling harps around."

"So you *were* at the concert last night?" Long's smile tightened. "A man hauls harps around for nothing, if that man is myself."

Very calmly Mr. Long stood up, and calmly he began

to empty his pockets onto the table. "Here is my pocketwatch, Mr. Stoughie. It is not made of brass. The works are by Patek Philippe, but that doesn't communicate anything to you, does it? That beside it is a manicure set I picked up in Belgium; I recommend it to you as leaving no unsightly lump in the jacket pocket. That flat case, also gold, is not for cigarettes, but credit cards. Allow me to show you my assortment; the airlines credit cards are not as impressive as the bank cards, are they? Rather too gaudy."

Stoughie glanced from one gold bauble to the next, hung between insult and fascination. Then Long emptied out the inner pocket hidden in his jacket lining. A flat, brown leather checkbook hit the desk, followed by another of green plastic. Long held the green one open in front of Stoughie's nose. "Here you see more or less the finances of Macnamara's Band. Not as bad as some. Solid, in fact, but perhaps in no state to engage in long-term legal jousting." He dropped the book on the desk and held up the other. "This, on the other hand, is the balance of the personal account which I am using for my expenses on the trip."

Stoughie looked at the neat, tiny figures and then he looked again. His eyes dilated, perhaps involuntarily.

"All of this could be faked, of course," continued Long, scooping up his possessions. "By anyone who wanted to pretend to a financial state he did not have. But when the goal is to convince you that I am a worthy adversary in the civil battlefield . . .

"Oh. Here's one more little toy that might interest you." From a pocket sewn into an unlikely place in his jacket pocket he produced a small square of green, which he tossed on the desk.

It was a stack of folded greenbacks, held neatly as the pages in a book by a clip of simple design, which shone brightly except for the tarnished image of a Chinese dragon which wound in waves and spirals along the length of it. The eyes of the dragon were bright.

"It is only bronze, of course," said Long modestly. "But I think the workmanship is clever."

Stoughie tore his gaze away from the denominations long enough to notice the workmanship. When Long put the clip back in his pocket, the agent sighed.

"Mrs. Macnamara, like the businesslike woman she is, will not permit any transfer of funds from the brown account to the green account. She will, however, accept a certain deposit from you. Therefore it is necessary that you write a certain overdue check, to clear the books."

Don Stoughie found that he had taken out his own checkbook, which had an elk on it, superimposed on imitation denim cloth. He watched himself writing a check, under Long's supervising eye.

"Ah, Mr. Stoughie. It is a little matter, but you have mistaken the month. Undoubtedly the heat of the season has led you to think of July, instead of June."

Stoughie's face had lost its mesmerized look. He shut his checkbook with a snap and he smiled. "Not really. I always pay at thirty days. Ask around, and consider yourself lucky you got it at all, after these shenanigans."

Now there was neither hummingbird nor pine tree in Mayland Long's cosmos, but only the shape of Don Stoughie on the other side of the desk. Still his voice was neutral as he said, "I needn't ask any further than our letter of agreement which specified payment last night."

Stoughie, facing a slight Asian man with a wadded tissue in his hand, flashed a bit of temper. "I'm tired of you, Long, with your . . . your ostentation," he said, putting the accent on the second syllable of the word. "And I'm doubly tired of irresponsible bands that are permitted to wreck my facilities, and that you can tell the Macnamara biddy."

The booking agent's words caused Mr. Long's face to pale and then darken again. The pupils of his eyes flashed like the throat of the hummingbird and in his ears came the same unearthly buzzing.

Stoughie, sensitive to none of this, went on. "Look. By the time you could make trouble for me about the check *or* about the accident, more than a month will be passed. And then, I promise you, I will make it so difficult for the band to collect that your little green checkbook will turn red over the whole deal. *This* way, you just wait a silly month, like people do all the time—and they get their money. If it isn't even a paying job with you, I don't see why you'd care."

Long's immobility encouraged the other to add, "So just admit to yourself that you don't get things your way this once and—" His words were cut off suddenly as he was lifted off the ground and dragged, by the neck, halfway over his desk.

Very close to his face hung the eyes of Long, bright gold and completely out of focus. A noise like a wind tunnel came out of Long's throat.

Stoughie felt a pen pressed into his hand. "Change the date. Change it or you're dead. . . . Now initial it.

"Now I want you to apologize for your language in reference to Mrs. Macnamara."

Stoughie uttered a croak, and was made to speak louder. All these things being done to Long's satisfaction, he dropped the agent back into his chair.

"My nose is bleeding," said Stoughie. "Bleeding all over my shirt! My God, I'm going to put you in jail for this."

"Are you?" Long's face showed no more than it had at any time since entering the room. "That will be very interesting, Mr. Stoughie. But not very profitable, I'm afraid." He turned to go and then turned back. "Why don't you just admit to yourself that you don't get things your way for once?" He walked out of the office, closing the door behind him.

And then Long ran, light and noiselessly, his style of darts and sudden changes of direction well suited to the crowded mall. He sprang up the stairs of the Bank of America, where there was no line, and very calmly he had the check put into Martha Macnamara's business account. There was no difficulty about it.

He was shaking. He leaned against the wall of the post office, coughing.

He had had no control over himself. He might have killed the man, sending both Martha and himself into endless trouble, over a silly bit of money meaningless to him. A surge of anger from within tried to say it wasn't the money, but he beat it down again. It hadn't been the money, but instead pique, at a small businessman who thought it clever to inconvenience and insult people. Reaction far out of proportion to action.

And last night? The episode with Marty. Could he trust his own senses about what had happened?

No wonder human beings were so reluctant to believe things. They spent their lives going from one confusion to another, and in general did not die with any greater perception of the truth than that with which they'd been born. Poor Marty: what was in store for that little spirit, born into this condition? Poor Mayland Long. Poor Martha.

No. There was nothing pitiful about Martha, not even—Long reflected carefully—when she had one shoe on and one shoe off. Not even with face cream. He leaned against the wall and thought about Martha until he felt well enough to walk back to the motel.

Elen followed Pádraig along the shore, wondering why, amid the cold winds and the fog, she should continue to do so. Her poncho whipped across her face. She missed some of the words.

". . . it's made of leather, and he made it on *The Brendan* herself, bobbing up and down in the Atlantic. He made a lot of them, I think, but this one he gave to me. I like it a lot."

"Which one was this?" she shouted into the wind. "Thor Heyerdahl?"

Pádraig gave her a very disappointed glance. "Trondur Patursson. On the leather boat *The Brendan*. That left from Kerry to—"

"Yes, I was listening. Just a confusion about the name," she said, in a voice heavy with her guilt.

"*The Brendan* itself is on display in a glass house. It seems to me a shame, you know? That it should only go out once."

Elen nodded vigorously. "Oh my, yes. A shame."

The stretch of wet sand was enormously wide here. The tongues of the waves lapped a hundred feet in from where the wave broke. Because the tide was out and the wind was strong, Pádraig had told her. Or maybe the opposite. Had the tide been in (or out), things would have been less interesting.

To Pádraig. It took nothing more than a piece of a left-handed shell to put Pádraig up. As little as it took to discourage him. Elen remembered yesterday afternoon and the making of the rope, which had ended in a quick clutch and kiss. She herself had set the situation up for it, standing too close and looking carefully elsewhere as she wound the slack toward her. But the vehemence of the boy's approach had startled her, and then he'd backed off in the face of that startlement. The end had been more awkward than the beginning.

And then the horrible moment at the concert for him, when he had known himself so helplessly off. Elen felt an impulse of pure malice toward George St. Ives. Too bad that little joke with the door had caught the wrong man.

And now the fine morning had gone cold enough to freeze Elen's ears and here was Pádraig, rattling on about *The Brendan* and fourteen-foot-dinghy competitions. As though nothing of moment had happened during the whole tour.

Elen wished herself elsewhere.

"Didn't you hear me?" Glancing up guiltily, Elen admitted she had not. Pádraig's hair was flattened by the wet air and droplets hung from the ends of it.

He was smallish and baby-faced and she wondered (having lost the ability to decide) whether he was good-looking at all, or whether her reaction to him was only the result of eight weeks of propinquity.

"I asked you how many brothers and sisters you have."

"Did you?" His eyes were the same color as the water out there, mixed into cloud. A very sleepy color. Elen yawned. "I don't have any."

"Not any? Not one?" He stared distrustfully, until Elen laughed at him.

"Not a one, sweetie. It's not an unheard-of situation."

"Not a what? Not rare? I think it must have been rotten for you." Pádraig had a wet slate in his hands. Waiting for the right moment, he skimmed it over a dying wave. It bounced four times before disappearing. "Here. You do it." He handed her another.

Without looking, she tossed it into the water, where it sank. "Most people I know spend all their time fighting with the sibl—with their brothers and sisters. How am I unlucky?"

He shrugged in exaggerated fashion. "You have to hit on somebody, when you are a child."

Elen smiled grimly and thrust her hands into her poncho. "You might also *be* hit on, Pat. And I had my parents to fulfill all such needs." She moved off along the strip of flotsam which marked the high-water line. The fog was so thick one couldn't see the boardwalk fifty yards away. Now Pádraig was following her. "You don't like your parents? I bet you ran away from home."

She turned in chilled shock. "He—who told you?"

Pádraig stepped back, stumbling over his feet. He dropped the last shell he'd picked up. "Don't be angry, Elen. Nobody told me. I was only ragging you."

She swayed away from him and toward the ocean, which had begun to soak into her shoes. It offered no comfort. "People don't really want to be teased, lover. Or at least I don't. But I did run away. I left home at the age of sixteen. I put myself through four years of music school. I *can* play Ravel, you know. I haven't been back to Atlanta since I was a freshman."

Ó Súilleabháin walked along beside her, gazing with a sort of awed curiosity. "At home that doesn't happen much—that a girl will leave home and then go to the university. It would be rare. You must have known yourself very clearly from the beginning."

Her laughter was bleak. "No such luck. If I had years to do over . . ." Then she laughed again, more naturally. "I *still* wouldn't go back home. I'm much better off as I am. Even after eight weeks on the road."

"Of course," said Pádraig, and he hit her on the shoulder lightly. "On the road there's me."

He sniggered. She sighed. "What about children, Elen?" asked Pádraig, with no shade of teasing in his voice. "Doesn't a woman want to have children?"

She gaped at him in real alarm, which soon dissolved into giggles. "Don't worry, Pat. You don't get babies by kissing." Then she ran into the empty fog, kicking wet sand behind her.

Pádraig went after, but the fog was so thick he missed where she turned off toward land. He stood and called. "Elen! Elen, stop fooling now. The fog is dangerous. Elen!"

"Here," she replied, coming to stand close to him. She touched a hand to his lips. "Stop talking. Listen."

He did so. There was the rush of the sea coming in and the growl of the pebbles. There were many bird cries.

"Someone's crying," Elen whispered. Pádraig opened his mouth to tell her it was a bird, but he changed his mind. Together they stepped forward, to the very edge of the ocean.

There was neither shore nor sea horizon. They held on to each other and Elen's ears started to ache from the cold. She shivered. Pádraig put his arm around her without self-consciousness. "It's very dark, for fog," she whispered. "Maybe it's dirty weather coming."

"No, it isn't. Be quiet, if you please." The crying was close now, and the cold bit into Elen's face. She could scarcely see Pádraig, next to her. His breath was steaming and his fog-colored eyes moving restlessly. "Where are you?" he shouted into the waves. Elen gasped as a voice answered him, a small, thin, very uncomfortable voice.

"Here I am."

She knelt down on the wet sand, and Pádraig knelt down beside her. "God and Mary with you, Marty! How did you get here?"

Marty was wearing her yellow trousers and no shirt, nor shoes. Her face was blotched with tears but when Pádraig picked her up she was warm. "Looking for Judy," she said, and all the way back, that was all they could get out of her.

As they turned toward the boardwalk, a blast of warmish wind blew the fog into rags, and they came to the motel under sunshine.

"If he's sick,
I'll wish him better"

Martha had her hands full of horsehair. Her fingers were slightly sticky from the heat and the long tail hairs were not behaving as they ought. She freed one hand and almost dropped the bow she was restringing. As she floundered after it, it came up and struck her smartly on the chin. Tears sprang up in her eyes, half from the smarting and half from self-pity, and then Pádraig and Elen came in. He was carrying Marty.

Martha, who had seated herself under the window with her back facing the doors of the room, looked over her shoulder before returning to her frustrating work. A moment later she looked again, more sharply. "Are you taking Marty out?"

"We are taking her in," answered Pádraig Ó Súilleabháin, and Elen added, "We found her at the beach by the boardwalk."

Martha stood up slowly. She dropped the bow, unclosed, on the windowsill. Birdlike, she tilted her head one way and then the other. "No. No, there must be some mistake. She's been in the other bedroom, with her crayons for the last . . ." She took a deep breath then, and shook herself all over.

"On the beach, you say? Alone? Dressed like that?"

Pádraig looked sideward at the carpet, as though it were he who was being found at fault. Marty herself wiggled down from his arms and, with a dubious glance at her grandmother, tried to fade from sight into the next room: the room with the unrumpled bed and the crayons.

Martha caught her, not harshly, in the doorway. "Marty, hon, did you go to the beach? By yourself?"

Marty's flaxen hair took the light of the window like Martha's own graying curls. She shrugged her small shoulders exactly as Elizabeth, her mother, might have.

"That's across a street, Marty. A big street. Did somebody take you across?" Martha's voice shook slightly, and the tears of five minutes before returned, making her blink. Marty looked away from her crying grandmother and said nothing.

"Why did you do it, Marty? Weren't we going to go to the beach when your Da—when Mayland came home?"

This penetrated through Marty's discomfort and confusion. She brightened. "Yes. I want to go to the beach!"

Martha sighed and ran both hands through her hair. She sat down heavily in the doorway in tailor fashion, hiking up her dress. "You just were at the beach, honey, and that wasn't good at all."

Marty's little face screwed up and she sought support from Elen and then Pádraig, but the two of them said nothing, only waiting respectfully for Martha to do whatever grandparents do. "It wasn't the beach. It wasn't like the beach at all!"

"Fog," offered Elen. "That's what she means. She was looking for this 'Judy' of hers in the fog. For a few minutes it was really thick out there."

Martha Macnamara blinked harder and glanced out the window at the blue sky. Elen giggled. "There was fog."

"Certainly there was," added Pádraig, a touch protectively. He took a nervous step that put him in between Martha and Elen. "We would not lie about it."

Martha, stone-faced, hauled herself up and walked toward him. Pádraig's shoulders slumped visibly and he looked again at the carpet. Martha's embrace was as hearty as it was unexpected, and she kissed him twice, once on the nose as he jerked his head up and once on the left cheek. Then, lest Elen feel slighted, she hugged and kissed her the same way.

"Thank you so much. For bringing her back to me. I am wonderfully grateful!" The tears standing in her delft-blue eyes became tears of relief.

"How I ever was so blind in my work as to let her slip by me . . ." She sat down on the end of one bed.

"Don't worry," said Elen, placing herself across from her, on the other bed. "I don't think she even got chilled."

"I'm not chilled," verified Marty, from the doorway. "I'm not dirty, either," she added, hopefully. "Maybe we can go to the beach?"

Elen and Pádraig left on that happy note, but Martha continued on the edge of the bed, gazing worriedly at Marty.

"Who is Judy?" she asked.

"Judy's kind of my friend," Marty answered, but she made a face as she said it. Martha thought very hard about what a three-year-old can understand and what she can't.

"Judy . . . isn't here, is she?"

Marty slumped down in the doorway and sat in the posture her grandmother had taken five minutes before. "Of *course* not. There's you and me here. That's all."

"Is Judy back at home?"

Marty's expression of bored patience flickered, as though Martha had finally asked a sensible question. "Not at home now. That's why I had to go looking."

Now Martha spent some moments considering what a fifty-four-year-old can be expected to understand and what she can't. "Tell me, Marty. Is Judy real? Real like you and me?"

Marty's tiny face drew into itself, until it bore a close approximation of her grandmother's worry. "I don't think so. Not like you and me."

Mayland Long came in to find Martha seated spraddle-legged on the bed, waving a long stick with horse-tail hairs at the end of it over her head. Her gaze was preoccupied. Though he was not in a bright mood, he made an effort at conviviality. "Here, madam, let me," he said, taking the tangled violin bow from her hand. "The mandarin does not shoo flies for herself. It would be a loss of prestige."

Distracted, she looked up, and what she saw in his familiar face brought her out of her study. "What happened with the agent, darling?"

He sat down beside her. Diffidently, he presented the deposit statement. She looked it over intently, and then chortled. "Hey! It's even for the right amount. And on time. Huzza, huzza! You're a miracle worker."

Long responded with no satisfaction whatsoever, and her enthusiasm leaked away. "Or . . . this isn't *your* money, is it, Mayland. You aren't trying to pay this out of your own . . ."

"No," he said, a bit harshly, and then broke into a fit of coughing. "No. It is Stoughie's payment." Disgustedly he added, "I almost killed him to get it."

She looked closely at him. "That would have been bad."

Long barked a laugh that almost set him off again. "It would have gotten me in a great deal of trouble. You too. And the worst is that it would have been . . . almost accidental."

"That would be the worst?" she asked in a small voice.

He turned toward her and at last he smiled. Touched her knee. "What I mean is that I assaulted the fellow with no thought. In a sudden rage."

Martha's answering smile was sly. "Well, dear, I've been telling you for five years now to be spontaneous."

Instead of growing, his grin faded. "With this sickness, I have no self-control, Martha. I'm afraid of what I might do through sheer irritation.

"And, I am not sure but that Donald Stoughie will have me arrested."

Martha sighed and bit her lip. Long coughed again. "This cold," he said. "Eight weeks," she said. They sat together at the foot of the motel bed, and he waved the broken violin bow over them both.

It was George St. Ives's curse, as it is that of every piper, that he spent a great deal of the time that ought to have been spent practicing, looking for a place where he could practice without having the police summoned. Today, at least, he had the empty theater.

St. Ives was seated on a broken-cane stool in the green room, and Ted Poznan sat on the table next to him. Ted was changing the strings on a blond guitar that shone with abalone inlay. He was smiling in sleepy fashion, and occasionally he gave St. Ives a pleased, proprietary glance.

St. Ives, falling victim to the other major piper's curse, could not get a single reed out of his box of reeds to work properly. They sat on a towel in front of him, while his treasured uillean pipes lay ungainly across his lap-leather, like some strange pet lobster.

"Hey." Ted leaned over. "I guess Martha was having the same sort of trouble this morning. With her bow. Maybe the energies just aren't right for putting little pieces together."

"Too dry," replied St. Ives, slowly fitting the shard of wood into its frame.

"Yeah. 'Swhat I said." Ted watched the tiny operation closely. He leaned forward and his guitar followed the gesture, vibrating the long feelers of its new strings.

George pushed the reed in and then pulled it out again. Very seriously he said, "I don't know whether it's tight enough."

Ted beamed. "Aw, sure it is, bro." He hit the piper on the shoulder, in the style of Pádraig Ó Súilleabháin, but with nowhere near the force.

St. Ives looked up, and the expression on his usually grim face was benign and almost shy. "Maybe it is after all," he said, and he let the chanter down on his lap. His voice was thick with emotion.

"Hey!" Ted said again, and repeated the affectionate

punch. "Hey, great, isn't it? I mean, really . . . it feels good, doesn't it?"

St. Ives put his hand into his beard and considered. He rocked ever so lightly back and forth on the stool. "Better than it's been in a long time, Pozz. I'll give you that." The brown eyes in his bison face shifted right and left through the dingy little room and settled on Ted's tanned young features.

"You know, you're goddamn pretty, Pozz."

The guitarist guffawed and made a face. "Gawsh, thanks."

"Naw. You are. Goddamn. You queer?"

"Gay, you mean," Ted corrected him almost unconsciously. "I'm not. Or not very. Not that I can really *say*." His eyebrows drew together and he huddled across the body of his instrument. "Or more correctly, I guess I should say my level of experience, so far . . ."

"You *are* weird, though. You gotta admit that."

Ted looked tenderly down at George and sighed. "Yeah. I gotta admit that, I guess." His glance sharpened. "Why did you ask, George? Are you . . . is the stuff helping you to find in yourself . . ."

St. Ives blew out through his beard. "Christ, no." He sat up straighter, and then on impulse he pulled his gray Icelandic sweater over his head. Underneath was a rag knit of the same color.

Ted watched the procedure. "Hey," he said one more time. "You took off your sweater."

"It's hot."

"Yeah, it's hot and so you took off your sweater to be more comfortable. That's a very good sign."

There was a little while of quiet in the room, which George broke with a sigh. "It's not perfect yet," he said, and he fished under the rag sweater. "In fact, in some ways it's worse."

"What's worse, fella?" Ted leaned perilously far out, following St. Ives's hands. When he saw the small plastic vial his eyes widened in owlish alarm. "Hey, George.

That's not the best idea. Don't crap the experience up with—"

"Don't get the idea I'm doing this for fun, Pozz. I need the pills." He shook two red dots into his hand and then clapped it on his mouth. Dry.

"Why. What?" Ted Poznan clambered down from the table, banging a protest out of his pretty guitar.

"Pain pills. I need them." St. Ives's voice was so very mild.

Ted on the other hand, was a bit disordered. "You mean narcotics? You're hooked?"

Very gently, and with only a hint of his usual irony, St. Ives corrected him. "I mean I have pain."

"Where?"

"Everywhere. In my joints. Arthritis. Old . . . injuries. Bad teeth." Before putting the vial away he looked down its throat.

"As a matter of fact, Teddy, I'm getting low on these. Very low. You'll have to get me some more."

Ted Poznan shook his multicolored head forcefully. "I'm sorry, George, but I think it'd be better if you just saw a doctor. A homeopath, maybe, or an Ayuervedic doctor. Narcs are not part of my realm."

George lifted his head on his bison-shoulders. This seemed to require effort. His eyes met Ted's. "Aren't they, Pozz? I had sort of thought they were. Narcs. Or had been."

Ted shied back with an astounded and slightly nervous expression. "Never, never, never."

St. Ives's smile was unshaken. "Well, maybe I was wrong about that, Pozz, but I *do* know you have the connections to help me."

"Not that way." Poznan laughed apologetically. He began to snip off the ends of the new guitar strings, which fell to the concrete floor and tinkled. "That's no kind of real help."

"It's what I need," St. Ives explained gently. "To keep playing. After all, playing's what I got left. And I think you'll help me, once you've thought about it." His eyes were dreamy and quite implacable. "I know about Cotati."

Ted dropped the dykes on the sound box of the guitar. They left a dent in the bright wood. He stood there staring at it.

Though Martha refused to take any money for the tour from Mayland Long, that did not alter the fact that he was a wealthy man, and would not by his own choice live under the level of discomfort usual to touring musicians. He liked to eat in restaurants—good restaurants—and he liked to take her with him. He said liking to eat in restaurants was a universal Chinese characteristic.

Their lunch at the Heavenly Goose had really improved the day for both of them. They had discussed yesterday's "accident" and today's altercation into insignificance. They had congratulated each other on surviving a very grainy tour.

And when they and Marty met Elen Evans on Pacific Mall, coming out of a sandwich shop in the company of Sandy, who was wearing overalls, she felt a twinge of guilt. She wondered whether garlic and hot sauce on her breath would give her away. Marty, seeing the woman who had dragged her along on errands all of the previous morning, slid unobtrusively behind the concealment of Mr. Long's legs.

Elen was wearing lavender gauze. "Kiss, kiss," she said, walking over to them with pointed toes and a great rolling of the hips. With every step her ubiquitous hand-knotted net bag knocked against her thigh, and the wooden handle of the wrench poked up like the head of a little animal. To Martha's relief, however, she did not kiss them at all, but turned her head to show a shocking red stripe down the back. "Today I'm being femme. Sandy, to achieve cosmic balance, has dressed utterly in butch."

"I have to dig a French drain," said the other woman, half-defensively. Her voice was slightly adenoidal, and she had very sloping shoulders, off which the overall straps threatened to slide.

Martha looked at the burgundy stripe. "Very . . . Santa Cruz, I'm sure. Is it permanent?"

"Oh, quite." Elen gave a throaty giggle. "I couldn't *help* but think of George all the while I was having it done. Won't he be impressed?"

No one gave her an answer.

Sandy, the babysitter, left them at the post office corner and went off to dig her drain. She looked rather depressed about it.

"Nice person, isn't she?" asked Martha as they walked along.

"Oh my, yes. Oldest friend," replied Elen. She had left her exaggerated walk behind on the mall.

"Why didn't she stop by after the concert last night? I forgot to thank her for lunch."

Elen blinked at Martha. "Sandy was at the Great American Thursday. She wasn't about to listen to us two nights in a row."

It occurred to Martha that perhaps Elen didn't know about Sandy and George. It was certainly not Martha's place to tell her. She kept her mouth shut.

They heard music as they entered by the back door of the theater, and they stood blinking in the cool, dark air. "What's that?" asked Martha. "Somebody practicing?"

Elen cocked her head. "Sure. It's George and Teddy, though what they're playing I don't know."

But Martha pursed her mouth and did not move. "I'll give you Teddy," she said. "But that's *not* George St. Ives on the pipes."

"Maybe Teddy's playing with a tape." Elen scuffed forward along the cracked hall toward the stairs. Long followed, holding Marty as though she were a bulky shopping bag. Her round legs drummed thoughtlessly against his perfect silk suit. Martha came last of all, frowning horribly with concentration and shaking her head as she went. "Not a tape, I don't think," she said to the steps in front of her.

They opened the door to the dressing room and stood

there all in a row, unnoticed by the musicians within. They listened for a long time.

"It's not right," Martha whispered at last, unhappily.

Long, who deferred to her on all questions of taste, shot her an inquiring glance. "Because it's not traditional?"

"Not at all that. Half what we do is not traditional, dear. This is . . . just not right."

Elen hissed into her ear. "Teddy's okay. He's just being Teddy. Following. It's George I can't believe. He's. . . He's . . ."

Martha sucked in her breath. "That's it! That's what makes it sound so unfinished. They're *both* following. No leader. No beginnings and ends."

"Perhaps it is a useful exercise. A discipline."

Elen snickered and stepped back out of the door. "More likely they're just stoned."

Marty, seeing one of her favorites sitting on the table, demanded her daddo put her down, which he did. Making a large, obvious circle around St. Ives, the little girl skipped over to Ted Poznan and began to talk up very loudly through the music. Long followed, to keep her out of trouble. Ted showed all his perfect teeth to Marty.

Elen was still standing behind Martha in the hall, as though she could neither bring herself to enter the room nor to leave it alone. "Actually, Ted's quite a nice-looking man, isn't he?" she said to Martha in tones of some surprise.

Though Martha immediately agreed that he was, Elen proceeded as though she said something different. "He really is. And he plays well and he means well, and he's responsible and kids like him. Never knocks things over or has moods and has to be placated, like young Trouble Himself.

"No. Certainly not."

"Much more attractive face and body than Pádraig's."

Martha had to nod.

"Then why is it that . . . that I . . . ?"

Martha didn't pretend not to understand. "I think it's

the mucus-free diet, Elen. I wonder if it doesn't depress sexual pheromones, or something like that."

Martha and Elen were called in by cries of gladness and so they had to come. They were pushed to get their instruments.

They found themselves in an uncomfortable sort of jam in that hot room—so uncomfortable that only twenty minutes later Elen dropped out. Ostensibly this was because her harp had faded completely out of tune with the others, but in reality because she could not discover what effect it was that George and Ted were trying to produce, nor what she had to offer toward it. Besides, she doubted very much the harp was being heard.

Martha stayed in longer, attempting a takeover of leadership with her fiddle, which failed. She left the two men playing and put her instrument away. Elen was still lounging in the doorway, looking at her quizzically.

"Ya can lead 'em, but ya can't drive 'em," was Martha's comment.

Without making any sound to indicate conclusion George St. Ives let his pipes fall. He grunted and took off his rag sweater, under which he wore a bleach-stained black T-shirt. Martha did not understand the applause this action received from Ted Poznan.

"Music from the heart chakra," announced Ted, holding both of his arms out into the air.

Elen, who had pulled a soda out of the refrigerator in the corner, lowered the can from her lips and whispered, "That's the problem! I should have been listening with my chakras, not my ears."

Muffled as the words were, St. Ives seemed to catch them. He leaned back until his neck touched the high table and he laughed very heartily. "Gawd! You said it, Elen. What a parade of sick cats! Music from the heart whatsit. Gawd!"

He straightened again, scratched his ribs, and looked at her. His small dark eyes were merry as Kris Kringle. "Elen," he stated. "Elen Evans. Who'd have believed you would grow up this tall."

Elen sat immobile. "Not so tall, George. Five-eight."

Right and left St. Ives swung his head, seemingly just for the pleasure of the movement. "You know what I mean, lady. Why hide it? Who is it gonna hurt to know?"

Elen was rigid, her sweating can clenched in a white hand. She opened her mouth but no sound came out. Ted, still on the high table, peered worriedly down at the top of his protégé's balding head. Martha, torn between wanting to stay with Elen and feeling the best help she could give her would be to go away before unwelcome revelations, paused half out of her seat.

"Why hide the fact that we had a thing, you and me. Once. A long time ago before you knew..."

"Anything." Elen finished the sentence for him, and then to make perfect her misery, there was Pádraig Ó Súilleabháin, standing in the doorway, looking from one to the other. "Before I knew anything at all. I thought, after all these weeks, that you were going to have enough common courtesy to keep your..."

He gave a massive shrug. "And what's wrong with it? Everyone begins somewhere. Me as an arrogant punk kid, you as a groupie."

In a quiet voice Elen called him something shocking.

Ted spoke louder. "You don't mean to insult Elen, George. I'm sure if you thought about it..."

Still with a gentle smile, St. Ives shook his head. "I'm not calling her a groupie, Pozz. I'm saying just the opposite. That she isn't a groupie now. Makes all the difference."

"Why is it"—it was Martha Macnamara who spoke, and with bitterness—"why is it that a woman with any interest in music is automatically...?" She sought control over herself, breathing deeply. "I do not like to recall the number of times I was asked, in my checkered career, who in the group I was married to or sleeping with to be allowed to go along with them. To be *allowed*!" Her voice broke. "Sometimes they were groups I'd put together too. Managed." She let out a shuddering breath.

"It makes me very glad to be on the slope side of fifty."

Ted Poznan, taking the opportunity to divert the conversation, chuckled too loudly. "It won't wash, Martha. 'Slope side of fifty,' like you were on crutches. You have the rowdiest personal life of the bunch of us."

Elen cut through. "As long as we're doing confessions here, George, at least you can tell it properly. We had a very brief thing, which was eight years ago. Hardly an affair at all."

St. Ives looked up at her from under his eyebrows. "Not to you?"

"Not to *you!*" she exploded.

"And you've hated me for it for all this time," he said evenly. "I know you have, you poor thing."

Elen sent the empty soda can spinning over the dirty floor. It was caught by Pádraig, who met her eyes. His glance was full of meaning but she could not decipher it. She was too upset to try. "I haven't exactly occupied my years with my disappointment, George. Let it alone!"

"I can't," he answered. "It's one of the things that won't let *me* alone anymore. I'm fifty-eight years old and I don't feel good about anything, in body or soul. It's got to be cleared out. All cleared out.

"You don't really know me, Elen. I'm not sure anyone does, least of all myself.

"I decided, when I was still a teenager, that I wasn't going to let friends or family—*any* personal relationship—stand between me and my music."

"Very convenient sacrifices," said Martha to no one in particular.

George wasn't listening. "Nor was I going to bend for money or popularity or any of those goodies. I know it's hard for you g—you women—to realize, but the lack of responsibilities was more than equaled by the years of deprivation!"

Elen blinked. "I'm trying to think of something you deprived yourself of, George."

"Home!" It was as though he had prepared to bellow the word and was as surprised as anyone that it came out in a sigh. "Home, family, security..."

"Not to be found on this earth," murmured Long to himself.

". . . everything the ordinary man has and doesn't know how to value."

Martha wanted very badly to ask George what he meant by an ordinary man. One who did not limit his sex to overnight encounters? She wanted to tell him that there were many people in the world who lived very stable lives and still wound up without fireplace, slippers, and the golden retriever. But it wasn't her argument, really, and George was going on.

"Maybe I was right and maybe I was wrong, but I've always tried to be straight about it. I never set out to hurt any human soul, Elen.

"And I'll tell you one other thing: what I'm going to do. I'm going to take care of all my responsibilities. That, and I'm going to make life give me what I need. That's why I broke open this ancient, abscessed secret of ours. It's a part of our—our histories which we have tried to pretend didn't exist. That's like suicide, woman. One might just as well die."

Ted Poznan, above him on the table, nodded to St. Ives's words like a happy Buddha.

Elen stood with arms crossed, as stiff as wood. "I'm not one of them, George. Not one of your responsibilities. Not much of your history, either, and certainly not your bloody business!"

George St. Ives considered her words carefully and granted them weight. "Not you. No, Elen. Perhaps I shouldn't . . ."

But she was already gone, brushing roughly past Pádraig Ó Súilleabháin. The young man stopped, uncertain, in the act of following her. St. Ives himself called the boy back.

"Pádraig. Come in. We missed you a while ago."

Pádraig looked as though he had been slapped across both cheeks. "Leave Elen be, George," he said belligerently.

St. Ives nodded agreeably. "I'm not going to chase

her. I know you two are close and I wouldn't do anything to hurt that."

When this didn't seem to soften the other appreciably, he added, "I won't talk to her again until she comes to me. How's that?"

Pádraig looked self-consciously from side to side. "Who said we were big with each other? I never said . . ."

Martha turned her giggle into a cough. George St. Ives also was smiling, with the greatest good humor she had ever seen in him. "You can't hide that kind of thing, boy. You've got puppy-dog-after-the-bitch written all over your face. Nothing wrong with it either."

St. Ives snarled both his hands in his hair in an attempt to push through it. So tangled was it that he had to pull the hands out the way they went in. "Gawd, Sully, you should be glad you've no gift for deceit. It's a bad talent to have. A bad talent.

"I called you back because I want to apologize to you. I've made this tour stinking for you, and there's no excuse." He rolled forward, rubbing the palms of both hands against his inflamed eyes.

"But you see, I wanted so much out of this tour. Dunno why. I thought, with the fiddling lady, Pozz, and me, we could really get down to something. Maybe an album. What you do wasn't part of it. In my head."

"You're forgetting Elen also," Martha interjected quietly.

St. Ives brushed flies away. "Yeah. That too. Not fair, just my . . . dream. I'm apologizing for it now. Hell, Pádraig, you've got your own problems, and the secrets that grind you up inside. Like me. Nationality's a bitch. Shouldn't have to have someone chewing up your tail on top of that."

Martha felt an alarming suspicion that George St. Ives was about to be maudlin. Perhaps Pádraig did also, for without another word he vacated the room.

Ted unfolded his legs with many winces and small pained noises. "That was great, George. Really giving. But I'm not sure that Pádraig *has* secrets grinding him up inside. He's only twenty . . ."

Martha asked the question that had been on her mind since she entered the room. "George, are you drunk?"

His howl of laughter echoed in the chamber. "Ah no, Martha. Not drunk at all. Just doped with smiles, from a little something-or-other from the cabinet of Pozz the Pusher, here."

Ted Poznan looked stricken, especially after the look Martha turned on him. "Don't call me that!

"Not drugs, Roshi. Just a perfectly natural substance that the body itself produces, which has a direct opening action on the heart chakra..."

"You mean like bee pollen? Yeast? Amino acids?" Her childlike brow was corrugated.

He choked. "Like that. Sure."

"How long?"

"It makes changes that last, Martha."

"How long?" she repeated.

He sighed. "Eight hours or so."

"And will he be... doped with smiles... for the concert tonight?"

"I certainly hope so," said St. Ives, stretching from side to side. "I'm looking forward to it."

"Probably not much," said Ted.

Martha stared intently down at her toenail at the tip of her open-toed sandal. "And you, Teddy. Are you doing this natural substance too?"

"Oh, no," he breathed. "This is just me. Weird Teddy. I'll take good care of him, Martha."

She gave him only half a smile.

Late in the afternoon it had become really too hot. Martha didn't stand such weather well, even when it was dry and the breeze was from the sea. She stayed indoors while Long took Marty to the beach.

But neither was the motel room very congenial, and there was nothing for her to do but putter about, picking up stray horse hairs that had gotten into the spread. "Music from the heart chakra," she said aloud, giving the headboard an unwarranted hostile glare. Were they going to have heart-chakra music tonight in front of a full house expecting Celtic traditional? She couldn't believe it of Teddy.

Still less of George St. Ives. Was it what they called male menopause going on there, she wondered. Or was it just the eighth week of tour? She picked up her battered black kapok-stuffed pillow and threw it into the middle of the room and sat on it where it landed. There she had a second zazen of the day: a fine angry sitting that lasted a half hour.

The sun left the window of the room and her irritation went with it.

It occurred to Martha that, under all the reverses of the day, the business of Marty was of highest importance, though adult tantrums had pushed it out of sight. But for Pádraig and Elen she might have come to harm.

It was possible Elizabeth had been right all along, and that following a group of not-so-adult adults from place to place did a child damage. She had been known to suggest that her own problems in life stemmed from that source (which had made it all the more odd that she had asked Martha to take her daughter for five days). Perhaps she trusted Long, Marty's self-declared daddo, to keep his eyes on her. More likely, she was just so used to using Grandma as a babysitter she hadn't thought it out.

Well, that situation was scheduled to end tomorrow, for they were leaving for Los Angeles and the last gig of the tour. Elizabeth would be at the motel by nine and they could sit down and talk about Marty's solitary expedition and about Judy and all. Elizabeth must be halfway down to Santa Cruz by now, if she were going to spend the night in the city, as she loved to do.

Martha felt a twinge of doubt. Her daughter was very reliable, but Martha didn't want to think of what would happen if she didn't come and it got later and later, with five hundred miles of hot road in the old, semioperative van in front of them.

She remembered the name of Elizabeth's closest friend in San Francisco. Elizabeth didn't have a large circle of friends, but those friendships she acquired were imbedded in concrete. If Shirley wasn't putting Elizabeth up for the night, she would know who was.

It took ten minutes to get the number from information, to put in her calling-card number, and to find the line open. Elizabeth was there.

Martha said that Marty was fine and they then talked about the house that Elizabeth and Fred were building in Mendocino. The insulation was just done and Elizabeth asked her mother whether she thought there was any chance of getting silicosis from the floating particles. Martha admitted her ignorance in the matter and neatly sidestepped the question of whether she'd be back in Mendocino in time to help put up the plasterboard.

Martha asked, very casually, who Judy was.

"I . . . I don't know, Mother. Some playschool mate? There are forty kids at the Montessori, and twenty or so at the day-care center that folded."

"This would be someone special. She talks about Judy a lot. Judy's unhappy. Marty went looking for her today. Alone." She told her daughter the whole story, not sparing her own responsibility. Elizabeth took it well, but could be of no further help. "Couldn't Judy be someone there? A friend of someone in the group, or a motel maid?" she asked. Martha denied it, and further added that the child had been exposed to neither television nor radio in the short stint with the band.

Elizabeth gave an oddly satisfied grunt. "Then she must be invisible."

"Uh . . . hey?"

"I've been waiting for that, Mother. Sooner or later, any child worth her salt finds an invisible playmate. In her present loneliness—"

Martha had called with the determination to remain humble and apologetic with her daughter, knowing well they did not always agree as to child rearing. But at this she could no longer restrain herself. "Loneliness? Dear one, that child has not had solitude to pee for five days!" Nor have I, she added silently.

"That's different. I remember well: hot and cold running musicians. Adults are not company to a child. Not that she'll be hurt by it," Elizabeth added quickly, perhaps remembering that she herself had suggested this vacation. "But I'm sure it's the stress of it that brought out this 'Judy' character."

In a different voice she asked, "By the by, Mother, do you still have that offensive fellow with you? The bagpiper? I think he alone might cause Marty a little bit of worry."

Martha tightened her hand on the grip of the phone. "George St. Ives is with us, of course. We'd be in deep yogurt if he left us: the group was formed to center on a good piper with an edge to his playing, and he's as good as we'll find. His manners and ideas aren't quite fashionable, perhaps, but he's had them for a good long while.

"As have I," she added, not mentioning that her own convictions, while equaling St. Ives's in seniority, were not at all identical to his. "But as for his scaring Marty, or inhibiting her in any way, he's welcome to try. She's unflappable, unfrightenable, and totally uninhibitable."

"She gets that from you," replied Elizabeth. "It skips a generation. Or from Fred, maybe. Did I tell you how he bounced around on the tops of the walls during the framing? He says he has natural talent as a carpenter, but I know it's just that he can't imagine himself getting hurt. Like any kid. On my bike I used . . ."

There was the sound of a door opening and closing in the adjoining room: the room where Marty slept. It was followed by a beating of energetic little feet against the bed frame, as Marty herself was set down. Martha heard a man's voice: not Long's. She stood up to investigate, but hearing Marty's "daddo" reply to it, she stopped in place.

Long was speaking in his deep, Oxfordish voice, which meant he was not happy. "You will not tell anyone at all, simply because you have promised me that you won't. Whether or not you agree with me. It is a matter of honor and I will hold you to it."

Was there threat in that tone? Martha thought about Stoughie, and Long's worry about the police. And about the black cable which had dragged Mayland Long almost into the hospital.

"Just a minute," she said, cutting off a story about broken spokes, a neighbor boy, and a pipe-rail fence. As she opened the connecting door she heard the outer door open and close once more. Marty was on the bed, pulling one shoelace out of its moorings in her tennie. Long stood beside the door, alone and impeccable, his dark skin shining against the rough weave of his jacket. His eyes were preoccupied and angry and did not offer confidences. "Hello," said Martha and she backed out again, returning to the telephone.

"And if he's dead,
I'll wish him rest"

The way Martha was shaking her head from side to side was intimidating, and more so was her silence. The musicians who had shown up glanced one to another. "I'm sorry as I can be," said Teddy Poznan, not for the first time. "But I really don't think this has anything to do with the MDM."

Her bothered blue eyes focused sharply on him. "MDM? Adam? But you said it was a natural substance, like bee pollen. Adam's a felony drug!"

Teddy couldn't help but wince. "It shouldn't be, Martha. And it *is* a natural substance, unlike most of what George shoves into his body."

Martha Macnamara turned away from him and he glanced around the small circle for support. Elen raised one eyebrow and looked down at her nylon-painted nails. Long's glance was flat and without pity. Pádraig Ó Súilleabháin was looking at the clock on the wall, which said seven-forty. Ted continued, "But the fact is, that stuff doesn't last so long in the human body. It's certainly not keeping him away now."

Martha's anger wore thin, curiosity taking its place. "Could he have fallen asleep somewhere? On the beach maybe?"

"Maybe he threw himself into the ocean," Elen suggested, hard-eyed.

Teddy started like a horse and rolled his eyes. "Wrong! Not after doing Adam, he didn't!"

She shrugged. "Then maybe someone with very good taste threw him in."

"Twenty minutes, yet," said Pádraig.

Martha grunted and slapped the dressing room table. "Enough. We have to plan what we'll do if he doesn't show."

Everyone around the table nodded, but apart from sitting expectantly, no one did anything for two minutes. At last Martha sighed and said, "It's a shame no one of us can sing. It's so easy to fake an accompaniment to a song, or just sit respectfully while somebody yodels. And it really uses up the time."

Pádraig, who was sitting next to Elen Evans, poked her with his finger, "Elen, can't you? You look like a girl who can sing."

"Like a very frog." The dark woman twisted her tendrils of hair around a pinkie.

"Well then, it must be that you can, Mayland. I bet you can sing like a church organ with that deep voice of yours." The young fellow's tone was teasing but he refrained from poking Long. In reply Mayland Long regarded him with eyes as pale as a parrot's and he blew his nose.

"Leave it alone, Pádraig," said Martha wearily. "None of us has enough voice to call a cab."

But Pádraig was in one of his antic moods and he would not. He wiggled and sniggered and blew a rude noise on his bass whistle. "My sister Órla can sing," he said. "Seannós."

Martha twitched an eyebrow. "She can? I never heard her."

"She sounds like this," said Pádraig. He narrowed his eyes and made a face, staring with great concentration at his hands in his lap. The sound that came out of him was startling: unrecognizable as his own voice. Elen and Teddy, who had never heard him speaking Irish, let alone singing, started visibly. The song was high in his throat and it sailed up and down in great ornate surges, without rest. It was formal, aloof, completely controlled, and as much like a cantor's invocation as any other Western music. It was, most of all, inexpressibly sad. Pádraig ended it with a great, rude laugh and punched Teddy on the shoulder.

"That's 'Caoineadh na d'Trí Muire,' 'The Lament of the Three Marys.' And then all the old people wipe their eyes and say, 'Live forever, Órla!' She is very popular with the old people, my sister."

Martha was shaking her head again, but in very different rhythm. "And I never knew. How many songs can you sing, Pádraig?"

The young man rolled his eyes at her. "No, no. I don't sing. I was imitating my sister, is all."

She took a breath. "How many songs can you . . . imitate your sister singing?"

Pádraig stared, snorted, and turned his face away. "Maybe three, but . . . aw, no, Martha. I'd feel like a grand ass out there . . ."

"Sounds wonderful, Pádraig," said Teddy, and he clapped him on the shoulder. "You can't ignore a gift."

The young man slid out from under Teddy's earnestness and sought Elen Evans's eyes. She saw a shade of real fright in his face.

The harper took Teddy's place beside Pádraig. He did not shrug off her hand on his shoulder. "My dear, you must remember that there is no one in that entire audience who knows you or whom you will ever meet again. Most likely there is no one who has any idea what this kind of singing is supposed to sound like, let alone being able to judge if you got it right."

Pádraig laughed at that and looked a bit braver.

"Don't bet on *that*," said Martha, but only to herself.

"But, but . . . I only sing on my boats, where it doesn't matter if I forget the words. What if . . ."

Elen's thin shoulders rose and fell. "Then fake it. Lilt. Sing scat. Sing vulgar curses.

"Do it for Auntie Elen, dear."

"Do it for Martha."

Pádraig glanced uneasily from face to face. Then he looked at the clock once more, stricken. With the resignation of the dying in his voice, he said, "Get me one shot of whiskey."

Martha watched the ruddy, late light that filtered through dirty glass and she listened to her own pulse. Ten minutes, now.

She felt the odd sensation that she was being flung down a tube into blackness: that she was vulnerable to forces she could not name. No stage fright, this. Martha was familiar with stage fright in all its permutations. And it was not just being let down by George. The terrible practical joke was responsible for some of it too. As was "Judy."

Bad feng shui. Bad interactions. Bad tour all around.

No. It was a very good tour, and one she'd be glad to have in her mental scrapbook, in years to come. And good musicians. She made herself say that aloud. "Good musicians, all of them!"

It gave her an idea.

"Hasn't Pádraig solved all your problems, Martha? You look so . . . so cornered."

When she turned from the gritty basement window to Long, Martha's face was still worried but it had lost the distracted look. "Almost, dear heart, but . . . I'd be grateful if you'd do me one more favor, in your endless series . . ."

Long felt an unworthy stab of disappointment. He had been kept in motel rooms every evening since Marty's arrival, and this evening Elen's friend Sandy had once again offered to take over, so that he could attend the concert. He did so like to sit in the front and watch Martha. But his face showed none of his struggle. "I am yours to command, madam. Does it mean I will miss the whole concert?"

Martha's eyes wrinkled up in laughter. "Oh, no. You'll hear well enough."

*　　*　　*

The warmth of the spotlights made him sleepy, and he had to remember not to blow his nose near the microphones.

Long felt no nervousness, sitting at his small and very nontraditional electric piano, waiting for the cues to put in his little bit of background. Not nervousness at the audience, at any rate. His very good eyes could make out the faces despite the darkness of the hall, and they affected him no more than so many faces of birds or rabbits. He would have rather had his sheet music, which Martha absolutely forbade him to take on stage, but that was not important. That his level of performance might disappoint his teacher, however, was another matter.

She didn't need him. She didn't need Pádraig's singing either, Long thought, however pleasant it was. And she had never needed St. Ives's intrusive piping. All alone with a one-pound fiddle she could hold this audience all night.

He watched Martha with quiet pride as she gave her little dip to the audience. He listened to her very short, very relaxed, and not especially witty introduction. He waited.

With a wild, ear-confusing burst Martha opened the concert, daring anyone to complain that the music was missing in some way.

Pádraig was nodding, as though he had made those sounds himself. He was wearing his bad-boy face and grinning like a fool. Oozing confidence, Long noted.

Perhaps he had just needed to be called upon to do something for which he was not really responsible, like singing, in order to feel at ease for the first time in the tour. Or perhaps he thought it was all too silly for nerves. His accordion came up in unison to Martha and, wonder of wonders, they were in perfect tune. So was Elen, on her cranky harp. And of course so was Mr. Long (no credit to him), when he added his simple runs and arpeggios.

Pádraig sang "An Bunnán Buí," but beforehand he stopped to explain how it was a poem about a bittern dead of thirst, and therefore a lesson to all not to stop drinking, no matter what the doctors might say. He got confused, and did not make it clear whether Raftery, the poet, had died or whether it was the bird, but he got quite a hand for the explanation.

And for the song.

It was working. Wonder of wonders, Pádraig Ó Súilleabháin seemed to be enjoying performing in public. Elen was beaming like the boy was her creation and Martha was making jokes with her fiddle. Teddy, still nervous and apologetic, was the perfect image of a self-effacing accompanist.

Long, himself, felt a surge of fellow feeling for the others which surprised him. Being the sort he was, he withdrew from it, and for the course of a set of reels, he played with mechanical severity. But it caught him back and held him. He exchanged a very friendly glance with Elen Evans.

Without George St. Ives, things were certainly more fun.

"Kid on the Mountain" went splendidly.

They came backstage after the first forty-five-minute set glowing and sweating. Martha looked half-drunk. She slapped both Elen and Pádraig on the back, gouging them with the butt of her bow. She gave Long an undignified, oversized wink.

Elen wiped her face with a rough paper towel. "My, my, Martha. This is a fine, big concert we have here. I feel like a child let out of school."

"It *is* a fine night," she replied. "Not well organized, mind you, but going very well. Now if we only don't have too many ethnologists in the audience . . ."

Elen stood with the paper still in her hand, breathing excitedly, when her eyes lit on the neatly stacked pipes on the table. "What a shame to feel so good just because someone isn't here."

Teddy, perhaps feeling outcast from the general high mood, mooched around the room. "I can't say for sure he hasn't been here, folks, but if so he surely left no traces behind."

Martha, seeing that all eyes were on the guitarist, gave Long a covert little hug and a kiss. She whispered in his ear a few words that caused him to explode into laughter.

"No, really. Very good," she whispered again. "And I can't let everyone out there wonder indefinitely." Louder she said, "Need brings out the best sometimes. That doesn't say anything against George's piping. It could have been any emergency."

No one replied.

There was a gentleman sitting in the front row. He had a huge handlebar moustache and thinning hair. It was Long's opinion that he was staring at Martha Macnamara with too much interest and not the proper respect. What did he think she was: a poster on a wall? Had Long's spare body carried hackles, he would have raised them at the gentleman.

But this preoccupation did not prevent him from catching his musical cues, and at the end of the first number of the second set, Martha made good her threat and introduced him, explaining to the hall that he had come in at the last moment to substitute for a sick performer. She added that he wasn't Irish, and that line got a wholly outsized laugh.

With great dignity Long stood and bowed, Chinese fashion.

Pádraig leaned over and stole Martha's microphone. "There is nobody here that is Irish. We ourselves are out of Minnesota."

After that it was all horselaughs and monkey business and a lot of very loose music which lasted until eleven. Teddy had room for two solos which were hardly tradition-al in style but were just what Santa Cruz liked to hear. Pádraig sang "Is Fada Mo Chosa gan Bróga," "Caoineadh na d'Trí Muire," and even "Casadh an t'Súgáin," of which he didn't remember quite all the words. He explained how it was about rope twisting, told them how that activity was done and what it meant as a courting ritual, and ended by advising all the audience that if they wanted to make money on visitors, they must thatch their guesthouses with straw.

In the end they were all a little silly, and Long could even forgive the man with the handlebar moustache for stopping to talk to Martha after the show.

"My, my, what a night." Elen gave a self-consciously limp-wristed farewell to the emptying hall. "Practice, preparation, and precision: my graven watchwords. La!"

Pádraig was at last too tired for either brooding or ragging. He gave Martha a shy glance, knowing he had pleased her.

She was swaying with weariness and Long stepped beside her, carrying her fiddle. Teddy, who had dashed off the stage ten minutes before them, came back out of the dressing room. "He still isn't there. Nor does he answer the phone. I'd better go find him, Martha."

Martha took a deep breath and shook her head to clear it. "Oh, yes. George. Well, I guess so," she said.

The white wickerwork in the lobby of the motel looked spidery under moonlight and the leaves of the potted tree like so many fat bellies of spiders. Martha walked through, turning her head away. "If he weren't such a . . . with his damn separate but equal accommodations . . ."

Long smiled thinly. "I don't think he would feel quite at ease bringing his lady friends into the sort of family situation we've evolved here, Martha. Nor would the young people have had as much fun together, had he been in the next room."

It was as though she hadn't heard him. "The worst of it is, we *can't* call the police for help. The man is out there somewhere doing"—and here she lowered her voice in a kind of desperate angriness—"some very illegal drugs, I bet. He wouldn't thank us at all."

"Perhaps some official agency other than the police,"

suggested Long. "Are there not telephone services for crises such as these? It occurs to me I have read about them."

The hall was too bright after the darkened lobby. They squinted against the light and made quickly for the door to the room. Martha sought in her small bag for the key to the right-hand door but Long opened the other before she had found it. He followed her into the room.

"Cold," she murmured. "Amazing how sharp the temperature differential when the sky is clear. Just this afternoon . . ."

The picture that met her stopped her flow of words by its quiet oddity. In the dark, lit only by the fluorescent light coming out of the bathroom door, sat two figures at diagonally opposite ends of the room. Their posture was the same, with arms wrapped around themselves, hands over their shoulders. Both were still, jaws clenched. One of the two, the one closest to the door, was Elen's friend Sandy, the babysitter, the digger of the French drain. The other was Marty, propped queenlike on the bed, and her face was dirty with tears.

The babysitter started, noticing them for the first time. She scrambled out of her chair. "God. You're back. I'm so glad." She stood very close to Martha but she did not relax her rigid arms.

Martha's glance, shifting birdlike from Sandy to the child on the bed, was curious and still a bit angry. "It's too cold in here," she said. "Do you still have on the air conditioning?"

Sandy looked down at her blue arms. As though appreciating her state for the first time, she shivered and her teeth began to chatter. "God. God, no. It's just her—uh—here, and I never knew that children had such a weird energy."

Martha stared blankly at the woman, who was young, thin, and slightly spinsterish despite the Egyptian gauze dress and Gypsy jewelry she had put on. Long, however, made a noise that was halfway between a hum and a hiss of anger. He slid past the two women and hit the light switch.

Marty's face wore a very concentrated, adult air, and she reacted to the sudden brilliance by screwing her eyes shut. She clenched her jaw harder and looked pained.

"Is she . . . is she within the bell curve?" asked Sandy. "I mean, is she normal?" She shrugged her shoulders apologetically. "I guess I don't know children very well. Probably I shouldn't have said I'd watch her. I don't know what's wrong.

"I gotta go. I'll call you tomorrow." The young woman was out the door and gone before Martha could think of a polite response.

Long sat on the edge of the bed and put his outsized hand against Marty's face. Martha joined him. "What's wrong, honey-lamb? Did Sandy and you have a fight?"

There was the noise of a siren in the distance and the light went dim. Martha raised her head and the sound became immediate: thin, metallic, keening. She thought at first that it was pipes, and a moment later changed her mind and thought it was a sea bird. Cold rose up from the bed and struck at her.

"Martha, look." Long's whisper was strained. He held Marty's face between his hands and it was not her face at all but the face of an idiot: lolling, slack-mouthed, and with a round, overhanging brow.

"Marty!" There was no recognition. She touched the horrible face and it was clammy, even to her chilled fingers.

"What is it, Martha?" Long's eyes were daffodil yellow and round-wide in the darkness. His lips were pulled back with either amazement or fear and he looked all eyes and teeth. "What is the truth of this happening?"

Martha's face, in its lineaments so like her grand-daughter's, almost mirrored the child's expression, so mystified was she. Then, in a moment, she was in a bright red rage. She struck the girl with both hands, left and then right. "No!" she shouted. "Stop it this instant."

Marty squinched her face together as the light came

up in the sudden silence. She took a deep breath. "You're back," she said, and then she lay down again under the covers.

"How could I tell you, Martha? Tell you what, that I heard a noise and the lights failed and for a moment your granddaughter looked like another person?"

"Yes, you could have told me that." Martha picked up her nightgown and put it down again. Having had to be strong for too many people and for too long, she was now in no mood to be reasonable with the one man she could trust.

"That would have made me seem a very timid creature, I fear." Long laughed. "But Martha—you know I do not have the right way of looking at things sometimes..."

"I know you *think* you don't."

He sighed and the sigh set off a fit of coughing. "What... what was it? A visitation? Possession?"

"Or an allergy. Or a nervous reaction to faulty electricity. I don't know, my dear. But I want it to stop."

He tried the sigh again, and this time it worked. "It seems to have. And tomorrow we leave this place, so the faulty wiring will be behind us. And her."

"She will be home, please God!" Martha frowned again, as she remembered the problem that had been subsumed in this one. "And speaking of things behind us, there's a missing musician to find. May I ask one more favor of you, Mayland? Will you stay with Marty while I look?"

The room being warmer now, Long had taken off his jacket. Now he swayed from side to side in his chair, in unhappy protest. "Martha, I am always at your service, as you well know, but I am really rather weary of being left at home to mind the baby!"

"Oh." Martha glanced at him with some surprise, so rarely did he fail to bend to her wishes. After a moment she began to grin. "Right on! I've been abusing you terribly. You must remind me."

He turned his head self-consciously away in embarrassment and Martha thought at that moment that his form and his features were very beautiful. "That is hardly the case. But I think in this instance I would do better to look than you."

For a moment she looked relieved. "What will you do if you find him, dear? If he's loopy on drugs or sick..."

"I have no idea, Martha. What did *you* intend to do?" She shrugged. "No idea. So you're as well off."

"Home safe," she called to the closing door.

Martha was putting on her nightgown when Marty went into the toilet in the other room. As there was a small-seat on the pot, and as Marty was quite proficient in her bathroom skills, there was no need for her grandmother to interrupt her own activity. Martha arranged her tousled hair in the mirror, wishing for the twentieth time that she had not had it cut short, and she heard the flush and then two doors closing. For five seconds more she played with uneven curls at her forehead and then her eyes widened and she made a dash into the outer hall.

"Marty! Where are you going?"

Marty's naked form disappeared around the turn of the hall and into the empty motel lobby. Martha scooped her up a few steps after and withdrew her own cotton-flanneled body as quickly as she could into her room. She slapped her granddaughter down on the bed.

It was a strained, preoccupied little face that met hers. "Where were you *going*, Martha Frisch-Macnamara, at this hour of the night?" Martha asked her.

The answer was slow. "To find Judy. Judy's lost and crying."

Martha took a breath. "Who is Judy, Marty?"

Marty frowned more deeply at adult obtuseness. "Judy's a kid, of course."

"Crying now? Is she crying now? Do you hear some-body crying at this minute?"

Marty closed her eyes, as though listening. Martha, too, listened, for she was not entirely convinced, as Elizabeth was, that this needy friend of the child's was made up.

After thirty seconds of sifting through the noises of the
lavatory and distant voices coming from another part of the
motel, she was still not sure whether there was the sound
of a child crying or not. She looked to Marty for verifica-
tion and found the girl sleeping, limp as seaweed.

Martha got up, went into the bathroom, and washed
her face in cold water.

It was four or slightly after when Long returned, and
he found Martha curled in an armchair, as sound asleep as
her granddaughter. All her gray curls had slid to one side
of her head and her neck was so crimped by the chairback
that she was snoring quietly. He considered picking her
up as he might Marty and depositing her on the bed, but
the lèse majesté proved too much for him and he woke her
instead.

"Martha? I have had as bad a luck as any feng shui
can offer. It does not seem our wandering piper is to be
found."

Martha stared up at him with the intensity of a person
who is not quite awake. He was back-lit by the bureau
lamp and looked impossibly slender. "Oh. What time . . . ?
Maybe Elen or Teddy . . . ?"

"Perhaps." Long walked to the bedside table, took a
fresh Kleenex, and blew his nose. "I presume they're out
looking also, as they're equally undiscoverable. Pádraig I
have found, strangely enough." Taking off his jacket and
his shoes, he sat down on one of the beds, took one of his
stockinged feet in either hand, and massaged it.

Martha whipped her brain awake. "Why strangely?
His room is two from ours."

He made a half-circle out of his back and stretched
left and right in a sort of unconscious yoga. "Certainly, my
dear. But I didn't find him there, but instead on the
boardwalk. In the Riva bar."

Martha sat upright. "Drinking? Our Pádraig? That's
twice tonight. I'm not really supposed to encourage that,
you know. I promised his mother."

"Enmeshed in conversation piscatorial—and drinking like a fish all the while."

She snorted. "What a line! Did you rehearse it?"

His yellow eyes seemed to glow for a moment. "Yes, I did. I'm not very original, you know, and so I have to cherish whatever comes to me. Can you guess what young Ó Súilleabháin drinks, when he's out for sport?"

Martha got up on legs filled with pins and needles. "Michelob?"

Long glanced at her, torn between amazement and disappointment. "Exactly. How?"

"It's the cheapest thing you can get, at the Riva bar," she said, limping into the bathroom. "I've been there." She put her head out the door again. "You mean he's not with Elen?"

"Not when I saw him," he replied.

"I thought they were a thing," she said, and her face looked troubled. "Just as well. Very strange pairing, those two." She closed the door again.

Long lay down on the bed, idly considering Martha's last words, until he began to laugh. "I can name you a stranger one," he called aloud at the bathroom door.

Had the land behind the Santa Cruz boardwalk been flat, the sun would have been over the horizon by now. But Santa Cruz was backed by little mountains, stamped black against the eastern sky, and the circus colors of dawn shone only on the wavelets far out in the bay.

The fishing boats were in and the cool air was pungent. Behind the counters of the open-air seafood vendors, a few men were moving back and forth in bloody aprons.

The patrol car drove the length of the pier very slowly, like a basking fish. The vendors waved to the clean young man behind the wheel with a great show of friendliness. Forcing a smile, he waved back.

There was nobody here yet except those who had to be here. The night shift had already ticketed the three cars left parked along the pier (one for the second night) and there was nothing to do. Officer Scherer parked at the end of the pier and got out.

How pink and coral and sky-blue the water was out there. Like Indian jewelry. It made him think of deserts. And how black straight down here, by the palings. The snarled lines of nylon left by the day fishermen made cobweb shapes. It was damn cold to be out in a cotton shirt.

Scherer would have liked a cup of coffee. If he asked at any of these places, one would be presented to him in a hurry. He didn't like to do that; it made him self-conscious. Officer Scherer had only been on the force for a few months, and was painfully aware of his uniform. Still, if he had a cup of coffee, he'd be in better shape to watch the sun colors spread from west to east, across the water. He walked slowly over the gray pavement, like a man with heavy issues on his mind. He was so tall that his poor posture could not diminish him. He passed between faded wooden tables and around the railed holes in the pier where people fed the seals. No seals at the moment.

He found something faintly interesting: a rope tied onto one of the uprights of the rails. A crabbing net. Such a thing shouldn't be there, down among the palings like that, and it shouldn't have been left overnight. It wasn't the concern of the Santa Cruz police to enforce the fishing regulations, but Scherer was a young officer and crabbing was a lot of fun. You never knew what you might find. He leaned over to haul the net in.

Funny, brittle sort of rope, and firmly snagged on something. As he hauled there would be give for a couple feet and then no more. Yet it wasn't the palings that had snagged the rope, for the feel swelled and ebbed with the water. Holding the rope in one hand, Scherer crouched down and pulled his flashlight out of his belt.

It was a very strange thing at the end of the rope, floating in the water of high tide. It was not like a log, nor yet like a large dogfish, both of which were occasionally washed under the pier.

A dead seal. A seal caught in the crab net and

drowned. Scherer, policeman though he was, felt the Ecotopian's surge of fury at the death of any sea mammal by the hand of man. He shone the flashlight at the place where the rope had caught it.

He started twice, and losing the rope and the flashlight, fell flat onto his back. Officer Scherer made a shrill sound and the fish vendors came running.

"It's horrible! Horrible," he said, his deep voice cracking. "Christ! And all blue!"

Hesitantly, they all stepped over to the hole.

It was nine o'clock and past time to be starting, but no one had begun loading the van. Neither George St. Ives nor Elizabeth Macnamara had shown. The California sun had touched the window only five minutes ago and was now crawling over the carpet to the bed where Elen Evans had put herself. The dark woman gave it no mind: she lay as though waiting for the funeral flowers to surround her and her motionless eyes were fixed on the ceiling.

Pádraig Ó Súilleabháin was in a chair, but hardly sitting. His legs were splayed out with the flexibility of an adolescent's and his arms dangled to the floor. His eyes were very red, as though he had been crying. Or had a hangover.

Across the tiny round table sat Mayland Long, his mug in his hand and the perforated tea-strainer spoon still in it. He was, if possible, more devastated by his cold than he had been the day before, but he sat straight, mindful of his spine. On the hard green carpet before the two Marty Frisch-Macnamara was covering the motel stationery with crayon marks. She favored purple over all other colors. The sun touched her fingers and she took note of it. She put her purple crayon down in the sun and stared at it.

"Surely we can survive one more day at this," offered Long. He was wondering whether perhaps Pádraig and Elen had had a falling-out. Unless they began talking, he might never know. That would be, for a creature of his curiosity, intolerable.

Elen turned a glowering face to him. "What do you mean, 'we,' white man? It isn't you going out there . . ."

Long's smile lit up his face? "White man? Inapposite, even as an insult." But her remorse outpaced his response. "Oh, God! I'm sorry, Mayland. It isn't true, either. You've had just as much misery on this tour as any of us, and you don't even need the money. I don't know why you didn't just go home three weeks ago."

The ghost of a teasing smile passed over Pádraig's face and was gone. "I know why he didn't. His girlfriend wouldn't let him!"

Long's fingers wrapped more tightly around the mug, showing he was not impervious to such remarks, but before he could open his mouth there came a knock on the door, and Teddy Poznan's voice saying something which was garbled by Marty's shout of "Teddy! Let Teddy come in."

Long stood and stared, his yellow eyes sharp. It was as though he would deny Marty's request, but after a moment he called, "The door is open. Come in." When the policeman came in with Ted, he alone in the room did not seem surprised.

"Mr. Stoughie sent you, I presume?" Still gripping his mug, Long advanced to meet them. The officer, a sandy-haired and very clean young man, merely blinked at the sight of a man with negroid complexion and mongoloid features, dressed in the height of tropical fashion and glaring at him with yellow eyes.

"I brought them," mumbled Teddy, rubbing his ugly-nailed right hand through his beard. And then the man with the handlebar moustache—the one whose attentions toward Martha Macnamara had been in Long's mind excessive only the evening before—walked into the motel room as though he owned it.

"George is dead," said Teddy, and he met Long's eyes. "He's dead: he died last night while we were all looking for him."

The room rang with silence.

After five seconds the man with the handlebar moustache spoke. "We can't exactly say when, Mr. Poznan." He had a very soothing voice.

Elen had sat up on the bed as soon as the policeman entered. Now she said, "No." Pádraig said nothing and he did not move in his seat, but the eyes of both, the brown eyes and the blue eyes, bore the identical blankness of shock.

"I'm sorry," continued the stranger. "I'm Detective-Sergeant Anderson. There is no good way to tell that news to people." He waited a respectful while, watching.

It seemed to him that they were behaving in typical form for having just heard about a death that concerns them, but doesn't concern them too closely. The girl (for Detective Anderson was fifty-five and to him Elen Evans was a girl) stared at the wall and she shuddered once. The boy that he remembered to have an accent had now begun to shake his head.

The black or Oriental man standing in front of him, though. . . . Who had sat at the back of the stage and played the piano. . . . One got no change out of him. He had had an uncommunicative face last night and it was no different now, except that he stared at Anderson himself with a peculiar intensity. It was as though *he* were trying to learn something important from the policeman's reactions, instead of the other way around.

"How did he die?" Long asked, very collectedly.

"They found him—" Teddy began, but a hard hand on his shoulder silenced him. The guitarist widened his eyes and the blond part of his hair fell in his face.

"I'd like to be able to tell it once, with everyone together," said Anderson apologetically. "And I believe there's one of your band that isn't here."

Long smiled grimly. "You know quite well that there is. The leader. Mrs. Macnamara is sitting zazen in the next room."

Anderson had thinning hair and a tan on the top of his head that was darker than that on his face. His gray eyes crinkled. "That so? How interesting. Not quite the usual thing, is she?"

Long did not reply.

"I'd still like to see her," continued Anderson. "It's really quite important."

The connecting door opened, causing everyone to start.

Martha Macnamara was cool in a blue print dress which matched her eyes and set off the pink of her complexion. Her gray hair shone silver in the window light. "Zazen is no kind of trance," she said quietly. "I can both see and hear things. Please sit down, Sergeant, and tell me how George died."

Anderson did sit down, on the chair that had been occupied by Long. Martha sat on the bed across from him and Elen came over and sat beside her, touching. Pádraig had not moved from his sprawl in the chair across the table from Anderson, though he withdrew to the far side of the seat. Long remained standing beside Teddy (who bit the nails of his left hand nervously), and the uniformed policeman, who seemed a bit nervous himself.

"We can't be too exact about either the time or the . . . cause of death at this time," Anderson said, glancing from one face to the other. Ted Poznan muffled a harsh cry that was like a laugh but not really a laugh at all. "All I can say to you is that he was found by Officer Scherer here at the pier at six this morning. It appears"—Anderson put emphasis on this word—"that he was—"

"Drowned?" It was Elen who blurted what was on almost everyone's tongue.

"Hung."

Elen gasped. Everyone stared.

"He was found hanging down from one of the openings in the concrete of the pier. Where people feed the seals, you know."

Pádraig Ó Súilleabháin made a muffled noise. His hand hit the table, hard. Now it was Martha's turn to shake her head. "Oh, how terrible! How terrible," she whispered into her cupped hand. "Where we fed . . ."

"It was a very unusual rope," continued Anderson, even more diffidently than before. "It didn't look capable of holding his weight. I cut a piece of it, but it immediately began to come apart. See?" And he offered for their inspection a length of twisted dry grass, with a loop at one end, very familiar to all.

"*Súgán*," stated Pádraig Ó Súilleabháin. "Hay rope. Grass, in this one."

"That's what I thought." The policeman nodded. "As you described in the concert last night? 'Twisting the Rope'?"

Parting Glass

It was Martha who broke the silence. "Yes, exactly. And it's our own rope, of course. You must have seen it coiled over the microphone last night at the concert."

Anderson's receding hairline made his forehead look very high, and his eyebrows ascended into it. "So you remember me? I'm flattered, Mrs. Macnamara. But no, I don't remember the rope. There are so many wires and cables—"

"It wasn't there, Martha." Pádraig spoke up. "That was the night before last we put it up. Last night it was . . . I don't know. In the cellar room, maybe." He turned to the detective, sullenly. "It is not *our* rope. It is my own. I made it out of the dry grass behind the hall, the day before yesterday. But not to hang George St. Ives. You are right; it is not strong enough for that."

Anderson's forehead reached halfway back his head when he widened his eyes. "I hadn't suggested that it was made for that purpose, Mr. Su-ill . . . Sull—"

"Patrick Sullivan, in English."

There was a stir among the musicians. "But that really isn't your name," said Teddy. "Martha told us to be careful . . ."

Pádraig waved the matter away with both hands. "That was my mother's idea. She is very big on Gaelic culture." He glanced back at the sergeant. "We are Irish speakers."

"Sometimes." He gave a rueful chuckle.

Anderson looked surprised. "Forgive me. But you mustn't, Mr. Sue-lowin, go racing ahead of me, or you'll come to grief over it. It's early days yet to talk about homocide. Let me ask my questions in their proper order.

"First, let's finish with this rope. The knot, you see, is not the most common thing. It looks like it was made by someone who knew what they were doing."

"It's a simple lark's head," replied Pádraig readily. "A knot you use to tie up to a stanchion."

"A sailor's knot?" asked the detective.

"All knots are sailor's knots," he replied.

Anderson nodded. "And I'm to understand that you're a sailor?"

There was an unsettled pause, as Pádraig stared at the detective. "You can understand that."

Anderson seemed not to take this admission, or brag, for more than its face value. "And was Mr. St. Ives a sailor also?"

Pádraig shifted in his seat. His knee fell loosely out against the chair arm. "He was from Cape Breton. Everyone knows that. But I think there's more than birth to being a sailor."

Again the detective nodded. "Was that 'lark' as in the bird? About the knot, I mean." He wrote in his little notebook with a ball-point pen.

"Okay for that. Now comes the great routine. . . ."

There was a rustle as Anderson's listeners either relaxed or straightened themselves at this news, depending on individual temperament. Long did neither one.

"Very dull, to begin with. I have to ask for identification from everyone here."

Martha stiffened momentarily and very carefully did not look at Mayland Long. Elen yawned and Pádraig began to haul his cheap cardboard suitcase out from under the table. Martha produced her purse from under the bed. "Driver's license and major credit card?" she asked tightly.

"I can do without the credit card." The inspector examined the license perfunctorily and then handed it on to his associate. "I see I have one year seniority on you, Mrs. Macnamara. I would have guessed ten or fifteen."

She did not reply.

Long was standing behind her, and he held in his spidery hand a driver's license and a blue American passport Martha had never seen before. Anderson took it.

"Born in Hong Kong," he murmured.

"That was a long time ago. I have been in this country for some years."

Anderson glanced up. With his cool gray eyes and high forehead he looked the picture of an academic. "I would have thought, to listen to you, that you had spent those years in England."

"Hong Kong is a British colony," answered Long evenly. Officer Scherer received the passport from his supervisor.

Elen Evans lay flat on the bed with her eyes closed. She threw the detective her wallet, and it hit his arm. Without rancor he leafed through it until he found the driver's license in its cellophane sheath.

"You have until the end of the month to get this renewed, Miss Evans. In case you forgot."

Elen gave a groan and did not open her eyes.

"Mr. Ó Súilleabháin?" This time Anderson got the vowel sound reasonably correct.

"A moment," replied the young man, who was fishing under his underwear in the cardboard suitcase. His passport was in much worse shape than Long's, and to Martha's great amazement, it was also American. She scratched her nose and looked at Anderson.

He examined the thing. "You also I would have guessed to be younger."

"I'm not a child." The reply was surly.

"That's not what I meant at all. So your mother was born in the States? That's double citizenship, isn't it?"

Pádraig nodded and let his hands dangle between his splayed knees. Martha, who knew Pádraig's mother, scratched her nose harder.

Anderson seemed impervious to the young man's rudeness. "Well, lucky for you. I've often envied people of double culture. I imagine it's a source of strength."

Pádraig let his unhappy eyes settle on Teddy, who had not moved from his position by the bureau. "I already showed them," said the guitarist, though no one had asked. "At the station."

"I'm sorry. I'll have to keep these things for a little while. I know it's inconvenient, but life without a car is quite workable in Santa Cruz, and we'd prefer that none of you left the city today. At least."

A glance of shared misery passed from Pádraig to Martha to Teddy. Elen seemed nearly asleep.

"Okay." The detective settled back in the chair that had belonged to Long. "I'd like to know when was the last time everyone here saw George St. Ives?" Anderson pronounced the name in perfect French, which drew a slight smile on Martha's face. "The uh . . . Québecois was a few generations back in his line, I think," she whispered to Anderson. "I never heard him called anything but Saint Aiives."

"And I try so hard," said Anderson, with a sigh.

"Elen and I last saw him at about two, in the rehearsal room—the dressing room, really—of the Hall. He and Teddy were branching out into new-age sound. That's two P.M., I mean."

"That goes for me too," added Elen. "I was with Martha."

Anderson had a spiral notebook, into which he wrote with a gold ball pen.

"And me," added Pádraig. "I was there, too, at the same time. I did not see him later than that."

Long felt Anderson's gaze, but waited to be asked. "For me it was a bit later, Sergeant. I last saw him walking down the hall toward the front door of the motel, at approximately three-ten yesterday afternoon."

"Approximately three-ten," murmured Anderson, his gray eyes reflective. "That's very close for an approximation."

Long smiled with his mouth closed. "There is a clock in the hall."

"Still, most people would not think to look at it, or would not remember."

"Most people," said Long dryly, "are not as literal-minded as I am. It is my handicap."

Teddy did not wait to be asked. "I saw him last. At five or five-thirty. Out front by the flower boxes. I tried to drag him to Right Livelihood for some soup, 'cause he didn't look good. He wouldn't go."

"He didn't look good?" Anderson's voice expressed only polite interest.

Teddy sat down on the corner of the mattress, by Martha. The bed bounced. "Well, yeah. I'd been worried about him. He'd been a bit run down."

No one said anything to this, although Elen glanced at Martha and Martha glanced at the rug.

"Which is St. Ives's room?" Anderson asked Martha.

She squirmed as she replied that she did not know. "He never stayed with the rest of us," she added.

He stared at her in clear disbelief, even when the others in the room corroborated her statement. "Well, we'll find out," he said shortly.

The sergeant was quiet for a moment, while all glanced from one to another. Then he asked, "And where did we all go last night, after the concert?"

The air in the room stretched tight.

"Out looking for George," said Elen. "Every mother's child of us."

"Except me." Martha spoke up. "I stayed here."

The sergeant's expression was neutral, almost dull. "Did you go out in groups?"

Long's grunt turned into a series of coughs. "No, Sergeant, we did not. Foolish of us . . ."

Anderson bit on the end of his metal pen and did not look up. "Unfortunate for me. And no one found him?"

"I did not."

Pádraig shook his head. "I really wasn't looking very hard. I was drinking beer."

Anderson glanced up, cheered by this news. "Where was that?"

"At a bar on the pier. White and green and blue."

"The Riva, Sergeant," explained Long.

Anderson nodded and wrote. He cleared his throat. "Now. St. Ives hadn't looked well, Mr. Poznan says? Did anyone else notice that?"

"Oh, yes," Martha replied. "He never looked healthy. He drank too much, and did—did not take care of himself."

"He had a liver problem, I think," offered Long. "His skin was quite yellow."

Martha let out a rough laugh. "Is that a joke, dear?"

"Of course not," replied Long, in confusion.

"Drink will destroy a man," said Pádraig, rubbing his red eyes with his many-scarred knuckles.

Anderson made a noncommittal grunt and kept writing. "What about you, Miss Evans? Did St. Ives look ill to you?"

Elen put two fingers to her mouth and spent a few seconds that way, silently. "It was more the way he acted. Irritable and depressed. A bear, in fact." She tilted her head and met the detective's eyes. "It's no secret that he wasn't getting along with us. Any of us, except possibly Teddy."

"Depressed." Anderson repeated that word heavily. "Do you all agree that Mr. St. Ives had been off-color and depressed in the last few days?"

Martha nodded. Long said, "Quite." Teddy shook his head, in pity, not negation, and Elen sat without moving. Pádraig alone spoke up.

"I don't know why you say that. Myself, I think he was happy making other people feel bad. And didn't he walk around with a smile on his face yesterday?"

"George was drunk yesterday," whispered Martha.

"I don't like George. I think he's nasty!" Marty came up from under the bed. Her purple crayon was covered with dust and the sun had bent it into a half-circle. Anderson's eyebrows went up to their full extension and his moustache stood out sideways.

"There's a child in here? Good grief, I didn't know. I am sorry," he said earnestly to Martha. "I would not have blurted all this out, had I known a child was present."

Marty stared at this outburst and Martha gave another snort of weary laughter. "Marty? It would take more than a policeman's interrogation to scare her."

"I don't like George!" repeated Marty stubbornly, knowing she wasn't supposed to say that in public. "He isn't nice to anyone. He made Pádraig cry!"

"He did not!" said Ó Súilleabháin hotly. "What a thing to say!"

Marty stared at her friend, deflated. "Well then, he made Elen cry!"

"Wrong again, little peeper," drawled Elen Evans. She leaned forward and pulled Marty up on the bed beside her. "Maybe it was actually Martha Frisch-Macnamara who cried?"

Anderson looked from the child to Martha. "Your daughter?"

"Granddaughter, of course," replied Martha, but the mistake didn't seem to offend her. "Traveling with us for a week. George St. Ives didn't have much of a way with children."

The uniformed policeman pulled on the knees of his trousers an instant before Detective Anderson moved to stand up. This interested Martha, and she was on the brink of asking him what cues he had used, when the terrible intelligence the officers had brought into the room weighed down on her again and she said nothing. Anderson looked around him, catching each pair of eyes in the most casual fashion. He sat back down in a more central position.

"I'm sorry the poor man is dead," he said. "And I'm glad that he wasn't anyone's son. Or lover, here. That it doesn't mean the end of the world to one of you people.

"But his death was an awkward one, and so it's my business, and I'm afraid I'm going to have to become a bit of a bother to each of you.

"It's my private opinion that no one ought to be allowed to run around by himself, ever. It makes my job so much harder. Just think how much smoother things would be if you all had done your searching by the buddy system. Now I'm going to have to get statements from each of you as to where you went and what you did, and you will become very confused and so will I. Also, none of the people you met will remember seeing you when my colleagues check them out. As they must do. It will all be strenuous and very depressing. Let's start now."

The statement-taking took thirty-five minutes and was, in fact, quite wearing on all. Pádraig was worst, for he had no notion what time he had gotten to the bar nor what time he left. Afterward he walked around the streets for some measureless interval and noticed neither direction nor living soul. He'd gotten lost.

Elen had some sense of order. She had walked the pier, and been to a few bars, not including the Riva. She had borrowed the van (she carried the spare keys) and driven out along the ocean, where she had had engine trouble for a little while. She had returned by four-thirty and was therefore very tired, and she had no corroboration for her story at all.

Long knew exactly where he had been, and when. He had started along the boardwalk and spoken to the clerk who was closing up the last souvenir shop. He had described St. Ives to her. By one A.M. he had been up and down the pier and had met Pádraig in the Riva.

Pádraig stared at Long, astounded. "Right enough! You *were* there. I thought it was my imagination. Was I drunk?"

Long looked tolerant and did not answer.

Finding no sign of St. Ives by the ocean, he had walked north and prowled the night places of the mall. He would give Detective Anderson a list of places that might remember him. He had gotten as far as the Ocean Street bars before giving up. He'd come home at four.

Anderson looked as tired as any of them. He cleared his throat. "Thank you, people. It sounds like a miserable night for all concerned. Except, perhaps, for Mr. Súilleabháin."

"It is the morning that is miserable," said Pádraig. Anderson smiled.

"Well, there has been no medical report on the body yet; we'd like to find next of kin first. But after the report does come in, the chances are good we will need to speak with each of you again. So, though I hate to have to repeat myself—"

"We can't leave," Elen broke in.

Martha thought of the calls—the explanations—she would have to make. She felt sick and knew that would only get worse.

Anderson's mouth opened, as though he were about to say something to mitigate those three uncomfortable words, but he took a slow breath before adding, "Only for a short while, I hope."

As the officials stepped toward the door of the room, Martha stood, and on impulse she said, "May I see him, Sergeant Anderson? May I see George?"

Anderson gave her a surprised glance.

So did Long. "I don't think there is any need for that, Martha," he said.

"My need."

Anderson nodded slowly. "Certainly, ma'am. A second identification would be very helpful. When did you have in mind?"

"Now." Martha spoke the word with such firmness the sergeant blinked. She led him out of the motel.

Teddy, Pádraig, and Elen were left in the room, standing, sitting, or sprawled over the beds: all alone together. Long was left holding the baby.

Anderson walked slowly beside Martha. The trees above their heads sagged with the weight of fluffy red flowers. Somewhere on the mall a jazz band was playing, heavy with brass. Martha kept darting glances over her shoulder.

Twice along the length of Laurel Street Anderson apologized for not having brought a car. "I find I move quicker in the central town without it," he said. "But I can call for one. . . ."

Martha waved this aside. "I have a van parked behind the motel, if I'd wanted to take it. I suppose that would be okay, since you're holding my license. Foolish thing to do,

though, in Santa Cruz. And I'm not in geriatric care yet."
She looked again over her right shoulder, at the uniformed policeman, who followed two steps behind.

Anderson mumbled that geriatric care had never entered his mind, but Martha interrupted him, stopping dead on the street. "Does he *have* to walk behind us? Because you're of higher rank? Or is it to prevent my running away?"

Officer Scherer, brought up suddenly, showed the whites of his eyes like a startled horse. Detective Anderson tightened his lips to control his expression. "I really don't know, ma'am. Why are you walking behind us, Dan?"

Scherer shrugged. "The sidewalk is narrow."

Martha considered this. "Oh," she said at last and continued walking.

"It was he who found the body?" asked Martha.

"Yes, at about six this morning," Anderson replied, gesturing over his shoulder. Martha turned around again, and her face was drawn with concern.

"That must have been terrible for you!"

Scherer brought himself up to his full height, and he was about to deny any such thing, but instead he found himself saying, "Yeah. It was pretty bad."

Martha turned her china-blue eyes on Anderson. "Do you really expect him to do a day's work after a shock like that? I'd think he'd be allowed to go home."

"I don't *want* to go home!" Scherer sought his superior's eyes, in outrage.

"Dan Scherer's a tough cookie," the detective said dryly.

Detective Anderson might have considered Martha Macnamara a dingy sort of woman, for she said the strangest things. So very distractible (or else operating out of a very different logic). Had she not played the fiddle the way she did . . . Had she not stood there in the motel room and said the single word "now" with that peculiar power, like the sound of an explosion far off . . . But for these things, her other unconventionalities might have put Anderson off.

He certainly might have found some quicker way to get this viewing over with. She was who she was, however, and he walked contentedly beside her and let her set the pace. Anderson liked to think and walk together, and he had a lot to think about.

As a younger man, he had been often afraid of his own reactions toward the people that made up the cases he investigated. He had kept a certain inviolate distance. But years had taught him that godlike objectivity, even if possible, was far too much trouble.

Especially when he wasn't sure any crime had been committed at all. Walking beside Martha, he found it difficult to believe there had been a crime. Musicians were not stable people, he was well aware, and the dead man had been depressed.

He wasn't at all sure it hadn't been murder, either. He remembered Theodore Poznan's attitude at the police station: self-righteous, martyred, more than a little hostile. And yet he'd come on his own. That indicated either innocence or intelligence.

"My own rope," Sullivan had said, belligerently. And he hadn't even tried for the appearance of being sorry. He was quite willing to admit his dislike for the victim (the deceased, Anderson's mind censored for him). Anderson suspected that the boy might have said more, had wiser heads not surrounded him. Well, there'd be time for that, should circumstances warrant it.

He remembered how Elen Evans threw her billfold at him. He hadn't liked it at all.

He did, however, like Martha: her face and coloring and the way she dressed. He also felt he could get along with the Chinese—Long—if the fellow ever loosened up. He wondered what the guy had against him that made him so clearly regard Anderson as the enemy. Of course, if he had put that cruel and fragile rope around St. Ives's neck, that would be enough reason to resent the police.

"I suppose this caught you in the middle of a dozen other things," Martha said, somewhat apologetically.

Anderson grunted, and then, feeling he had been too

brusque, added, "A dozen little things like purse snatchings, maybe. Two auto thefts today. Not things that interest the detective force a lot. One missing child."

"Oh, dear!" Martha's eyes went round and then narrowed. "Do they think it's . . . was it . . . ?"

"Molested? No, we don't think so. It was a retarded kid. From an institution." Seeing her face, he felt compelled to add, "We suspect a custody sort of thing, and the boy's all right. He's been getting visitors lately, and . . . well, I wouldn't worry."

Or not about that, he added to himself.

They turned onto the mall itself, where silk trees made a pattern of lace on the bricks of the walkway. The star jasmine was in bloom and the air was full of the scent of it. From here the jazz band was very loud.

"You like kids?" Anderson bellowed over it. "I've got three." And two ex-wives, he added silently.

"I like some of them," answered Martha without excess enthusiasm. Her steps grew slower and slower. Officer Scherer had to shy off to the outside to avoid treading on her heels.

"I wonder," said Martha, and after a few moments, added, "I think there's something that might be relevant to this. Only might, Sergeant. It happened the day before yesterday."

Anderson came a very little bit closer and made a responsive noise.

She told him about the trick with the cable and the door. She spoke concisely and tried neither to exaggerate nor to minimize its importance. She did not forget to mention the fact that St. Ives's pipes had been in the back room.

When she was done, and had described Long's small injuries, Anderson said, "Ah. Yes. That's an old fraternity prank. Helps if the victim is drunk."

"I'm glad he wasn't!"

"Miserable trick," muttered Don Scherer behind them. "I'd be p—tee'd off." Martha spared him a grateful glance.

"Well, the bit about the double coil of rope under the

door isn't part of it," admitted the detective. "Not in the best frat houses, anyway. You say it was a length tied out of the middle of the cord?"

"Closer to this end." Crimson fuzz fell from the trees around Martha's face, like a light, bloody rain. "We wondered if that might have been nothing but an oversight on the joker's part."

The detective shrugged and blew flower bits out of his large moustache. "One would hope so. But no one admits to this cuteness?"

Martha sighed and shook her gray curls. "Not then, they didn't. I didn't think of it this morning. Maybe the shock of George's dying will open them up. Of course, it *could* have been set up by some complete stranger."

Anderson walked silent for a few steps and then asked, "Is this the sort of thing musicians generally get up to, on a tour? I mean, one reads stories..."

"It is," admitted Martha. "It is."

She identified the rope, and then looked at the ugly, dead face. "Yes, that's him," she said. She put the sheet back over him herself and turned away. "I knew him years ago. What a miserable end for a hard life."

Then Martha remembered the moment two days before, when the door had opened and Elen and Pádraig had burst in on them, fresh from their experiment and bringing sunlight with them. She touched the soaked and brittle knot of grass he had brought to show her. "And for a good rope," she added.

She fixed Anderson with blue eyes strangely calm in her sad face. She touched his hand, lightly. "I will find out how this happened," she said to him, as if in apology to the detective.

He had to smile. "I'll hold you to that promise, ma'am."

Elen Evans walked over to the air conditioner and turned it on. "Well," she said, and sat down on the bed again.

Long, blank-faced and with eyes unfocused, followed her movement with his head, causing Elen to laugh. "My dear Mr. Long, you certainly are limber for a gentleman of your age and sedentary habits." Her voice went distinctly Georgia.

"His what?" Pádraig straightened in his chair. "I didn't understand a word of that."

Long remained expressionless and staring. "Actually, I do get my exercise, Elen. Last night I got quite a lot."

The silence was cut only by the growl of the fan. At last Long went to his customary seat at the round table. And then there was a rattling knock at the door and Elizabeth Macnamara burst in, sweaty and breathing hard.

Elizabeth was a young woman of unusual height and unusual beauty. She dressed conservatively and with good effect, today in a soft-green cotton wraparound that had a French flavor. Her honey-colored hair waved softly around her face.

Pádraig found himself on his feet, though surprise and not manners had moved him. Teddy Poznan found himself smiling.

"Good morning, Elizabeth," Mayland Long greeted her.

"Mommy!" cried Marty, jumping hard on the bed.

Elen Evans said nothing. Her eyes were fixed on Pádraig.

"Damn! You're all here waiting for me. I knew it!" Elizabeth grabbed her daughter and swung her off the bed. "Hello, Queen of the Universe! How ya been? Mommy's missed you!"

Marty took about ten seconds of swinging before she said, "That's enough, thank you," and sat back on the bed, looking complacent. Elizabeth glanced up again.

"It was a radiator hose, and if you're pissed at me, imagine how everybody else on Highway 17 feels? What a mess. Ninety minutes and I didn't dare get out of the car. I should have changed them all months ago; why are computer engineers invariably useless around cars?"

No one answered her, but then she had not given

them a chance. Elizabeth took one more deep breath of the cool indoor air and looked around her in more collected fashion.

"Where's my mother?"

Long stepped forward. "Your mother is at the police station, Elizabeth."

She had been standing with her left hip cocked and her face tilted, looking over her shoulder at Long, and in that position she froze. With her elegance and height she resembled a mannequin from some expensive department store. "The police station?"

"George St. Ives is dead," said Long. Elizabeth gasped and put her hand down on her daughter's flaxen head.

"She felt she ought to go."

"He . . . killed himself," offered Teddy. "It's so sad."

Elizabeth did not care for Ted Poznan. She did not care for many people. But it was not scorn that made her look through him completely.

"He was—he was found at the pier? This morning?"

Ted opened his eyes very wide. "How did you know that?" asked Pádraig.

Long guessed. "The police towed your car?"

"The Highway Patrol. It was back and forth on the radio. But"—Elizabeth gave Marty a nervous little hug—"I didn't suspect who it was. They didn't know!"

"Yeah. He didn't have any identification. I'm the one that told them," said Teddy. It was a plaintive admission.

Elizabeth raised stormy eyes to Long. "What are you going to do about it?"

Elen, still curled on the bed, laughed outright. "What is he supposed—"

"*I* do? Martha is there," he began.

"That's what I mean!" Elizabeth set her jaw. "Why should she be the one?"

" 'Cause she's da boss lady." Elen spoke to Elizabeth with no great warmth.

"She knows what to do," said Long.

"Goddamn it!" said Elizabeth to them all, and she sat down on the far bed with Marty on her lap, glaring.

* * *

The liquor bottles behind the bar at the Riva glowed with a fantastic play of light, bounced from the sun to the sea to the slanted windows of the building and hence inward. It also glanced off the round face of Pádraig Ó Súilleabháin and put corrugations around his blue eyes. Had Detective Anderson been there, he might have recanted his estimation of the man's age, for Pádraig, this afternoon, had a terrible squint which added years to him.

Mayland Long sat beside him at the bar, and perhaps because of the affinity of color, his yellowish eyes were fixed on the tumbler half full of Glenlivet Scotch in his hand. Pádraig, too, had a double Scotch, because Long was buying.

Elen Evans, seated at Pádraig's other hand, propped her chin on her hand heel and drank coffee. It seemed to have no power over her.

"Did I show you this?" Pádraig reached his many-scarred hand into his shirt and pulled out the limp leather cross.

"Yes, you did," replied Long politely.

"Yes, you did," said Elen.

He let the memento slip back under his shirt. There was an uncomfortable silence.

"Perhaps we should have gone someplace else," Long whispered. "For us to parade up and down the pier today shows a certain lack of feeling."

Pádraig lifted his eyes out of the bar of sunlight. "I don't know any other places in this city. Not on the water."

Elen gave a yawn which dwarfed her face and left her almost unable to sit up. "Excuse me," she said. "This daytime wake is a bit too much for me." She picked up her purse and headed toward the back of the restaurant.

Long rubbed his face with both hands. His suit rustled like dry moth wings. He gave a chuckle.

"My, but three Macnamaras can fill a room. One would think they were much bigger women."

Pádraig nodded sagaciously. "Women. That is the important word in what you said. Myself I have five sisters. And they wonder why I love to go out in small boats!" He took a long sip of the drink before him and made a face. "Smells like a smoking stove! Whisky can kill a man," he said.

"You say that frequently."

"It is what my mother says. She brought us all up as Pioneers."

"Then why are you drinking alcohol?" asked Long in simple curiosity. Pádraig did not answer.

Long drank his Scotch without grimacing.

"Many things can kill a man, *Fear Uí Súilleabháin*. Sickness, for one. A rope, for another."

Pádraig whined.

"I want the truth," said Long. He blew his nose on a cocktail napkin and slapped his big hand down on the bar. The bartender glanced over casually and then went back to cutting lemons. "I'm old and I'm tired and my nose hurts abominably! I want to have the truth now!"

"I didn't kill him," said Pádraig, daunted. "And I don't think that knowing who did will help you with your cold."

Long grunted. "You don't understand."

Pádraig drank the drink Long had bought for him and agreed that he didn't understand.

"You're too young," Long said. Again Pádraig agreed.

Long noticed his glass was empty and he raised his head. Within five seconds the bartender had refilled it, as well as Pádraig's. "They treat you good," the young man said.

Long nodded ponderously. "That is because I am *not* young." He paused and exhaled the smell of Scotch.

"And I have a secret which gives me a certain . . . edge over others in getting my way."

"Ah? What's that?"

Long gave a display of teeth. "If I told you, it wouldn't be a secret anymore."

Pádraig thought for a moment, and then admitted the veracity of that statement. "I have my own secret," he said. "But I'm willing to tell you, my friend, because I trust you. Anyone would trust you! It's that my father is not really my father."

"That's a common one," Long said with sympathy.

"*Óchón!* But my mother is not my mother, either, and that's less common, I think."

Long folded his hands and considered this.

Pádraig spoke again. "Does Martha have a secret, do you think?"

Now the mouth full of teeth closed in a frown. "A great secret, that she would tell if she could. The secret of Zen. But other than that . . ."

"I meant a power over men, Mayland," said Pádraig. His snigger bubbled through his nose. "That makes you follow her around the way you do." He punched Long on the shoulder, and then massaged his stinging hand, for the shoulder was harder than expected.

Long groaned and put one hand over his face. That hand stretched easily from ear to ear. "You are being frivolous, Pádraig. You should not be frivolous regarding Martha." He took a sizable drink of Scotch and let his eyes wander out the window, where the waters of Monterey Bay lapped and gulls stood in rank on the concrete sill. "She is truth incarnate!"

"She is a very nice lady," agreed Pádraig. He watched Long watching the gulls. "Tell me, *a chara*. Did you hang George under the pier last night, God have mercy on his soul?"

Long opened his eyes exaggeratedly wide. "Did I? Why on earth would I want to kill him?"

Pádraig laughed. "Because he was a pig. He made fun of you, the same as all of us."

"He didn't make fun of Martha," replied Long complacently. "And I am not sensitive about my musical ability. Or lack of it."

Pádraig stuck his nose into his glass. "Let's not start in on that," he mumbled to the melting ice cubes. "Ability or . . . lack of it." He raised his face again and took a deep breath, seeming surprised at the quality of the air.

"No good to complain about a man who is cold and dead right now. He can't do us any harm."

Long looked honestly surprised. "He never could."

Pádraig Ó Súilleabháin's smallish mouth tightened. "You think he couldn't? Maybe not to you. But forget that. He is dead, and it's Máirtín—little Marty—I worry about now."

Long blinked at this quick change of subject. He leaned over. "Worry about Marty? Why? What do you know about . . . about that?"

Pádraig raised his head from his drink to the cold sea outside the window. He rubbed his hands together. "When she was by the water yesterday, and it so dark. Not all the strange old things are gone."

"As H. P. Lovecraft was so fond of saying."

Pádraig shook his shiny dark head in dismissal. "I mean with the sea. I am a young fellow, but I know the feelings of the ocean, and it didn't feel nice, around her. In fact, it felt worse than George's tongue on you. We should do something to help Marty."

It was Long's turn to look surprised. "What can we possibly do? Are you suggesting something of a preternatural order, or . . ."

"If you are going to speak English with me, make the words short. I am saying we should say a rosary for her. We should be saying one for George already." He sneaked a half-humorous glance at Long. "I'll bet you don't know how to say the rosary."

The dark man arched in his chair. "I'll bet I do!" he answered with heat. "The sorrowful, joyful, or . . . ?"

"All three kinds. One for Máirtín, one for George, and one for all the rest of us." Pádraig peered around into the dim room. "Where is Elen? We really need women for a rosary."

Long looked also, his body twisting from the waist as he looked around the corner and into the white-tabled dining area. A small, absentminded hiss escaped him. "Perhaps she went out the back way."

Pádraig sighed in disappointment. "Too bad. A rosary

would be good for that girl! I like her. I like the way she talks."

Long nodded ponderously. "Very decorative, both visually and audiall . . . auditory . . . and to hear. I think that is because she has learned many of her mannerisms from gay men."

Pádraig Ó Súilleabháin looked closely at Long. He opened his mouth to ask the other to repeat what he had said, but then he closed it again. At last he shook his head portentously and said, "I think she has not been too happy, Mayland. It's a pity."

Pádraig pulled the white plastic beads with the silver cross out of his jeans pocket, and very slowly and carefully he led Long through the five sorrowful, the five joyful, and the five glorious mysteries, all in the Irish language.

Though time passed and the Riva filled up, their end of the bar remained empty, save for themselves.

Long saw pale blue out of the corner of his eye and there was Martha, sitting next to him. In front of her was a glass half the size of Pádraig's and his own.

"Have you been there long?" he asked her.

"Three decade's worth." She pointed to the Scotch in front of her. "I had them put it on your tab."

Long rubbed his eyes and sneezed. "The least I can do, after ignoring you so long."

"We were full of religious feeling. Like Saint Theresa," added Pádraig. "We could not even see you."

Martha smiled agreeably. "It makes me wonder what Saint Theresa's capacity was. And whether Glenlivet was her drink of choice."

Hangman's Reel

The sun hit them hard as the bar door closed behind them. "Like coming out of church," Martha said.

"I wouldn't know. I've rarely been in a church. One of your churches, that is."

Long peered through the many-paned door behind them to where Pádraig still sat, reduced to drinking Michelob. "I don't think it is really a desire to drink, with him, as much as it is an indebility—inability—to stand the heat."

"Poor boy." Martha answered mechanically and gave her consort a sharp glance. "Can you talk—that is, make sense, Mayland?"

"Rarely," he replied, rolling his word. "Compared to you, Martha, I am a walking bundle of misconceptions."

She snorted. "*That's* your only misconception. But I'm asking you how drunk you are."

Long straightened his spine and looked up at the sky. "Only moderately. I presume you wish to ask me whether I killed George St. Ives."

Her face went entirely foolish and she stood on the crowded sidewalk of the pier, staring at him. "I did not! It never . . . *did* you kill him?" she whispered. She remembered the strained conversation overheard the day before and she bit her lip.

"I don't think so," he answered composedly. "Though with this virus I cannot be quite sure. I can say I have no memory of killing him."

"That's enough for me." Her voice failed.

"I don't suppose you did either?" Long's normally

128

excellent eyes were having difficulty focusing. He moved his head back and forth in an attempt to find the focal distance. It made him appear quite inhuman. Martha rubbed her eyes and looked away.

"Don't do that. It makes my knees weak. No. I didn't kill George, unless I did it in my sleep."

Long's teeth gleamed in the summer sun. "Good. Then we can be comfortable again!"

"Comfortable? My God!" Martha started down the sidewalk toward the beach. "I almost liked him, you know. When we played together, I liked him very much. Despite what he was."

"You like the policeman, too, don't you?" asked Long with an effort at nonchalance. "Despite what he is."

She slapped her forehead with her palm and energetically ruined her hairdo. "Why the hell shouldn't I—

"Hey, fella!" She stopped. "Where did you get that passport?"

"What does it matter?" He seemed completely sober now, looking down at her rumpled head.

"They'll check up on it."

"That's fine. It's a valid passport." His smile was too broad for beauty.

"You were born in Hong Kong? Sixty-three years ago?"

"No. Of course not."

Martha gave an exasperated sigh and a gull dove close over her head. "Well, I hope you know what you're doing. Then I'll only have to worry about Pádraig's."

"Ah!" Long watched the gull and let his gaze drift to the water. He had become vastly more tolerant of things oceanic in the previous five years. "So you picked up on that too? A young man whose mother is not his mother. You are subtle, Martha. I suspected nothing until he told me the riddle just now."

"Suspected? Bullshit! I *know* Peig Uí Súilleabháin! She's no Yank! The boy's here on a false passport." These last words were spoken in an angry growl as she threaded her way among the bright-shirted holiday-makers of Santa Cruz. Long followed, touching no one.

The little man with the beard and the double-headed crystal pendant was acting nervous, but that was not too surprising, for Elizabeth Macnamara often made people nervous. She had sat him down on the chair beneath the light, more by command than invitation, and her inquisitorial attitude was combined with a general feeling that she shouldn't have to become involved in the affairs of Teddy Poznan.

"He calls you late yesterday and says to be here by nine this morning?"

"I'm late," the man mumbled.

"Late, hah! Tell me about it!" she answered angrily, but did not explain why the simple statement roused her so. "Why did he wait till yesterday? He had plenty of time to contact old friends in Santa Cruz during the weekend, and they would have been off long since, if this mess hadn't happened."

The visitor, who was from Cotati, and who had had a long drive, shook his head. "If I know Teddy, it was something of a spiritual nature. Or dietary. I am his counselor on such matters."

She sneered in most unladylike fashion. In self-defense he brought both hands down around his save-the-humans belt buckle and breathed from his center. "Find him and then maybe we'll both know," he suggested. "Didn't he say where he was going?"

"To me?" Elizabeth straightened to regal height. "Hardly. For all I know he's back at the police station."

". . . —lice station?" he echoed and he stood up, scraping the chair. "Gawd! Teddy? What kind of trouble is he in?"

"Murder," she said almost viciously. "He finds a body and dumps it on my mother."

"Dumps? On your . . . ?"

Elizabeth took hold of the telephone receiver as

though she were wringing a neck. "I'll try the station for him. What's your name?"

There was no answer at all, and when she turned, the room was empty.

The road was covered with white dust which coated the windshield of the Dodge van almost beyond usability. The awkward old vehicle bucked at every dry rivulet and pothole in the dirt, and when she floored the accelerator to pull her out of the ruts, the air was touched with the ominous smell of slipping fan belts. The van had taken the whole crew of them, plus instruments, luggage, and sound equipment, from Massachusetts to Santa Cruz, breaking down completely only once. Elen doubted it would ever make such a trip again.

Redwood trees, flanking the single-lane road, were coated in dirt ten feet off the ground. Elen parked the van where last winter's rain had washed the remnants of the road away and walked the last hundred yards to the cabin, picking dirt out of her nostrils. The windows were caked in dirt also, but she could see Sandy's head moving behind one of them.

There was noise as she got closer. Sandy opened the door and Elen stepped into the darkness and found a chair. "It doesn't smell good," she whispered.

"I'm sorry," said Sandy. Her green cotton harem pants were stained down the front. "I'm not very good at this kind of thing. I told you."

Elen shrugged and slumped forward. "I had no right to speak. Just tired." Her friend's arm helped her to her feet and she went to make sure everything was all right. "How many people would do this for me?"

The thin woman wrung her hands. "I just feel so sorry. . . ."

Sandy waited for Elen in the front room of the cabin. Steller jays outside the ceiling-high window made a great racket. She sat with her hands tightly folded, and when Elen came back, she said, "This is terrible, isn't it?"

Elen Evans choked, caught her breath, nodded, and started to cry.

Detective Anderson read the preliminary medical report under the light of the window. He wore bifocals to read, and he adjusted his focus by wrinkling his nose. "No great surprises, so far," he said to Officer Scherer, who had folded his long body into the scoop of a plastic chair. "Neck broken. That's a mercy, at least."

Scherer came to half-attention. "Neck broken? Quite a strain on the rope."

"I know. Ugly, wasn't it? Could be"—and the detective's words slowed to an uncertain pause—"a weakness in the vertebrae. Or if—if he flung himself off headfirst, the angle would be more likely..."

Scherer grimaced and turned his face away from his superior. From the thing that happened to him whenever he closed his eyes, he guessed he was going to have trouble sleeping.

Everyone got depressed. Scherer himself got moody, when he thought about his job too much, or the divorce. It would be so easy to go off one night after too many Seagrams, full of anger at Kate's family or his own. To take a dive, literally: a good dive, as in the local pool, to fool one's reflexes... To come to one's senses too late. In the air.

Don Scherer shuddered, shaking the chair.

Anderson watched quietly, thinking the Macnamara woman might have been right. Perhaps the boy should have been given time, after finding the body. He wasn't even on the detective team. But he'd asked, and it was only fair. Besides, time for what? To go back to his apartment in Capitola? Scherer was alone, he seemed to remember. The usual divorce.

Let him shudder his shudders in company.

"Other things," continued the detective, flat-voiced as though he hadn't noticed. "A crack in the skull at the back of the head. Don't think we can do much with that; it was right where it would hit the square post. Some needle marks. Not a lot. Not a heroin habit, I'd say. Jaundice. Isn't that what the Chinese guy said? Jaundice. Hey, Scherer, did you know Orientals could tan like that? I always thought they just went darker yellow."

"I never thought about it," answered Scherer in the jaded-cop tones he affected very poorly.

"Big bruise on the left arm. Broken toe improperly healed. Poor sod. Five teeth missing. Poor sod, what a list of miseries!"

"Did anything come back about his relatives in Canada?" Officer Scherer mumbled. He wasn't in any position to know such things, having been with the detective all morning. What was more, Anderson knew the man wasn't, but he asked anyway. He turned on the intercom and asked again, getting a negative reply.

"Shame, when there's a body and no one left who cares."

Scherer's mumble grew fainter and he rolled his eyes away from Anderson's.

"Aside from Macnamara, who is going to discover what happened for us. By some Buddhist rite, perhaps? Dunno.

"But it's easier on us this way, huh? No more 'I am sorry to have to tell you' and fried-egg stares and weeping and wailing and then us going home feeling like shit? And why haven't we caught the guy already? All that." Scherer nodded blankly, obediently, as his superior wandered on.

"Do you think it was murder?" He threw the question at Scherer without warning and the young officer shied like a horse.

"Murder? No. My idea is he did it himself," Scherer said. "Seems obvious."

Not to me, sonny boy, said Anderson to himself, and spared one nearsighted glance for Scherer's brooding face. "It wouldn't shock me either way," is what the sergeant said aloud.

It was only five minutes later when Pratt, on front-desk duty, came in with Donald Stoughie.

"This is kind of odd," he said to Anderson, "but it

might tie in with this—uh—strangulation case." He spoke very softly, for the sergeant's ears only, and then gestured the reluctant complainant forward. "Tell him the story, as you told me, Mr. Stoughie."

"Again? The whole thing?" Stoughie's face fell and it seemed, for a moment, that he would turn and walk out of the station.

Pratt's eyes flickered from Anderson to Stoughie. "Sure. If the guy tried to kill you, it's worth telling twice, isn't it?"

Anderson's face went expressionless by habit. "Who tried to kill you, Mr. . . . ."

"Stuffy, S-t-o-u-g-h-i-e," he replied. "It was a man named Maxwell Long. Chinese."

Anderson stared more blankly than ever. He motioned Stoughie to a chair. "When?" he asked. "How?"

'It was yesterday morning, in my office. He claimed I owed him money and he tried to throttle me. I barely escaped with my . . . with my health."

Anderson's regard was unwavering, and Stoughie, turning his head, found that Officer Scherer was also looking at him. The policeman looked very like a cowboy, with his long jaw and sideburns and his large, loose-framed body, and he looked at Stoughie as though the man were some dubious horse. Stoughie didn't find either of them supportive.

"This was Mayland Long?" asked Anderson.

Stoughie stirred. "Yes. That's it. You already know about it? You were listening when I told—"

'No, Mr. Stoughie. I merely know the name."

Stoughie relaxed as much as one could into the plastic scoop-chair, for he had never regarded it as a mark in one's favor to have the police know one's name. Unless, of course, one is connected with the police. With this thought, he sat up straight again.

He explained at length how the man Long had come raging into his office with a demand for payment for services not even rendered, let alone payment due, after wrecking the premises too. How he had refused to listen to reason, but picked the agent up by the neck—by the neck itself—and flung him about the room, doing damage thereby both to the room and the person of Donald Stoughie. Which was no more than to be expected out of someone who went about wrecking theaters.

Anderson listened, and the expressionless quality of his face faded before a sort of mystified concern. He rose, pulling on the knees of his trousers, and stepped around his large desk. He squatted on the floor beside Stoughie and put one finger to Stoughie's neck. The man stopped in the middle of a sentence.

"Here, let's see." Anderson's voice was that of a solicitous nurse, but Mr. Stoughie still flinched as he felt the touch.

"Isn't the mark obvious?" asked Stoughie bitterly.

"I *think* I see a red mark," replied Anderson. "Probably it was much worse yesterday, though. Why did you wait so long before coming in?"

"I was afraid," said Stoughie, balling his hands in his lap. "He said if I dared go to the police . . ."

"Yes, don't leave it like that. If you dared go to the police, what?"

Stoughie's jaw clenched and relaxed. "He'd be back for me."

A sudden gust of wind blew the curtains in and filled the cubicle with salt smell. Both Anderson and Scherer followed the movement with their eyes, and Scherer took a hungry breath of the outside air. Anderson sighed.

"Long is . . . what? About five eight? And you're maybe four inches taller and forty pounds—"

"What has that got to do with it? Is it okay to assault people that are bigger than you? I'm not used to violence." Stoughie wrapped his arms around himself as a sort of protective casing, and his eyes of bathtub blue puckered around the edges.

"I was just wondering how he managed to pull you over the desk, Mr. Stoughie. That's quite a feat for a small man."

The booking agent's face tightened even more. "I think it was karate."

"Karate?"

The gauze shirt billowed with Stoughie's exhalation. "Or something. Some martial art."

"T'ai chi maybe," offered Pratt, who was standing behind Stoughie, casually reading the morning's report. "Considering Long's age—"

Stoughie rose angrily from the chair. "Enough! I don't need to suffer this, as well as getting beat up."

Anderson forestalled him with one arm. "No, Mr. Stoughie. I'm sorry. We *are* taking your report seriously. Very seriously, in fact. But before I move on it I want to make very sure we have the whole truth here. It may be more important than you think."

Stoughie turned, half-mollified and half-frightened. "What's more important than somebody's trying to kill somebody?"

"Somebody succeeding," replied the detective. Stoughie sat down.

"I don't know. Some hippie friend of his," said Elizabeth to her mother, offhand.

Martha sputtered a laugh and sank gratefully down into a chair by the air conditioner. "You don't know how funny that sounds, coming from someone your age. I think you just do it to be shocking. Besides, what *is* a hippie, in the year 1986?"

Elizabeth was cleaning an unexpectedly dirtied pair of child's panties and her voice was barely audible over the flush. "It's a guy with beads and a headband and too much bare belly. As well as tatoos. And drugs."

"What drugs?" her mother asked languidly, but her relaxation had become no more than a pose.

Elizabeth emerged with her hair in her face and her nose screwed up. She dried her fresh-washed hands on a motel bathmat. "I don't know what drugs. I'm not a walking pharmacopoeia."

"A walking *Physician's Desk Reference* is what you mean, dear," said Martha faintly.

"I'm not an authority on drugs. But I know the type; my God, how could I not, after Stanford and living in Silicon Gulch? The guy called himself a counselor or something, and that usually means—"

"Teddy's on a mucus-free diet," said Martha, as though that proved something.

"Well..." Elizabeth dabbed the damp mat on her face. "What does it matter? He was looking for Poznan and the creep isn't here."

Martha turned her face from her daughter, just as Long emerged from the next room. Both women looked up at him.

"She's still crying," he said. "But I think she is almost asleep."

"God!" Elizabeth invoked heaven with both arms. "I'm so sorry I did this to her. And to you," she added, with a guilty glance at her mother.

"If I had really remembered what it was like, on tour..."

Martha said nothing. "A murder is not the usual climax of a tour, I don't think," said Long gently. "At least, not with Celtic traditional music."

Elizabeth looked at him askance, but she was chary of contradicting her mother's dignified suitor. "Is she still on this Judy trip?"

"Yes. 'Judy's lost.' "

Elizabeth's mouth tightened and she sat down on the end of a bed. "I don't know. There just isn't anyone by that name that she knows! I ... have a friend in San Rafael who does regressions. Maybe—"

"Hippie!" called Martha genially. Elizabeth showed a glint of anger and then buried it.

"Where's Pádraig?" she asked the air. Long and Elizabeth glanced at each other expectantly. Long went out the door and was gone for perhaps a minute.

"He went into his room," he replied, coming back quietly.

"Is anyone else here?"

Long shook his head. Martha looked very sad. "My dears," she said. "We've got to think about this, and it's very confusing. We have to figure out how George died."

Elizabeth showed the whites of her eyes, looking as though she'd rather do anything but. Long, without a word, sat down cross-legged on the carpet, close to Martha's feet.

"Either George killed himself last night, which is too terrible, or some stranger killed him, which is worse, or one of our close friends killed him, which is..."

"Quite possible," Elizabeth concluded with a snap of her jaws. Both Martha and Long stared up in surprise. His eyes were cold yellow.

"It's true!" Elizabeth took a step back before the combined gaze. Her beautiful face was stony. "Mother, you trust the weirdest people!"

"Sometimes they prove very helpful, when I need help," replied Martha, very angry. Long looked away.

Elizabeth wiped the hair off her face again, and at a noise from the next room, all heads rose. But Marty settled more deeply into sleep, and Elizabeth filled her lungs for argument. "Sometimes very rarely, and usually they eat your savings and run. These particular weirdos—"

"The finest traditional players I could get together!"

"Whoopie! And one of them's a murderer, isn't he? Or she?" Elizabeth's mouth was tight and she glanced repeatedly from the door to the bedroom where Marty slept to the face of her mother, and the same concern and resentment showed. "You're just lucky it wasn't you found with a hand-knit rope around your neck."

"No one is going to hurt Martha," said Long softly, and his face was a set of angles in tarnished bronze.

Martha, fully enraged, stood next to her daughter, staring into the face six inches above hers. "Who, then, is your candidate for the position of murderer?"

"Teddy," came her reply, and as at a signal, Ted Poznan entered the room.

"I hear at the front desk there was someone looking..."

he began, but then he read the emotion in the faces before
him and fell silent.

The phone rang and Martha went to answer it. She
stood before the object with her eyes half-shut and breathed
heavily for a few seconds before picking it up. "Hello?"

There was another knock at the door and Detective
Anderson came in, looking apologetic. Looking at Long.

It was Sandy, Marty's babysitter of the night before,
on the phone. Her message, delivered with trepidation
and hardly intelligible, was that Elen Evans was at her
house and too sleepy to make it back to the motel. She
was, in fact, asleep already.

Martha listened with half an ear and finally cut her
off. "When she wakes up, dear, you might tell her that
Mayland's been arrested for murder. She'll be interested."

The response was an explosive gasp. Martha found
she was listening to a dead line and she hung up the
phone.

"Not arrested, no," Anderson was saying. "But we
really would like to speak with you at the station. Not
about Mr. St. Ives's death, however."

"Not about the murder?" It was Martha who spoke.
Long merely stood, looking patient.

"No . . ." There was a sort of drawling qualification in
Anderson's word, making it an almost-no rather than a real
negation. 'It's about a complaint filed by Mr. Donald
Stoughie."

"That?" Martha gaped and even Long gave a start and
a short laugh, followed by a series of coughs. "I am made
to see again that all one's acts return home. When . . . one
least expects, always." He took out a Kleenex and held it
to his mouth for the racking coughs would not let him be.
As his cold was starting to loosen, they were very unpleasant to hear.

Anderson looked down at the glossy black head and
wondered if the man dyed his hair. According to the
passport he was older than Anderson by a good five years,
and what hair the detective had left was more salt than

pepper. At least, he reflected, he was in better health than
Long, whose bony fingers were cupped around his mouth,
half-hidden in the tissue. They looked like dead spiders,
those hands, and Anderson could see the points of Long's
spine through the thin fabric of the suit jacket. His
sympathy with the unappealing Mr. Stoughie reached a
new low, and he wondered if Long had tuberculosis.

"Of course, Sergeant. I expected some such action
from Mr. Stoughie yesterday or this morning at the latest,
and this sad business drove it completely out of my mind."
He patted his pockets methodically, checked his gold
wristwatch (it was one-forty), and said, "Quite ready now."

"Wait. I'll need my purse!" Martha snapped her
fingers and stooped under the bed. Long gave her a wary
glance.

"I don't believe the gentleman asked for you, Martha,"
he said.

"Not just yet," said Anderson, and his tone suggested
that maybe this entire business could be settled without
fuss, if no one *made* a fuss. His tone suggested that, but
gave no promises.

"That's because he doesn't know I'm relevant to the
matter. Very relevant, since it's my band you are manag-
ing, and that Stoughie was prepared to rip off. And
since . . . well, we'll talk about it there."

Long remained standing in place, with Anderson,
staring at the wall beside him. "It isn't worth your trouble,
Martha."

She snorted. "Don't give me that. An accusation of
assault, following closely on the discovery of a body, is
nothing to sneeze at."

Long wiped his nose on yet another tissue. "Inapposite," he murmured and glanced expectantly at Anderson,
who shrugged.

"I can't tie her to the bedpost," the detective said,
and followed them both out of the room.

Pádraig Ó Súilleabháin was in the hallway, looking
like the bad beginning of a hangover. "Is there any aspirin?" he asked Martha, and then he saw Anderson and

noticed the intent progression of the group. "What is this?"

"We're off to the police station again," answered Long, trying to sound bored.

"*Mar sinn é?* Is that so?" The boy caught up with them, stumbling on the pile of the carpet, and he blocked their way at the doorway into the lobby. "Who is going, and why wasn't I told?" Anderson took him by the upper arm, to keep him upright, and felt the unexpectedly heavy arm harden belligerently. For just a moment, he wished he had brought Scherer.

"It's not about George at all," said Long. "It's about the tour business."

Pádraig blinked and made a face. "I'm not that drunk. At least, not anymore. What have the police to do with the music business?"

Martha pushed past Pádraig, clearing the way for the rest of them. "That horrid booking agent has filed a complaint against Mayland. That's all."

"*Mar sinn é?*" said Pádraig again. His shoulders swelled in his nylon polo shirt and he stuffed his fists into his trouser pockets. "That *gaimbín* man? I'm with you, Mayland." And Pádraig would not be dissuaded.

Anderson and Long, silent and dressed in sport jackets, got into the unmarked car. Martha got in beside Long, but Ó Súilleabháin had to walk.

"Be careful," said Anderson, in the privacy of his cubicle. "I have not asked you for any admissions, and if you are going to start throwing them around, I will read you your rights."

"I merely admitted to having lost my temper," said Long judiciously. He sat curled into the plastic bucket seat as though his spine had been made for such curves. His arm was over the chair back and he looked more at ease than he had yet in Anderson's presence. The detective guessed the fellow was glad to be alone with him. "That is not always a violation of the law. But I think it will save much time if you do 'read me my rights' so that the truth can come out."

Anderson smiled. Closing his eyes he quoted the précis of Miranda v. Arizona very clearly, following it with the traditional injunction. Long nodded with appreciation of the ritual. "And you did not have to read."

"Not for years." He touched a button on the machine on his desk. "Anytime, Mr. Long."

Long cocked his right foot onto his left knee and pulled it up to his hip. The left foot remained on the floor. He straightened up and lay his curled hands in his lap, and in that hybrid Eurasian position he began:

"In February of this year I contracted with Mr. Donald Stoughie for the group called Macnamara's Band to play at a hall he manages in Santa Cruz. Landaman Hall. Mrs. Macnamara warned me that Stoughie had a very bad reputation in the field for paying late or not at all, and so I took the precaution of getting a written agreement to pay after the first of the two concerts. Had it not been for the location and the very good acoustics of the room, we would not have bothered with the man. And as it turned out, though the acoustics were good, the location was inauspicious after all."

"I would agree to that," answered Anderson solemnly.

"Friday last they gave the first of their two concerts, and he did not show up to pay." Long fell into a moment's brown study. "You know, had I not made that agreement for a flat fee, we'd have been better off, for the house was more crowded than Martha expected."

"Good music," murmured Anderson and Long glanced sharply at him. "That's right. You were there."

"I came to Mr. Stoughie's office on the following morning, and it became clear he had no intention of paying at that time, if at all. He claimed that one of our party had worked some damage on his property, though he had no proof, nor even anyone in particular to blame."

"I know about the practical joke," said Anderson. "Mrs. Macnamara told me this morning."

Long's teeth showed in a grin. "Well, then. It was not

the time to play such a game with me, for I was not feeling well. This virus ... Then he made comments about Mrs. Macnamara I had no choice but to regard as slighting."

Anderson's expression brightened for an instant. He chewed absently on a pencil and almost smiled.

"And I lost patience with the man. I laid my hand on him." He fell to brooding again, his hands a circle in his lap.

Anderson raised his eyebrows at this unusual gallantry. "Hand? Singular?"

Long glanced up in amusement. "Yes, one hand. I put it around the man's neck."

Anderson grunted without surprise. "And did you lift him out of his chair, by the neck?"

There was a ten-second silence. "I ... may have. I was quite angry for a moment. My memory is hazy."

"Do you remember flinging him about the room, also by the neck?"

Long's jacket rustled like dead leaves. "I could hardly do that! And if I had, he'd surely be dead now, with a broken neck!"

"Like St. Ives," added the detective.

Long pushed back into the chair until his back reflected the arch of it. His neck and head, too, continued this serpentine curve, and he contrived to rear over the taller man. "But Donald Stoughie does not *have* a broken neck, because I did not fling him about the room. Nor did I hang George St. Ives up by Pádraig's *súgán*."

Anderson nodded to Long with a wealth of sympathy. "But you must admit it was a bad time for such an incident to come up. It is difficult to believe that two acts of violence, coming together in time so closely ..."

"Are unrelated. I admit it readily."

"*Are* they related?"

Long seemed offended momentarily. His narrow chest swelled. "Of course. All actions are related. Some in the human sphere of dharma and others in ways beyond. I am quite aware how this particular series of events appears to the observer's eye, and I agree that the response of a reasonable official must be to arrest me."

Anderson looked out the window and scratched a silvery stubble on his face. A reasonable official. Who on earth aspired to be "a reasonable official"? He thought of the meaty face and bathwater eyes of Mr. Stoughie and felt very unreasonable. "Tell me, Mr. Long. Have you ever studied karate?"

Long's astonishment at this question resolved itself into laughter, and then to roaring coughs. "Karate! Never! Can it be you think that every person of Asian—"

"Or perhaps another martial art," the sergeant pressed. "Even t'ai chi?"

"Such studies have never come in my way. They were not necessary. Zen sitting, however, I do study. Martha is my teacher."

Anderson nodded, as Long had merely agreed with an opinion that he, Anderson, had stated. "I regret it, Mr. Long, but as you say, I am going to have to keep you here with us."

"On a charge of murder?"

"On the charge of having assaulted Mr. Donald Stoughie and worked battery upon his person."

Long's resigned nod was formal.

Rights of Man

Teddy Poznan slumped miserably in the chair that was usually Long's. "Oh, friends and neighbors!" He stared at his hands in his lap as though they were the key to his perplexity. "That's an act that will come back on somebody. What goes around, comes around, you know, and to do harm to such a very old soul as Mayland will really set the gears to meshing.

"Still, I don't know what Wolfie's visit had to do with the Dragon being arrested."

"Don't call him that."

Elizabeth snapped this out in quick fury and then turned away from Teddy. She went through the connecting door into her daughter's bedroom.

Teddy's oxlike brown eyes wrinkled all around the edges. "I left a message this morning for him not to bother. Coming, that is. That . . . we'd be leaving before he could get here."

"Didn't you know that when you asked him to come?" Elizabeth said, having stuck her head back through the door. Teddy flinched away from her. "He . . . was supposed to be here yesterday, not today. He gets things screwed up."

"Swell kind of a spiritual director, I think," called Elizabeth, and then shut the connecting door between them.

Martha sat in the nicely appointed lobby of the Santa Cruz police station, listening to the sound of Dixieland jazz from Cooper House and swinging her feet. She had swung her short legs over the carpet when she was three and she did the same at the age of fifty-four. Especially when she was nervous.

Was Pádraig even now jogging the half mile or so between the Bright Sands Hotel and the station, or was she expected to carry the ball alone? Carry it and do what with it?

What a mess. Mayland had had every right to bop that miserable, wormlike Don Stoughie, who had spent twenty years doing her friends out of their pay, and George St. Ives was quite within his rights (though completely deluded), in deciding not to watch the sun rise anymore. But putting those two things together . . . what a mess.

She couldn't even blame Sergeant Anderson, though her enthusiasm for him had certainly cooled. When one of the suspects in a suspicious death turns out to have committed a minor act of violence the day before, it is natural to make a connection. Though a really *good* investigator might have seen that the sort of person who would become outraged at Stoughie was exactly the opposite of the sort who would . . .

No, that wouldn't wash, for Martha knew very well that her dear and closest friend was exactly the sort to kill a man in cold blood, if he thought the man's death a good idea. Despite the jokes paid out regarding his docility with Martha, Long was no tame beast.

(Cooper House sure had a fine trumpeter. Listen to him!)

The way to remove the suspicion from Long was to find the killer, of course, if there *had* been a killer, or elsewise discover a note or something. She had already promised Sergeant Anderson as much. She had a few ideas already, but nothing of immediate help.

Officer Scherer walked by, saw Martha, and recognized her. She saw him take an involuntary step away from her, and she suspected it was because he suddenly recalled her boyfriend had been arrested and she might press upon him, asking the kind of help a police officer was in no position to give. Martha smiled and nodded and stared blandly ahead again. Her indifference pulled the tall policeman closer.

"Anything I can do to help?" he found himself saying.

Her blue eyes were cool but not resentful. "The only thing I can think of is to prove somehow that George committed suicide. Or if he didn't, find me out who killed him. It wasn't Mayland."

Scherer said nothing, but Martha answered as though he had. "I say that not because he's the sort who couldn't kill, but because he's the sort who couldn't tell a lie. Never. And he told me he didn't kill George."

Officer Scherer's shoulders started to crawl upward "Murder isn't what he was arrested for, ma'am." He had a funny, cowboyish way of saying "ma'am" that caught Martha's ear. It made a whole with his rangy size and a peculiar rough tan he had, even darker than the detective's. She wondered if the effect was premeditated on his part.

"No, sir, but murder is what is at question here, all the same," she said very calmly. "If George did not kill himself, someone killed him."

Scherer shifted in his chair and gazed vaguely up at the fluorescent lights. "But you, Mrs. Macnamara, think he killed himself."

Martha straightened as much as she could in the bucket chair. "I didn't say that, Officer Scherer. It seems unlikely to me, in fact. But I don't claim to have understood the mind-workings of George St. Ives." She regarded the tall policeman closely, noticing that all his underneath aspects (the only kind she could see at close range) were pale and all the upper surfaces a brickish brown. Except for his forehead, which shaded smoothly down from fair to dark.

"Where did you get that striking farmer's tan, Officer? Surely a patrol car is no place to catch some rays?"

Scherer blinked, both embarrassed and inordinately pleased by the observation. He fingered his nonregulation belt buckle. "No, ma'am. I guess I picked this up doing endurance racing."

Martha wasn't sure what sort of race an endurance was, whether of horses or autos. Or feet. She said in exploratory fashion, "That must take up a great deal of your spare time."

He nodded and his wary face grew positively animated. "It does, I'll tell you. And I can't be regular about the training, either, and that's really rough on a horse. . . ."

Horse, echoed Martha in her mind.

"Sometimes I'm up riding her in the first light and then the next day nothing and the next it's the heat of the day or moonlight."

"That sounds like a lovely life," said Martha sincerely. "Though I know very little about riding."

Scherer cast her a glance of surprise touched with distrust, for rarely did people admit to him that they weren't au courant with horses, even when that was proved lamentably true. He reminded himself that this woman was from the East, and that might make the difference. "Well, it's wearing, for sure, but I guess I wouldn't do it if I didn't like it. . . ."

Pádraig pulled into the shadow of the station blowing much like a horse himself. His child-featured face was shiny and his shirt stuck to his back. He wondered how it was that people could live in this unforgiving climate. It was almost eighty out there. Standing within the glass doors, his eyes adjusting to the light, he remembered his errand and turned from ruddy to pale. He made for the front desk, hoping his shyness would not rise up and embarrass him, and he asked for Martha.

There she was, sitting in a pink plastic chair in the lobby, looking all rosy and fragile, while a terribly tall policeman loomed over her. Pádraig, not too tall himself, felt a hot ball of protective anger grow in his chest.

"Now, 'English' people might say I'm too big for her," the *garda* was saying. "But actually, if she was any bigger, she'd have more work in pushin' herself along. I'm easy on her, telling her to ease off, when by herself she'd die in a headlong rush. She's a girl that works *hard*."

Pádraig Ó Súilleabháin stopped dead, his fine anger leaking away into puzzlement. What was the man confessing to, in front of Martha that way? And what by seven saints had the opinions of English people to do with California? Two round fists unfisted, and their scarred palms were clammy and cold.

"Now the English-type people do a lot worse to their big bruisers, whippin' em over fences. There's more sound old endurance racers than there are hunter-jumpers, believe you me!"

Martha nodded agreeably, looked up and saw Pádraig. "Hello. You remember Officer Scherer, don't you, Pádraig? We were talking about horses."

Slowly the young Irishman nodded. "I think I knew that. It was either horses or your wife."

Scherer sputtered appreciatively, then remembered his wife and went sober. "I have to talk to you, Martha," Pádraig said, nervously. Martha met his eye.

The policeman excused himself with a word and a gesture and unfolded from the little chair. Pádraig took his place, and from the way he yanked his trousers up in sitting, he seemed to be prepared for a job of work.

"What evidence do they have on him?" he whispered to Martha, who leaned over to catch his words.

She looked even more pink and fragile as she answered. "He admits to being there, of course. It's all a matter of whether what he did was excusable under law, or an outright crime."

Pádraig stiffened in place. He was grayish white and he mouthed words that might have been an invocation and might have been something else. "Excusable? How could it be excusable?" He shook his head and the silky black hair floated about. "I don't believe a word of it. I don't believe he was even there. I will tell them better—"

Martha sensed his mistake. "We're not talking about George's death, Pádraig. Don't make that horrible error. Mayland's arrested for assault only."

The child-face had no expression, but color returned to it. *"Cén fáth?"*

"For beaning Don Stoughie, or shaking him, or whatever. Saturday morning."

Now Pádraig collapsed into the chair, until his wet back made noise slipping against the hard plastic. "Is that so?"

Martha nodded. "Stoughie was trying to do us out, as expected, and since Mayland wasn't feeling too well, he lost his temper."

Pádraig beat a rough hand against his knee, though whether the act was in irritation with Long or in sympathy with him, Martha had no clue. "It's a bad time for them to be worrying about that, with George after dying."

Martha's back did not quite touch the back of her chair. Her feet began once more to pendulum as she replied, "They think it was a bad time for him to lose his temper."

"It's a bad time enough!" Pádraig's voice was heated and just a bit too loud. The policeman at the desk looked up warily, as did a woman in muslin sitting at a word processor. Pádraig did not notice, for he was so slumped into his seat that the top of his sleek black head was all that was visible from the front. He hit his thigh with his hand once more, for good measure, and he gave a sigh that bounced his torso.

"You'll feel better if you sit up," Martha said, hesitantly. Half-sullen, half-tolerant, he obliged her. "What can happen, if he is convicted of this beating?"

Martha shrugged. "A fine, I hope. He looks so harmless, no judge could take the complaint too seriously."

Pádraig made a rough and disbelieving sound.

For another few minutes they sat there, side by side, each busy with solitary thought, and then Martha glanced over once again. "Pádraig? What were you going to tell them, if they *had* arrested him for murder? About his not being at the place at all . . . ?"

Pádraig straightened again and made a grimace. "Not so. I was confused. I would have told them that I know this man could not kill a man. That I *know* it."

Martha sat in the embarrassed silence she always felt when someone told her what she knew to be a lie.

The jail cell looked out to a four-lane street, with the multistory parking garage beyond. Not picturesque. Nor was the cell as comfy as the police station had seemed to promise. It was neat, the walls were freshly painted, and there was a W.C., but it was not a place to either rest or delight the spirit. Worst of all, in Long's opinion, it was not wholly his.

He had to share it with a very unappealing stripling with great blackheads all over his cheeks, who hadn't said a word in response to Long's greeting, nor had he met his companion's eyes in the hour since forced to share the domicile.

But that was just as well. Unlikely the boy's conversation would be entertaining, and with the involvements of eye contact removed, Long felt free to examine the fellow. He sat on the edge of one bunk (better mattress than the motel. Solid) with one leg drawn up and his head moving almost imperceptibly from side to side in slow rhythm, and he stared at the boy all he liked.

A runaway, Long surmised. From an institution, rather than a family perhaps. That particular brand of calm sullenness was rarely of home brew. Not a street thug or a gang member: he lacked the necessary rude dash. Long doubted also that he was a drug pusher, for who would buy anything to be put into the body from such a dirty fellow?

He might have been a petty thief, of course. It was even possible (but not probable, Long qualified carefully) that he was an honest soul unjustly accused of something. Who had been unfairly goaded to violence upon someone richly deserving violence. Examining the boy's eyes and nostrils closely, Long ascertained that he did not have a cold, so that particular very good excuse did not apply, but there were various sorts of torture in the world.

Thought slid toward the personal. He reviewed his interview with Stoughie with real regret.

He ought to have killed the fellow and disposed of the body. Out of a window, or into a suitcase. Better, a pair of suitcases. Thence into the ocean, like fishbait. Would the local fishermen accept indeterminate chunks of red meat? Lovely for rock cod. Surely the gulls would dispose of the offal.

But Martha would disapprove very highly. She had considered a similar act of five years previous as philosophical error of the worst kind, albeit effective. And who knew but that Don Stoughie had an aged mother at home, whose sole support he was. Long, being Chinese, had a great respect for family.

No matter, he had made his decision there by the agent's desk, and had gone halfway in action. Now the consequences would wash over him. What goes around, comes around. Who said that? Dogen? Weird Teddy?

Blue hell. Sometimes the game wasn't worth the candle. It was all because he wasn't a natural, Long knew. With human life, as with music, he hadn't the intuitive grasp, and needed much study. Human life, however, was far less comprehensible and therefore more important to him than was music.

With a thrill of fear and elation and horror he felt himself as what he was: an aging human man wearing clothes and sitting on a hard mattress under electric lights, waiting for others to decide his future. And with a terrible head cold. What awesome truth was concealed in that he did not know. But he wanted so much to know, that he began to tremble.

Since he had been with Martha he had most certainly approached that knowledge. He had seen the footprints of the ox of enlightenment, at least. Sometimes, in the past four years, while talking with her or walking alone in Mendocino, he believed he had had visions of the animal itself. Not that Martha was in any sense oxlike. . . . But he found it a fragile understanding, and wiped away by confusion and the body's pain. He wanted more. Right now, he wanted aspirin.

He took out a Kleenex. He glanced once more at the

unappealing youth, to find that one staring with unhealthy fascination at the center of Long's body.

Long recoiled, but the boy did not notice, for his gaze was impersonal, almost unfocused, and directed two feet down from Long's head. It was hungry.

Long felt the repulsion many people feel for snakes. He curled his knees to his chest. He turned away. Now he was facing the door of the cell, half glass and wire-reinforced, like that in a grammar school. Peripherally he could see that the reptilian scrutiny continued. Very nervous-making.

He forced his mind to constructive effort. Nothing would happen here until Mr. Alexander, the lawyer, arrived from Palo Alto. Then he would be let out on bail, unless Don Stoughie could convince them all he was a continuing danger to him. That was not likely. Long coughed into his Kleenex with a touch of self-pity.

The very idea of pity reminded him of St Ives's death, for Long, though he had no reason to like the man, did feel sorry that he had been killed in that way. Ugly.

There was little doubt in his mind that the death had been murder. From the little he had known of the piper, he had decided that although St. Ives was more than a bit cruel and dishonest in method, he was not a creature of wild moods. And a generally sour attitude does not lead to suicide, Long believed. St. Ives had taken drugs that day, and drugs could certainly affect the moods, but Long had never heard of suicide as a side effect of MDM, and he kept up with every major news weekly, as well as *The New York Times*.

Fear, shame, despair, or ungovernable pain: those could lead to self-destruction. St. Ives didn't seem governed by any of these. He *was*, however, governed by a need to cut at people, and he had given all five of them good reasons to want him dead in the eight weeks of the tour.

Pádraig was the obvious one, goaded like an elephant with an ankh-man on his shoulder. Long smiled a slight, sweet smile at the thought of small, round-faced Pádraig with hardly any nose) as an elephant. Though his ears *did* stick out. Had St. Ives tried to ride Long that way, he would not have survived the first week. Of course he would not have continued trying, after the first time. . . .

Elen was almost as good a candidate, with her long brooding grudge against the man. Though Elen, also, would have done better to kill him early, before he revealed the history she found so distasteful. Dispassionately the dapper Mr. Long considered St. Ives's appeal, or possible appeal, to women.

He must have cut a better figure as a young man.

Teddy Poznan seemed further out in the running. If he killed St. Ives for the cumulated insults dished out to him, then he had had a marvelous gift for concealing his irritation. What did the piper have as ammunition against Teddy? His dislike of the guitar, of course. His contempt for the counterculture. What else?

Ted Poznan had supplied him with an illegal drug. A drug that made St. Ives very happy at least for a while. Did that, perhaps, cause an equal and opposite reaction, after the drug wore off?

What was it St. Ives had said, under the influence of Adam: about being done with secrets? The piper had stored quite a trove of unlovely secrets. Long thought of one that he himself had shared with St. Ives and he grunted aloud, more certain than ever that St. Ives had not died by his own hand.

Although he was only moderately sure that he himself was not the murderer (what with this cold and the lack of intuition and all), Mayland Long had no doubt that Martha was completely innocent of the affair. What she was and what she said went clear through. Simple and perfect. She had spent the night of the death watching over Marty. Poor Marty, who was doing such odd things. Long's face grew grieved, for he had a long-standing fondness for children, especially little girls.

Yes, Martha was accounted for, but the other three rooms . . . Not that there was anything especially incriminating about the musicians going out to "sport" (as Pádraig would put it) after a concert. They were young, unlike Martha and himself. But it made a pretty problem.

Mayland Long had no qualms about casting any of his friends into the role of cold-blooded murderer. He would think no less of them for it. He might even, with mind and money, be able to help, but not while he was kept ignorant. And not while he was in jail.

Martha was the only one in a position to find things out at the moment, and he had complete faith in her. Complacently Long considered Martha's ability to find things out (things interior and exterior) as he gazed vaguely at the half-glass door, his hands folded in his lap. Given a little time, she would pick out the murderer.

But wait. Murderers, by definition, were people that killed people. And Martha, he had reason to remember, was a breakable treasure, alone out there, but for her daughter.

And Pádraig. And Elen. And Weird Teddy.

Long sprang toward the door and pounded on it, calling quite forcefully for his lawyer.

It didn't look as though Sunday was going to be as warm as Saturday, and Martha, sitting on the bus-stop bench, grew a little chilled. Or maybe her thoughts were not pleasant, for she sat with her hands balled in her lap and occasionally she shivered. When this happened, the canary-yellow paper in her hands crackled and her wrap-skirt (the only thing left that was clean) threatened to slide open.

Though many of the shops were closed, there was enough going on to keep the mall busy in this fine summer weather. The jazz band had taken a break, but there was a cowboy singing in the doorway of Leask's Department Store, playing on a plywood guitar. Three people, neither young nor old, passed, wearing army surplus. Their hair hung in the kind of dreadlocks that only great filth produces in those of Caucasian ancestry.

She looked up to find a blue and white bus stopped before her. Though she had known this was a bus stop, she had not expected the arrival of a real bus, and gazed at the driver with such vacancy that he seemed on the verge of making his hydraulic suspension kneel for the old lady. She waved him on and the bus sighed and went, its rack of bicycles bobbing behind like a bustle.

Martha was not sure her errand would bear fruit, nor that the produce would be edible even if it worked. She had been sitting on the wooden bench for a half hour, and it was now the middle of the afternoon. With George dead and Mayland in jail it seemed that active work of some kind must be called for, but she didn't know what to do about George, and David Alexander was probably already getting her friend out on bail.

Teddy had nothing to say, except "What goes around, comes around," and that got no one any forrader. Please God that he didn't do anything to set Elizabeth off. Just being Teddy was enough, really. (If only Elizabeth would forget family loyalty, take her daughter and drive home!)

Pádraig was in his room alone. Theoretically asleep. He had lied to her.

No word from Elen.

Many pairs of feet passed behind her, until one pair stopped. She turned her head and shoulders, but instead of the man she sought, there stood a slight young black woman holding a dangly leotard and a wasp-waisted drum. Martha got up anyway.

"The door," she said to the woman. "It's locked and I couldn't get anyone to answer."

"Likely they can't hear you, dear," the dancer answered amiably. "Who're you looking for?"

"Don Stoughie." Martha smiled her rosebud smile, which was answered by the other.

"Him?" The single word was followed by a snort. "Well, I'll let you in, but you mustn't go assaulting him."

Martha just raised her eyebrows, so the woman added, "But then, you're probably too young. It seems to be the really senior citizens who get that urge." The dusty door opened and Martha heard jazz guitar coming down the dark staircase. A recording, she noted, but the floor-thumps that accompanied it were live.

Martha put on a sweet-little-old-lady voice and said, "No promises." She followed the dancer up the stairs with an exaggerated stiff shuffle and turned left when the other turned right. The jazz guitar shut off as the young woman entered her studio.

Stoughie's door had a white-on-black plastic plate bearing his name, with a much more ornate brass sign below it that read REALTY. For a moment Martha read it as REALITY and wondered why such a sign should be so pretentious. Once she knew the subject was property, she understood.

Light seeped under the door; she knocked on it.

"Who'sere?" The words came out almost as one syllable. Martha mumbled.

Silence. Scraping. He asked again, this time from right behind the door, and Martha's mumble was more carefully indistinguishable, as well as a little querulous. He cracked open the door and she put her foot in it, having thought to come wearing heavy sandals. The hard sole rang when the door hit it.

"Oh, don't do that! I only want to talk to you."

"Well, I don't want to talk to you! When I do it will be in court!" He threw the door heavily at the jamb, but it bowed around Martha's Birkenstock and bounced back, hitting Stoughie smartly on the fingers. Martha interpreted the following sounds as cursing, dancing around, and sucking on knuckle joints.

"I doubt you really want to take it to court," she said judiciously, not moving her foot. "What with the terrible publicity, and the strength of our suit for malicious persecution, I suspect it will put you out of business."

"Malicious persecution?"

"And slander, of course. As well as attempt to defraud. Your insurance won't cover you for this, you know. Mr. Alexander thinks we have a case cut out for us with pinking shears."

This was not strictly true. Mr. Alexander had been

much more guarded. He had ideas for the defense, but Martha, legally uneducated, still preferred the sound of hers.

The crack of gray daylight wavered, as Stoughie moved about on the other side of the door. Then Martha yelped at a very sharp attack upon her instep and she withdrew her foot. Laughing in the most unpleasant way, Stoughie thrust the pointed iron ferrule of an umbrella through the crack as though teasing an animal before he slammed the door once more.

"Swine," whispered Martha, adding louder, "You *are* out of business for that, Stoughie. I have here a list of names of musicians who are willing to testify that you were either grossly late in your contracted payments, you underpaid, or you did not pay at all! Listen to this:"

Stoughie made a rude noise, but Martha ignored it. "This last hour I've called Hector Galleux, Máirtín Dunning and his brother Lou, Robin Petrie and Dan Carnahan, Sister Frye, Chris Caswell, Earl LeBeau, and the manager of the Riverside Synco-pates. And you know, not one of them failed to offer to help? How many of them do you think said they only wished they had hauled your ashes years ago?

"Don, you do not have either hard evidence or a basis of business goodwill upon which to build something. Mayland, on the other hand, seems to have no enemies to speak of and just oodles of time and money with which to insure his constitutional rights." The word "constitutional" sounded funny to Martha, coming out of her own mouth.

Her words had an effect on Stoughie, though not exactly the one for which she had hoped. "He can rot!" the man roared, sending the door into a tremble. "He can rot, rot, ROT in jail!"

Martha's ears rang. There was a shift in the air of the hall, as though a door had opened, but not this door. Overwhelmed, she took breath to say, "Oh, I doubt he will, Don. I imagine he's out already, in fact," and she turned to go, her list of names a bit crumpled in her hand.

At the end of the hall the door to the dance studio

was open, and eight wondering eyes stared out. The woman with the drum was at the top. She gave Martha an encouraging smile.

"Hey! I could string fishing line across the top of the stairs, about eighteen inches up, and then shout 'fire' for a while, till he runs out. . . ."

"Thanks. Let me prepare my alibi first," Martha answered, and she limped down into the daylight.

Searching for Lambs

The sergeant's string of curses began with a "goddamn" and ended with "bugger," the middle being both more imaginative and less clear. Officer Scherer looked up from his typing in mild alarm.

"That Long character. Every new bit messes things up for him worse."

Scherer frowned. "So why should that piss you off?"

Sergeant Anderson heaved back into his desk chair. "Dunno. But it does.

"Here—look. Five years ago. Robbery and a dead man. Neck broken, of all things. Found by the Coast Guard on the water, just to make an extra tie-in with this thing here." He flung the computer-generated report at Scherer.

Who read it, with his superior's simmering silence as a background. "I don't know, sir. This comes out with him smelling like a rose. Almost killed, along with the old lady—I like her—and—"

"Then don't call her an old lady," said Anderson snappishly.

Scherer raised his innocent red-brown eyes. "Well anyway. Just because he happens to be there when one crook kills another crook—"

Anderson made a noise like a teakettle coming to boil. "Just happens to be there. Just happens to lose his temper and almost strangle someone. Just happens to be there again when another gentleman decides to end it all with a rope. Are you asking me to believe that Mr

160

Mayland Long has a gift for attracting this particular kind of violence? Like honey to bees—our Mr. Long for broken necks?"

Scherer was only half cowed by this eloquence. He shrugged. "It's like that, sometimes. My mother had her car smashed by pickup trucks five times in three years. Always while parked on the street too.

"I wonder what happened to the daughter in the case?"

Anderson snorted, his interest not extending that far. "Ask Records."

Anderson asked Long about it.

"My memory is not perfect," said the very composed gentleman, sitting cross-legged on the padded and ortho-pedically sound green chair in the cozy room where they had taken him for interrogation. "I had lost a lot of blood."

Anderson nodded, grudgingly. He pulled forward the single hard chair in that padded room and sat down on it.

"Mrs. Macnamara's story is that she came to to find this man Threve lying dead and you in very bad shape and Rasmussen coming at you with a . . . wrench, or some-thing."

"Mayland, my advice to you is to say nothing."

"It was a gun," Long answered as if he had not heard the lawyer.

"You don't have to answer *any* of these questions, Mayland," said Alexander. Turning an almost icy regard to Sergeant Anderson, he continued. "I hope, at least, that you're prepared to apply these questions in some way to the matter for which my client has been arrested?" The lawyer was leaning against the window, his tie at half-mast, looking coolly from Anderson to Long.

"Prepared seven ways from Sunday!" Anderson spoke with heat.

"Don't worry about it at all, David," said Long to his

attorney. "The sergeant is naturally interested in coincidences."

Alexander was unmoved. "Coincidences are well within your rights, Mayland, and this man is not a social
acquaintance, for your standards of politeness to—"

"I will worry about my rights when I feel threatened,
David, and I will decide my circle of acquaintance."

Alexander tightened his jaw and sighed. He fixed the
detective with a glare like that of a hound held back from
attack by the word of a too-trusting master.

Long continued, "The quicker we finish this, the
quicker I will be able to take care of Martha, and that
is what interests me now."

"Famous last words, my friend!" David Alexander
pulled his knit tie through his collar and wadded it in a
ball in his hands. He sat down on the edge of the soft chair
opposite to his client's.

Long spoke over his lawyer's voice. "It was a gun. He
aimed it at me, but he did not shoot me. I was looking at
him."

Anderson's trick eyebrows went up. "Beg pardon?"

'I was looking at him. It is much more difficult to do
harm to a person who is looking into your eyes. This,
experience has led me to believe."

"But the man had just killed his partner, hadn't
he?"

Long sighed, unhurriedly. "That I cannot answer. I
was very dizzy. But it could well be that his partner was
not looking at him."

Anderson stared. "And then he let you knock him
down and tie him up."

"Evidently he did."

A thought brought a fleeting smile to the sergeant's
face. "But wasn't *he* looking at *you* when you did
it?"

"I am not bothered with that handicap," answered
Long, simply and without noticeable pride.

"And the San Francisco police believed all this?"

Long nodded. "After consideration, they did."

"You must have had a good lawyer."

"Thank you," said Alexander, very dryly. "May we go now?"

"One more question." He looked very sharply into Long's eyes, as though disputing that the Asian was immune to that sort of influence. "Is there, in your knowledge, any connection between these three incidents? The one five years ago, your . . . interaction with Don Stoughie, and the death of George St. Ives."

Long leaned forward toward the sergeant, and when he answered he seemed more interested than defensive. "I can think of none, Sergeant Anderson. But you should ask Martha."

Anderson blinked. "Are you . . . suggesting she may have some kind of involvement . . . ?"

"I am not suggesting but telling you a thing: that Martha Macnamara sees what is really there. She will see a connection, if one exists to be seen. And she will tell you what it is.

"Nor need you look at me that way, Sergeant, as though I am throwing her to you: a sacrifice in my own interest. There is nothing you or your police force can do that could do her harm. Except remain in error, of course."

Anderson signaled for the door to be opened and the three of them walked out: first the sergeant, then the lawyer, and finally Long. He turned to take a final glance down the hall in the direction of the cell where he had been incarcerated.

He caught up with Anderson. "Tell me, Sergeant. Who was that boy in the cell with me?"

Anderson's brooding expression vanished. He snickered silently and rubbed his hand over his mouth to wipe off an undignified grin. "Oh, Jerry? Jerry Carver. He's an old friend of ours."

Long took three steps and then ventured: "He . . . stared at me in the oddest manner this afternoon."

Well he might, thought Anderson. Well anyone might.

But then the explanation struck him and he giggled again, audibly.

"That would be your suit. Jerry's nickname is 'The Silkie.' Not a sea monster: he's got a thing for silks. He steals them. Usually underwear, but I guess a raw-silk jacket is good enough for him. Sometimes he puts his booty on all together, panties in layers and brassieres and stockings with old-fashioned seams, and he goes walking in the mall. Sometimes he burns them, in a pile. Dangerous, this time of year, what with the dry hills.

"He's in and out of institutions, our Jerry. Harmless, at least so far, but completely unreachable."

Long turned to Anderson. On his very dark face was building a kind of outrage that neither his arrest nor the extensive questioning had been able to elicit. "And you dared to put *me* in with..."

Alexander, the lawyer, pinched him sharply by the skin of the elbow. Through his silk jacket.

Martha did not feel successful as she walked the six blocks back to the motel. It had not been her plan to get Stoughie irrationally angry at her. She had not intended her reading of the list to sound so very threatening. It had never entered her head (and this would serve her right) that he would stab at her bare foot that way. She limped and staggered across the cobbled mall, and she wished that whoever had borrowed the van, hadn't.

That jazz band, again. She passed it and wished she were playing there, with people in the audience buying her tropical drinks with a little bit of rum in them, and with the sound of the bass guitar and the trumpet. How carefree they were, compared with being the head and founder of a now-defunct Celtic traditional band with one member dead, a manager in jail, and maybe a murderer among the remaining players.

Halfway down the next block the buildings blocked the sound of the brass and changed it all, and for a moment Martha forgot her problems and even the misery of her bruised and blackening foot. For the sun through the leaves of the blossoming eucalyptus made a comforting and domestic play over the pavement, all peppered with ants. Martha took a breath.

Three notes of the obscure music behind her snagged in her brain and met a memory, and Martha closed her eyes and heard again Pádraig Ó Súilleabháin singing "An Caoineadh na d'Trí Muire," "The Lament of the Three Marys," in the practice room at the Hall. Only last night.

Martha herself had played the tune on her fiddle many years before someone first sang those words for her. And told her the terrible meaning of the Irish words:

"Who is it, that fine man there on the tree of suffering? O grief, O my grief. Mother, don't you recognize your son? O grief, O my grief."

And as great sorrow drives out lesser, this old song quieted her restless spirit as it stung her sun-brightened eyes. George was dead. All the sour caring and all the pain and all the music of him departed from them. Silent. Nor was there mother, lover, or even aunt left to grieve for him. Unless it was Sandy, who had been with him Friday evening. But no, Sandy had seen Elen this morning, and had called and didn't seem concerned. Not about *that*. There was no one but Martha, the leader of the band.

For one still minute Martha Macnamara stood on the sidewalk, favoring her left foot and marking the passing of George St. Ives. The brass band at Cooper House rang around the angles of the stucco buildings like distant war pipes. Martha went back to the motel limping, but with a peaceful face.

She was only a minute behind Long, who had parted from his frustrated lawyer at the same Cooper House jazz patio. She heard the storming of Elizabeth through the door.

"I went down the hall because this . . . this turkey had a phone call. On *our* phone again. And then he just doesn't answer, so I stand there pounding like a fool . . ."

It was Long she addressed, but Teddy Poznan was the "turkey" in question. He glanced in appeal from Long to Martha. "I was meditating."

This was not the politic thing to say to Elizabeth. "Meditation? Hah! What drug do you call 'meditating'? You don't even know what the word means!"

Long attempted to placate. "It has endless meanings, Elizabeth. And it doesn't matter what Theodore was doing. How long was Marty left alone?"

Martha started. "Marty?" She bulled past them all and limped furiously to the connecting door.

Elizabeth wailed in anger and worry. "Yes, yes, she's gone! Out the door unnoticed! I've been all around the streets. That sweet little Pádraig's been out looking for a half hour and nothing. She's gone!"

Martha, in her shock, could think of nothing but the fact that women certainly liked Pádraig Ó Súilleabháin. Even Elizabeth, who liked so few. Martha looked into the bedroom where the child had been napping (too well behaved by half) and she saw the truth of it. She let her head sag sideways into the doorframe, none too gently. "The same nightmare," she whispered.

Long spoke, coughing. "Let us remain calm. First, I will go down to the beach. Wait here for me."

Martha turned to say she was coming along, but she stopped herself. She knew she couldn't move like he could, cut the crowds like he could, or dodge the traffic. Not even if both her legs were sound. She knew a moment's blind jealousy of that sinuous, athletic form, and then she almost laughed, for he went down the hallway coughing like a dying man.

"To the beach?" Elizabeth remembered what her mother had told her about Marty's escapade. "Oh, dear God! The traffic. In the middle of the day!"

Elizabeth sat down with the receiver of the phone in her hand, but she did nothing but stare at the green wall, holding the receiver in her lap. Martha sat down and eased out of her shoes.

O grief, O my grief.

"What'd you do to your foot?" asked Teddy, wandering over to her.

She kept her eyes closed. "Oh. I just put it where I shouldn't have. Not thinking straight."

He squatted at the end of the bed and took the foot in his hands. It was square and the toes had not known polish. Not even much trimming.

"I can help the swelling to stop. Maybe even keep the bruise down?"

"How's that?" Martha worked hard to sound politely interested.

"With acupressure."

Martha nodded that he could try. Teddy was on his feet and moving toward the door with energy. "I need my mosibustion sticks," he said, and was gone.

Martha opened her eyes and saw the ceiling. Without moving, she said to her daughter, "I think you should apologize to him. You've been rude since you got here, and Teddy hasn't done a thing wrong."

"Unless he killed George St. Ives." Elizabeth dangled the receiver and suddenly winced, sending her perfect forehead into wrinkles. "Okay, okay, Mother. I'll apologize. It's just been such a stinking day."

The dial tone from the telephone was making harmonies in Martha's head, but when she turned to ask her daughter to put it back, she found Elizabeth dialing. "The police?"

In another second or two the connection was made, and it was obvious her guess was the right one. Elizabeth was very good on the telephone; she gave her story and the necessary information reasonably and without excess emotion. Well, why not? She was a bright and well-educated professional woman. Forceful.

An officer would be right there.

"They're certainly going to know us well at the police station," murmured Martha.

Elizabeth stifled a sob. "They're allowed to know us as well as they want, as long as they find her."

Martha sat down beside her on the little bench of the

desk. "Remember, Elizabeth? You ran away. We were living on Riverside Drive and the policeman took you in and you wouldn't answer questions."

Elizabeth's perfect lips grew very tight as she resisted the analogy. "I didn't run away. The cop was an overbearing pig."

Martha nodded. "When we ask Marty, I'm sure she'll say she wasn't running away either. Kids always have their reasons."

But Elizabeth shook her head, slowly and as though it carried a great weight. "There's something... something hurting her today. I think she feels I abandoned her, and so she's—"

"I think you're full of shit," said Martha, and Teddy came in with the moxybustion sticks.

The boardwalk was not as crowded today, as it was cooler, and there were fewer human forms speckling the white beach. A stiff breeze blew inland and the blue sheet was wrinkled. Long squinted against the wind.

There was a black shape at the water's edge, made shapeless and glossy through soaking, and with something frilly, like hair at one end. He ran through the sand to it, scraping the polish off his black leather shoes, but it proved to be only strands of kelp, with their little blond bladders bunched around them. The moving ribbon of brightness where sea met shore was otherwise unbroken.

That lump on the sand was a man, and the far one, which had looked promising, turned into a yellow dog. Damn—were his eyes failing him too? The forced run had brought the phlegm up and he was coughing repeatedly.

He jogged back to the boardwalk. His shoes were full of sand. He was in front of a souvenir shop: the place where Marty had waited with her grandmother while he found her flowered sunglasses. The place which closed last at night. A clerk, young and female, was gazing vaguely out over the street to the vague blue ocean.

She hadn't seen a little girl, she told him, but the

entranced boredom in her face made her words lack value. He went down the boardwalk.

Someone shrieked on the little roller coaster: a gratuitous noise, Long thought. People should be more considerate. He shut his mind against all sounds of disaster and went on.

No one at the hot-dog stand had seen anything. The words of the Wild Mouse Ride ticket taker were swallowed by wind, and he had to shake his head to be understood. The man at the Ferris wheel said he shouldn't be expected to remember.

Long walked back the way he had come. His hair blew in his face and that bothered him more than it would have bothered most people. He looked west and out, over the beach and to the high concrete pier.

That was an ominous place to lose a child.

But Marty had never shown any interest in getting from the beach up to the pier. Indeed, it looked very heavy and uninviting from below, like this. She would have had to cross over back at Front Street, and a little girl heading toward the beach couldn't be expected to think of that.

He looked down the uncompromising length of it, feeling less and less inclined to believe she might have tried to make her way there, when he spied a little knot of people clustered around the end of it. Where St. Ives had been found hanging.

Full of dread and coughing, Long made the trip down the pier.

It was only a marketman, his hair slicked back and his apron pink with fish blood, explaining to the visitors how the body had been discovered. Long asked—not this vendor, but another one—if he had seen a little blond girl in a sundress, walking alone.

The man raised his heavy square face and stared at Long, seeming to ask what this dapper and very dark Asian had to do with such a child, but he only shook his head and went back to wrapping salmon steaks in newspaper. His hands were not bloody, but stained with printer's ink.

When Long returned there were four people in the motel room, for Pádraig had returned and was slouched in his accustomed place by the table. There was a smell of incense in the air.

The all looked at Long with a painful hope, and he looked only at Martha. "I don't think she went that way."

"She is not by the motel," stated Pádraig. "I looked everywhere. Even in the dustbins."

Long went into the bathroom and washed his face. He wished he could wash his lungs as well, for they felt both filthy and abused. The desire for a cup of strong tea swept over him, but he ignored it. There was no time.

"Did you call the police?" he asked, coming back into the bedroom. Its paint and polyester, white, green, and lilac colored, hit him as though he had never seen them before.

"Of course," said Elizabeth, who still sat at the bureau by the telephone.

"Sergeant Anderson was out," her mother murmured. "Because of the other missing kid—the one from last night. But they sent Officer Scherer again."

"The other missing child?"

Martha shook her head, forestalling either hope or new worry. "Not like this. They think it's a custody kind of thing. Institutionalized kid stolen by the parents who originally gave it up and can't have it back. Or I may have it wrong. He told me about it before.

"About that and some purse snatchings."

Long looked at her closely and in silence, as though her incomplete thoughts would communicate themselves if he were patient.

"It was the string-bean cowboy with the Tevis Cup buckle who came," added Elizabeth in a voice drained of feeling. "He said they would all look for her."

Long was tired and the sand had made his shoes uncomfortable. He took them off one at a time and emptied them into the wastebasket. "I'm sure they will," he said, and added, "I'm going out again."

"Where?" It was Elizabeth who asked.

"I don't know. To the mall, perhaps. Perhaps only to run in circles, uselessly. But I feel impelled to movement."

Martha raised her foot, which was now sausagelike both in shape and color. She cursed using words Elizabeth hadn't believed her mother knew.

Elizabeth herself made fists in her pockets. "I . . . I feel that way, too, but I'm terrified to leave the phone."

"I don't think you should," said Long. The afternoon was now advanced enough that the shadow of the wall darkened the window, and Elizabeth's face was full of haggard shadows. "When the police find her, she will surely be tired and upset and then it will be important that you are near."

She bit down on her own hand and looked away.

"I'm going with you," said Pádraig, almost belligerently.

Long opened his mouth to say he would rather not have the company, but the very young Irishman stood in front of him, hands in pockets and head bulled out in front of his shoulders, ready for anything.

Was this the boy who had begun the day with a shock, continued by getting drunk, fell asleep, woke with a hangover, and ran to the Santa Cruz jail to rescue him? Heavens, but youth had a magic to it. Long decided he'd be a fool to turn down such aid. Pádraig might have to carry him home.

Teddy Poznan had not said a word since Long's arrival. Now he uncoiled himself from his yogic seat on the carpet. A moxybustion stick fell from his shirt pocket and broke. "I have a little idea of my own," he said. "I'll go out and give it a go."

"What's that?" Elizabeth's question was harsh.

Martha sighed. "I can't imagine it's anything that could do Marty any harm, Elizabeth."

"I'm going to knock on doors." Teddy moved his shoulders in circles and took a deep breath alternately through each nostril. "I'm going to go from door to door and ask every person in the neighborhood if he or she has seen a pretty little yellow-haired girl.

"I'll probably get arrested, but maybe I'll just find Marty, seated in front of someone's television, happy as a clam."

"Rotting her brain," murmured Elizabeth, but her heart wasn't in it.

"Even if they haven't seen her," added Martha, "you'd have the perfect opportunity to tell them about the values of acupressure. Or a mucus-free diet. Or even colonic cleansing!"

Ted's face reflected massive resignation as he followed the other two out the door.

The sea wind had blown the sky gray, and Long kept both his hands in the pockets of his jacket. Pádraig didn't seem to notice the sudden chill, not even when his hair snapped around his eyes.

"Did you ask the woman at the bus stop?" Long asked him, standing as yet undecided on the street in front of the motel.

Pádraig tucked his round head between his sizable shoulders. "I didn't talk to anybody," he said, making his sudden shift to shyness.

She was heavy and dressed with orchids on polyester. She hadn't seen a child.

Long looked left and then right. On the one side was Chestnut Street, blank and busy. Down the block on the right side was the south end of the mall.

How could a child ignore the appeal of the blossoming red eucalyptus in its rows, or the crazy brick walkways? Long turned right, dragging Pádraig in his wake.

At the corner the wind hit them, and it was wet. "It's starting to drizzle," said Long in disbelief.

Pádraig Ó Súilleabháin made a triumphant noise. "At last the drought has ended!"

Long turned and stared at him. Though they were almost of a height, he managed to tower over Pádraig with arched neck. "What drought?"

Pádraig took a step backward and bumped into the cowboy guitarist of the mall, who was making a dart for a shop doorway. The guitarist was protecting his instrument from the rain with his fringed jacket. He had drops beading his droopy moustache.

Long turned the encounter to use, and to his satisfaction the guitarist admitted to having seen a little girl with yellow hair about an hour previous. All alone. He mentioned particularly the daisy-rimmed sunglasses, which gave her "a Lolita sort of look."

Long didn't approve of the allusion. Pádraig didn't understand it. They went along the mall in the rain.

Pacific Mall in the rain had a very different look to it. Less tropical. The bricks on the street shone with a more conservative, cityish rust, and the red fluff of blossoms was battered to the sidewalks.

"Look at them," said Pádraig, pointing quite rudely at a cluster of pedestrians packed into the alcove of a jewelry store. "They might melt, they think."

"They might," answered Long, without looking. "Rain in June is an aberration. A disgusting one."

"Hah!" Pádraig hopped in place at Long's side. "In this heat it's nothing but a good face-washing." Indeed, the water on his face seemed to brighten Pádraig's color and his mood until he seemed to Long much like the rowdy boy who had begun the tour in Massachusetts, eight weeks (only eight weeks?) before.

"My mother had a cow that did like Marty—would run away. She ran off every day, and you know where she'd go?"

"Is it relevant?" asked Long in return, wiping his face with both hands.

Pádraig opened his mouth at the unfamiliar-sounding word, but decided to let it go. "She would go into Ballyferriter and stand in front of the hostelry. There she would stand and drop her little piles against the window. The barman would be wild!"

Long said nothing. The rain came down with force.

"It wasn't anything to eat that she got there, because

no one would feed her. And before we got the telephone in, he'd have to call next door and a lad would come over with the message she was out and in front of the bar. Then it was me to come and get her. Me and the dog."

The air was suddenly filled with the smell of coffee, heavy enough to sting the nose. Mayland Long was not a coffee drinker, but he was not immune to the invitation of the smell, associated as it was with sweet pastries and other foods he did like. Searching about him through water-sparkled lashes, he found the establishment whence the odor came. It had an especially good door alcove, containing three backpackers in semi-Indian garb and a hammer dulcimer player.

He stood without and asked his question, this time adding the sunglasses to his description.

"I saw her," said the woman with the dulcimer. "I won't forget her in a hurry either. The little thing stood right in front of me quiet as a mouse all the time I was playing, and when I was done she said, 'Planxty Irwin,' clear as a bell."

"And was it 'Planxty Irwin,' then, that you were playing?" asked Pádraig, grinning.

"No. It was 'Arkansas Traveler.' But still . . ." Her gray-blue glance sharpened. "'Scuse me, but are you Pat Sullivan?"

Pádraig admitted as much, lackadaisically. He was made to wonder how many of that faceless audience last night had been musicians. (And how many knew how he'd made a fool of himself with the *seannós*.) He read a surmise in this girl's eyes, and predicted she was about to suggest he get his instrument. Or to go somewhere. He couldn't, of course, and as a matter of fact, the idea struck him as boring. But he always made such a mess of turning people down. Pádraig sighed.

"I thought so," said the dulcimer player, doing a sort of juggle of her knobbed sticks. "I saw you race once, in Brittany. *The Tiger Cat*, wasn't it?

"I have a little boat out here," she continued, casually. "Fourteen foot. Nothing competitive, but . . ."

Long had to drag him away.

Someone had seen Marty drift off to the east. Another
lounger was sure she went back down the mall. The
dulcimer player herself hadn't noticed. At last Long and Ó
Súilleabháin stood uncertain at the end of the mall and
looked around them.

On one side of the street was a bakery. On the other
was the coffee emporium. To the north, across a bleak and
busy intersection, was the Santa Cruz clock tower, which
was of red brick with an open arch underneath. A fountain, protected by the clock itself from the rain, spurted in
lively fashion within the arch.

"She'd have to!" said Pádraig. "Any *páiste* would have
to. I think I have to myself." He led the way across to the
tower, oblivious to the honking traffic. Long followed, his
face set into worry at the thought that Marty might have
breasted this same mindless metal flow.

It was such a pretty little fountain he was forced to
agree with Pádraig. A child could not see this place
without coming to it. He felt a surge of anger that the
builders had put the thing here: a bait of bright water and
cobalt tile in the center of a murderous trap.

Pádraig, still being a *páiste*, sat on the edge of the
fountain and waited to see what would draw him on next.
But the next step was not so clear.

"She didn't go back or we'd have found her," said
Long, leaning against the bricks. "And left and right are
only streams of traffic. I venture to suggest she went on."
He looked up in surprise, for it had abruptly stopped
raining.

On the far curb was a telephone kiosk. "We should
call in," Long said, and felt in his pockets for change.
There was only his elegantly thin checkbook and his
money clip, containing a large number of twenties. At the
lintless bottom of the pocket were three pennies.

"I have ten-cent pieces," said Pádraig, digging out a

jingling handful. "My mother told me always to have silver in a strange place."

Long took two dimes. "Your mother told you correctly," he admitted, and out of a new feeling for the woman he had never met, he added, "What did she ever do about the cow?"

"She sold it and bought a used washing machine," said Pádraig as Long picked up the receiver.

For a moment the thought that he was about to find that Marty was home and it was all over was so overpowering that Long could not dial. He had not realized he had become so attached to the child. It made him almost unable to act. But his face showed nothing and he blew his nose discreetly as his other hand punched out the now-familiar number.

The conversation was short.

"Nothing," Long said to Pádraig, who didn't need to be told.

From then on the way became a matter of guesswork, but Mr. Long was a very careful guesser. On the streets north of the mall there were fewer street people, and the pedestrians going to have vacuum cleaners fixed or to buy bagged almonds were not likely to remember the presence of a small solitary child, passing an hour or a half hour before.

But the rain had left puddles in the sidewalk, and out of one of them ran a track of footprints of the proper size. These might have been left by Marty, and if so, she was not too far ahead of them. Long decided they were meaningful, and he and Pádraig continued north.

It rained again and stopped again, for the wind was blowing new weather in from the southwest. Pádraig's heavy black hair, straight as an Indian's, straight as Long's Chinese hair, collected diamond beads. So did his eyelashes, but he didn't seem to mind.

Long felt chilled and hot together, as they came out of River Street and came to the wide swath of Highway 1.

The traffic was heavy and fast; it was difficult to see pavement in between the cars. He opened his mouth to say, "No, she can't have gone this way," but the words didn't come out.

But Pádraig heard what was not said. "Terrible place. But there's a light, isn't there?"

Yes, there was a traffic light, and pedestrian boxes too. Would a three-year-old be strong enough to push the steel button, and responsible enough to go through the work of it? Long found he was shaking his head.

"Either she did or she didn't," Pádraig was shouting into his ear, for the roar of traffic was formidable. "And if she didn't, then it must be that she walked along the highway here."

"That's almost worse," said Long, glowering as though it were somehow Ó Súilleabháin's fault.

"I know it," answered Pádraig, on the intake of breath. His small nose wrinkled at the stink of exhaust and he stepped out into the street. "We can go see, at least."

Long yanked him back as he pushed the recalcitrant steel button that controlled the pedestrian box. "We, being adults, can do it safely."

"Naw, but it's such a long wait!" But Pádraig waited, scowling, Long's hand heavy on his shoulder.

Both men glanced furtively at the gray pavement as they passed across the highway. No blood in the damp road.

On the other side they discovered another little cause for optimism, for the same muddy little footprints led in and out of the puddles leading away.

"Perhaps it is not Marty," murmured Long, "but it is the same foot we've been following."

Pádraig leaped into the air making fists above his head. He gave a good imitation of a hunting horn. Mr. Long, though he himself was heartened by the discovery, viewed this without enthusiasm. "My granddaughter is not a fox *or* a hare, Ó Súilleabháin." But Pádraig had already dashed ahead.

Youth. Mr. Long did not feel very well, and this out-of-season rain had left him worse. There was something he remembered, about being sick and in an unexpected California rain. As he walked on, he breathed with effort and tried to remember.

There it was: the memory. Sick and bleeding and cold, under the scrub trees of a house lot, while two vulgar characters made ready to kill Martha Macnamara. One of the worst times of his extended life. One of the best, too, in retrospect.

Surely a head cold could be endured. . . .

Certainly it could, in exchange for Marty's being found safe. His granddaughter, Long had called her, and it was doubtful he remembered at the moment that she was not, in fact, his blood relation. She was little and perfect and full of trust in him; Long was her Chinese daddo: ready to destroy whatever creature came between them to do her harm.

But of course there was nowhere to focus his anger, for Marty had simply wandered off by herself. There was no villain in this piece at all. Perhaps he could vent his rage on "Judy," the imaginary playmate she could not forget, but that would not be much to the purpose.

They were passing the garden of the Salz Tannery, and the sour, dry smell of leather hit their lungs. Then Long felt a much harsher assault: an assault of cold that seemed to have malice of its own, stronger than the warmth of anger. He gasped, tripped on the sidewalk, and staggered into Pádraig.

The young man's mouth hung open, and his blue eyes squinted in confusion. "Fog?" he said, his word leaving a cloud of mist in the air. He shook his head like a dog. "Isn't. No fog. But like yesterday, on the beach. It was bad like this."

Long heard him without understanding. "Listen," he whispered, and the two stood huddled on the rainy sidewalk, while the traffic going by made scissor sounds. After only five seconds, the cold went away.

"Did you hear anything, *a chara*?" asked Long. "Like pipes? Or a sea gull?" Pádraig shook his head.

"Nevertheless," said Long. "Nevertheless." He strode forward, his face set in hard lines.

"And to think I said there was no villain."

*   *   *

Martha was looking out the motel room window, which had a view of the parking lot, the enclosed patch of dry grass beyond it, and the backyard of a row house beyond that. There was a tricycle made of pink plastic upended on a tiny square of green, and a small boy with an orange popsicle on the concrete stoop. Martha felt a rush of envy that made her knees weak.

It was not that she wanted to be that boy with his frozen confection (she hated artificial orange flavor) any more than she wanted to be a pink tricycle. She only wanted to be unconcerned.

Óchón, agus mochón Ó!

The dead grass in the little field sparkled with drops from the unaccountable rain. So dry was the grass that the rain could not soften it, nor the sea wind ruffle it. How awkward a play the two young people had made out of that dead grass; the old play of courtship. Which is just about the best play in life and yet—she considered Elen and Pádraig—sometimes a mistake. . . .

And how strange a murder weapon. Murder is always a mistake.

As though conjured, Elen Evans came in the door, slumped from weariness and with her fringe of hair in untidy strings, but still perfectly in command of herself. "Where is everybody?" she asked. Under her dark hair and dark tan, her face shone pale. The painted walls put a green tint to it.

Elizabeth lifted her head from the glass-topped bureau table, where she still sat by the phone. She had the red imprints of her knuckles on her cheek. She focused with difficulty on Elen, decided she was inconsequential, and put her head down again.

Martha was not looking at Elen's face, but at her hand and what she held in it. "You brought back my van?"

Elen blinked and glanced at the key ring herself. "Oh. Yes. I'm sorry. I . . . borrowed it."

"You didn't tell me."

Though Martha's words had been free of rancor, Elen flinched. "I'm so sorry about that, Martha. Especially after I heard they arrested Mayland for this damn George thing. But I didn't expect to be gone more than—"

"Oh my, that's right." Martha raked her hair with both hands and she walked over to where Elen stood in the doorway. "That's what I said to your friend on the phone. And that's what I thought at the time. But it wasn't for that. He was arrested for shaking up Don Stoughie."

Elen's mouth sagged open, her shoulders sank down, and she swayed on her feet, but such was her self-possession that all these seemed only conscious theatricality. "My dear! For shaking the who...?"

"Assault," said Martha. "It's claimed that he used some... fairly mild strong-arm tactics in order to get Stoughie to release our money."

Elen threw her purse on the bed, following it with herself. "Really? How frivolous! And what marvelous timing."

She stared blankly at the blank ceiling, and after sixty seconds, she added in quite another tone, "So there's no evidence to say George's death was anything other than suicide, is there?"

Martha sat down beside her. Her hair stood out in a wing on one side and she wore an owlish, tired expression. "None that I know of. But I don't think it *was* suicide. Do you?"

Elen merely stared.

"Besides, we have another problem right now. Marty's gone off again."

Elen sat up so fast the bed rocked. "Oh, no. The beach!"

Elizabeth spoke, and her voice was phlegmy with suppressed tears. "We tried that. Both Mayland and the police. She's not there.

"According to him she went north, this time. He found footprints. Some people saw her. I wish he'd call in again."

Elen squeezed her head between her hands. "Slow down. Too much to digest, here, and I just woke up. That sweet idiot Sandy thought I needed my sleep too much and I woke up and came blasting down here thinking they had our manager on a murder rap. . . ."

Martha took a breath to collect herself. From where she was sitting she could see the distant backyard, but not the little boy. Nor the tricycle. Just as well.

"He's out on bail for the assault charge. He and Pádraig went out along the streets, looking for Marty or for someone who might have seen her walking along."

"Pádraig may very well find her," Elen interrupted. "He has an affinity for children. Like calls to like, I guess."

Martha considered this and a slight smile touched her lips. "Mayland has an affinity for Marty herself. Like calling to unlike."

"She went looking for Judy, again," Elizabeth said, and her voice was ragged. "God, I wish I knew where that one came from! I ask her and she just cries."

The blond woman's face was patches of white and red and her bones stood out both in face and shoulders. Elen Evans stared at her silently, as though she were afraid of her, and indeed, with her size, passion, and Valkyrie face, Elizabeth did look dangerous. Martha glanced again at the van keys.

"I'm going to follow them," she stated. "Give me those keys and all the dimes you have." She turned to her daughter almost fiercely. "I think you should come with me, Liz. You're falling apart here."

Elizabeth made a floundering gesture to rise, but then fell down onto the stool again. "The phone. I have to stay. . . ."

"I can do that." Elen slipped off the bed and her eyes, like Elizabeth's, were wet. "It's the least I can do for you, after running off with your only transportation all this time." She dispossessed Elizabeth of the seat. "I won't move from here till you come back.

"With Marty."

Teddy came in without knocking, for the door was not completely closed. He found Elen in the comfortable armchair, for she had dragged the phone to the breakfast table. Her eyes were swollen.

"Wet through," he mumbled. "And for nothing. At least not on the material level." Then he remembered Elen had not been there before.

"They tell you? About Marty?"

She nodded and yawned. "Yep. And that Mayland isn't really arrested for murder."

"If it was murder," he said.

Elen made a casting-away gesture: remnant of her usual smooth manner. "La! But Martha believes it was murder. And who is the prime suspect, I ask you? He shows up dead the very day he blows the gaff on our very embarrassing shared past. . . ."

There was silence, broken only by traffic, bird song, and faint footsteps in the hall. Teddy broke it. "Hey, Elen, did you see a friend of mine here this morning? Little guy with a headband?"

Elen squinted at him, irritated by the non sequitur. "No, I didn't."

The reply was daunting, but it did not satisfy Ted Poznan. He wiggled in his damp shirt and gazed at his own face in the mirror behind the bureau. The footsteps became louder and then someone knocked.

As Ted had left it cracked, the door opened by the force of the knock to reveal Sergeant Anderson standing there. "Hello again," he said. "Where's Mrs. Macnamara?"

"Out looking for Marty," answered Elen, rising. "You do know about that, don't you?"

Stepping into the room, Anderson nodded to Teddy. He revealed a patrolman, who stood outside.

"I heard it on the radio, but I was out investigating— oddly enough—another missing child."

Elen sighed, rubbed her eyes, and looked around for a chair. "That seems to be the trendy thing now. Pictures on all my shopping bags of missing children. And the coupon packages . . . Horrible. Do sit down, Inspector."

"Sergeant," he corrected her amiably. "And I'm afraid I'd like a little private conversation . . ."

Elen's face froze and went white. Teddy rose and looked uncertain whether perhaps leaving Elen would be an act of cowardice.

"Go, Ted," she whispered.

"But the conversation I had in mind was *with* Mr. Poznan," said Detective-Sergeant Anderson apologetically.

Teddy's brown eyes went very wide.

The Bear Went Over the Mountain

The two men stood at the dripping edge of the forest. "Shit, what a strange place," said Pádraig reverently and he took a step back onto the sidewalk.

Long stepped into the briars that edged the road and they clawed at his cream-colored trousers. He called over his shoulder: "And it has a strange reputation. It's a state park. I would rather find that Marty hadn't gone in here, but that deer path is the sort of thing that would attract a child."

"I would like to see a deer. A wild deer." Pádraig took another step back and lunged forward, making a single leap over the bramble barrier. He landed hands and knees on wet redwood mulch and sent a spatter of mud onto his companion. He apologized, grinning.

The light was dim, not merely because of the wind-blown and dissolving clouds in the sky, but because of the trees. The perfectly straight and even trunks of the redwoods seemed to be holding up a blue-green and furry ceiling far above. Sound faded. There was no undergrowth. A few yards in, it was perfectly dust-dry.

There was a streak of paler dust scoring the mulch from behind them and into the distance ahead. "This has been disturbed recently," said Long. "Perhaps only by deer . . ." He straightened again and looked up. "Or dogs." The silence of the place fell like drapes around them, and Long continued in a whisper: "Older than human. Older than the hairy creatures: these redwood trees. Even as a sapling, a redwood feels old. They do not compromise, and they do not care for us or for our problems, a Phádraig."

"Then you're like these trees yourself, Mayland," said Pádraig, walking very close beside him and looking all around. "It's just this morning when we were at the bar I began to wonder if you were human, with your talk about the age on you and the power. Maybe you have the soul of a redwood."

Long stopped and snorted. "By seven sages, I remember that conversation! And if that was any indication, I have the soul of a drunk. And I—well, I won't brag my age under a redwood tree. Most inauspicious.

"But it isn't the redwoods that give the park its odd reputation. The strangeness I mean is of human kind." His breath made a thick, phlegmy sound and he winced as he cleared his throat.

"This place is too big and too dark and hilly to be patrolled. And it is too near a pleasant town like Santa Cruz. It attracts those who can neither live in cities nor in complete wilderness. I read about it too often in the San Francisco papers: criminals and crazy people. The poor park has more than its share of crazy people." Long's steps raised little beige clouds. It sounded as though he were walking on foam. "Of course a man may be only pleasantly crazy—some of the finest men are *called* crazy—but people have died here."

Pádraig now stepped so close beside Long they bumped shoulders with each step. "*Óch*, you have more than your share of craziness all over this country, I think." His foot slipped into a hole concealed by shed redwood sprigs and he went down with an outsized squeal.

Long caught him under the arms and pulled him up. "Why you would call me a part of this country, I don't know. It's you who have the citizenship by birth, isn't it? Through your mother?"

Pádraig's glance was doggishly sly. "Aw, but that didn't fool you, did it?"

"Indeed it did, a Phádraig! Are your papers forged, then?"

Pádraig gave a completely childish skip over the redwood mulch. "They're real papers for a real Pádraig Ó Súilleabháin, but I'm not him. He's my cousin of the same name, who does plastering and has no use for his passport, so I've been him since I came out for my first race.

"Did I really fool you? And Martha? She must have known better, for she knows my ma. I made the mistake of telling George, worse my luck."

Long stopped still in a cloud of forest dust. "St. Ives knew? I'm surprised he kept his mouth shut, since he was not your friend at all. . . ."

"You can believe he wasn't! It was his idea that I should go home in the first week, and he said if I was still with the band after that, he'd turn me in to the immigration men. But it seems he forgot again, or was afraid what Martha would do, because I heard no more about it."

Pádraig stood beside Long, grinning unrepentantly and with his hair in his eyes. It seemed he attracted more dirt in his passage than did the other, and a large part of it was on his face. His shirt front had come out of his trousers. His raffish, unfinished appearance led Long to thinking.

"One question, a Phádraig. Are you the same age as well as the same name as your cousin?"

The grin grew broader. "That would be asking too much out of chance. I'm three years older. Couldn't you have guessed that?"

"I could not," answered Long very firmly. "And I think this trick of yours is going to do you no good, lad. The police aren't stupid, and if they find out you are traveling under false papers—and it would have been so easy to get you a temporary visa for the tour—they'll feel obliged to poke further. You've put yourself into a corner where you have a reason to have killed that man there.

Worse for yourself, you made the very rope that took his life."

Long, the complete linguist, often slipped from English to Irish in speaking with Pádraig, and such was the influence of the boy's history that the more he chided him the more he tended to use Irish.

But before Long was finished talking, Pádraig had finished listening, for there was a shimmer of metal at the floor of a valley below them, most unaccountable in the forest. The young man plunged with renewed enthusiasm down the slippery hill. Mr. Long followed more sedately, for the dust had set him to coughing once again.

"Don't worry, Mayland," Pádraig called out as he slid. "I need that passport for the autumn, when I'm going to be teaching the sailing classes by Boston. And why should it be questioned a bit? No one knows now but you, and you won't tell."

Don't depend on that, my boy, said Long, but only to himself. He stepped delicately in Pádraig's wake, wondering why the young fellow who had been so cowed by St. Ives (and by his father, if Martha was to be believed) could be so hard for Long himself to influence.

Perhaps his personal authority was waning. Why not, when his body's constitution let him down so easily? At one time the affair with Don Stoughie would not have dragged out to its cat-fight end.

But watching Pádraig Ó Súilleabháin bounce, high-stepping down the dry slope in front of him, full of determination and unthinking confidence, Long decided that it was not his own senility, but only that the boy reminded him too strongly of Marty for him to use discipline.

"Look what we have here!" Pádraig kicked the fallen needles aside, covering himself in aromatic compost. "It's iron. A train rail, out here in the middle of the wilderness."

Long stooped down and picked among the litter less wholeheartedly. At this distance, the smell of the cast redwood twigs was heady. "Right enough. It's an old, narrow-gauge railroad line. In remarkably good preservation too. The top shows almost no rust."

"Well, what would you have, in this desert?" said Pádraig, and he added, "I think that she came down here. Look how it's scuffed all along the side. She went along the track, probably walking *on* it, down between those two hills." Pádraig started off at a trot. Walking on the rail.

"It isn't a desert in the winter," said Long, again following. "And I'm not at all sure this track wasn't made by deer or dogs."

Pádraig shrugged, not bothering to turn. "But I'm confident we're close behind her, Mayland, and sometimes I know things I can't explain. Isn't it so with you?"

Long chuckled, and for easier conversation, he stepped onto the other shiny rail. His balance was at least as good as Pádraig's, and he bounced less. "Not at all, my friend. I know only what I am told, or what my eyes and ears tell me. I loathe the confusion of the occult. It does not lead to the truth."

"Now you sound like the priest." Pádraig's progress faltered, for he had led Long around a bend into a very intimidating scene. To the left of the old rail rose what might have been a brush jam in a creek. But the branches were the trunks of massive trees that rose in splintered majesty forty feet up. A circle of earth and root the size of a small asteroid clutched at the air. Only half-aware of his action, Pádraig slipped from the rail and retreated five steps to the steep undercut of the right-hand slope. "Jesus! What hand did that? It darkens the sky!"

Long came beside him and pointed. "If you look a few yards away you can see the bed of a stream, though it's dry."

"That little thing?"

"I told you there is some rain here in the winter. It's odd that slide didn't block our path entirely. It looks like it's been cleared. But why would anyone go to the effort of moving all that?"

Pádraig continued flattened against the crumbly wall, shaking his head from side to side in awe of the fallen monsters.

"Well, let's go on now, if you've still got your feeling.

I wouldn't want the child to be caught by the dark in here."

As if in response to Long's unhappy thought, the air filled with a lonely keening. In the hush of the trees, it was very loud. It got louder. There was a menacing rumble.

"I hear it this time, all right," Pádraig stated. "Very like the pipes. Not the elbow pipes, but the Scottish pipes, I think. And it's no recording, for—"

Long had been staring into the dusky distance, frozen with what seemed a supernatural horror. Now he locked his spiderish hand around Pádraig's upper arm. "Jump, Pádraig! Jump!" As good as his word, Long flung himself off into the tangle of fallen branches, carrying his astonished companion with him. It was a heavy, bruising fall.

Five seconds later, the train shot through, its under-sized steam locomotive puffing gouts of smoke. The three little cars behind it were filled with wondering faces as the tourists took in the scope and size of the root ball on the fallen redwood. Long and Ó Súilleabháin were too far down amid the detritus of the stream bed to be seen, or to note how dear was the tiny antique train that had nearly run them over.

Pádraig lay flat on his back with a burled tree limb sticking out from behind his shoulder like a second head. His shirt gaped over a midsection that gleamed against the black earth and his belt had caught a branch and pulled his trousers half down over an equally white rear end. First he covered himself again, and then felt himself over for injuries.

He groaned and scrambled up painfully, saying: "I am the donkey with the longest ears in all Kerry. *And* California, I think. The sound of the Scottish pipes. Listen to me!"

Long was already seated cross-legged on a flat splinter of redwood in front of the mammoth root ball. He was dusting off his jacket sleeves, and such is the magic of silk fabric that his apparel had suffered minimal damage. "I was quite fooled too, Pádraig. Though the rails were in suspiciously good repair."

He sighed and straightened his spine (as Martha would have him do). The circle of earth and spread tree roots behind him became a sort of halo around Long, like that found around statues of the dancing Shiva.

But Mr. Long did not feel like dancing. He rose slowly to his feet and coughed, experimentally. "I wish I had know there was a train serving Santa Cruz," he murmured. "I wonder if it makes connections to Amtrack?" He climbed back up to the tracks, on his hands and knees. Pádraig followed him with more noise and effort.

"Has your feeling about Marty's direction faded with all that excitement, or are we still going on?"

"I feel nothing but embarrassed," Pádraig said, kicking leaves at his feet.

"What's that?" Long broke in. "No, don't kick dirt on it. Let me see." He swooped over something white that lay between the tracks.

"It is her sunglasses." Pádraig came forward to touch. "But they are broken!"

Long's fingers, almost as black as the forest earth, tightened on the remaining stem of the glasses. His eyes, searching forward and backward along the tracks, were hard and pale. Then they softened. "I think they got stepped on by an animal," he said.

"Now, how could you know that?" Pádraig's blue eyes, startling as a Siamese cat's in the darkness, were wide with wonder.

"By the biggest donkey in California, I mean." Long bent down and slapped Pádraig on the shin until he picked up his foot like a horse. Long examined the shoe. There in the sole of the cheap, aged tennis shoes were trapped fragments of plastic that had once been tiny daisies. "So I did," said Pádraig. "Please God she's come to no more harm than that."

They went ahead, trusting that the forest train did not run too frequently. The way grew more difficult and deep-layered with winter castings. Those few patches of sun they passed were heavy in briars, and everywhere grew the bright, oily tendrils of poison oak. Long knew the stuff, though he had never gotten a rash from it. Pádraig, despite warnings, plowed through the bushes.

But this same hard footing meant a dearth of choices; they were forced to stay by the tracks, and no doubt Marty had been also. It was definitely darker than when they had entered the woods, and as the railroad tracks climbed up from the valley floor on a trestle of heavy redwood, it cast an unhappy shadow over the two men who trudged dustily underneath.

'How much can a three-year-old do in one day?' asked Long of the world in general.

"Everything," answered Pádraig. "They don't know they are tired until their feet fall off them. My sister Sióbhán would go out with her dolls in the morning and—"

"Peace to your sister," Long whispered. "What's that?"

Pádraig stood quiet and listened, either for pipes or steam locomotives, but what he heard brought life to his weary face. "It's singing, Mayland. It's a *child* singing."

Weak and treble as a bird's, but without doubt human, the small voice cut through the thick silence of the trees.

Slowly, in relief, Long closed his brown-glass eyes. "It's Marty, a Phádraig. Didn't I teach her that song myself?" He broke into a run, just as the tracks came down to the valley floor, which was rising. Up a steep incline they came, Pádraig with heavy feet and much energy, and Long occasionally coughing.

"What is it, Mayland?" called Pádraig. "A Chinese song?"

Long chuckled soundlessly. "Not exactly. It's called 'The Bear Went Over the Mountain.' "

They crested the hill and expected to find Marty there, so close had seemed the voice. But they saw nothing except what the bear saw in the song. The tracks went right and the ridge itself continued left, but straight ahead of them, down through the perfectly vertical display of redwood trees, was a khaki stripe in the forest with a square dark blotch beside it.

A road. A house.

As they made out that much, the singing ceased.

"Mr. Poznan." Sergeant Anderson sank into the only chair in Teddy's own, much smaller room. Teddy himself stood before him, his hands behind his back as he leaned against the wall radiator. As he heard his name his body straightened as though hung from a string.

"Gawd! Even the banks don't use 'Mister' anymore. I'm Teddy." His voice, though almost too cordial, was shaky.

Anderson made a face that pulled down on his nose and up on his eyebrows. "I, however, am still required to. I don't have anywhere near as much money as a bank. That must be the difference." He glanced casually behind Teddy's shoulder, assuring himself that his subordinate had entered the room behind them, and he pulled out a large manila envelope. "You did not tell the officer at the station where you made your initial statement that you are presently on probation."

'I'm not," said Teddy. "My probation ended just before the tour began. That's how I could go."

Anderson stared sharply at Ted, whose face was pulled into a half-placating smile. Then he took from his pocket a pair of rimless bifocals and positioned them over his nose. He read. For thirty seconds no one spoke, but the officer in the doorway cleared his throat. Teddy carefully didn't look at him.

"My sincere apologies," murmured Anderson. "That slipped right by me. Three years ended as of April eighth." He sighed and rubbed his nose. "They say this sort of little error will disappear once we have the *entire* records system computerized, statewide, or nationwide, or whatever. I suppose then the mistakes will be much wilder." The glasses went back into their case.

"No matter. Though the courts must ignore the fact

that you were convicted of dealing in narcotics on this scale—"

"Wrongly," said Teddy. His hands thrust him away from the table he had been using for support. His dark eyes shone like buttons under his sun-bleached hair. "Convicted wrongly, if you're interested."

Anderson looked up. Obviously he was interested, but what he said was: "I can't be, Mr. Poznan. Because what we're investigating is a murder in 1986, not a bust in—"

Teddy's face flushed and he dropped down on his heels in front of the detective. "A moment ago you were about to tell me that my conviction was relevant to George's murder. In the next breath you say that the fact that the conviction was—was completely screwy . . . is not." He pulled on the neat beard which was so much darker than his hair.

"The truth is I was living in a house where another guy was growing and dealing, and the Feds were sweeping through with a helicopter, and it was an election year! There was no more to it than that. And though the roots of the miserable experience probably lie somewhere back in this life or a past one, I feel more than a little bit bitter about the California police! Everyone who knows me knows I don't do drugs."

Sure that the burly officer was placed within reasonable distance of Teddy, Anderson leaned back in his chair and closed his eyes. "All right, Mr. Poznan. I'll let it be, except to remind you that there is no such thing as the 'California police.' I represent Santa Cruz, not Cotati, and have no more influence with the FBI than you do. As a matter of fact, they scare me.

"Let's just push through a few questions here, which don't in any way touch on your unfortunate past. First. Did St. Ives do drugs?"

Teddy grunted and settled back on his haunches. "All the time. I think. Alcohol I'm sure of. Pills, too, though I can't tell you whether they were legal or not. Doesn't matter."

"Doesn't matter, Teddy—Mr. Poznan?"

"Doesn't matter at all. They were shit! He'd take them at about noon and spend all afternoon in a thick daze, being sleepy and surly at the same time. Then in the late afternoon he'd perk up for an hour or so and bring himself down with booze until time to work. In the morning he'd be sicker than a cat.'"

Ted swept both his hands through his hair, pulling out the elastic band in a crackle of static. His long, straight, and very clean hair fell, separate in its colors, all over his shoulders. Though Sergeant Anderson had worked in Santa Cruz for twenty years and more, he still felt a disorientation, as Ted Poznan suddenly looked like a woman to him.

"I noticed. From when we got together first in Mendocino, I knew there was something wrong with George. I don't know that anyone else did. Notice, that is. Unless maybe Martha."

Anderson took a breath and longed for a cigarette. He had a pack in his jacket pocket and smoked perhaps five a day, saving them for times of weakness. He reached into his pocket and then stopped. "You say you don't do drugs, Mr. Poznan? Not even...aspirin?"

"Nothing processed. And not marijuana, either," he added, glaring resentfully at the expressions passing over the detective's face.

"Tobacco?"

Teddy looked quite fierce. "Enslavement of the body by bodily poison itself!"

Anderson let his hand slide out again, empty. "So. St. Ives started each day badly, took codeine and morphine to kill the pain, went to bennies, moderated by alcohol, to allow him to work, and then got to sleep by the light of phenobarb. Am I right?"

Teddy shook his head vaguely. "I don't know if he took exactly that...."

"We do," said Anderson. "We searched his room. There were little bits of this and that, but mostly morphine and codeine."

Teddy's face, under all the hair, was almost invisible

to the sergeant, but his attitude was one of dejection. Almost grief. "He told me, the day before—the day before he died, that he was in almost constant pain."

Anderson nodded as though this did not surprise him.

"Drugs will do that," said Teddy, not raising his head. "It's a bad cycle. After the health is ruined you have to keep taking them to prevent your feeling just how bad you're off. If you guys would only learn . . ."

"Learn what?"

"That education, not laws, is the way to keep people from doing things to damage themselves. It's all ignorance."

Anderson glanced up from Teddy to his own assistant, and his face expressed a potent combination of amused and weary disbelief. But it was not the sensitive Scherer he had brought along this afternoon, and his colleague met his eyes with a stare most bovine. Anderson sighed.

Very calmly he asked, "What about the little plastic bag we found among his stash? With your fingerprints on it."

Now Teddy raised his head, brushing the hair out of his eyes with his left hand. He looked to Anderson much like an attentive Indian brave, naked to the waist and evenly sun-bronzed. Except that Indian braves weren't usually pictured with beards. "The one with bee pollen in it? Or the kelp? I gave him a lot of things."

"But no drugs?"

"No drugs," answered Teddy after a pause.

Anderson was forced to admit the envelope had been empty. He glared absently at the top of Teddy's head and bit his lip for a while. At last he spoke. "Was there anything specifically wrong with St. Ives, when he died? Any disease or . . . trouble?"

Now Teddy straightened full up, clawing back his hair with an ugly, taloned right hand. "What do you mean?" he asked, dry-voiced. "You want a name for ruination of body? Will a name make it any better?"

Anderson cogitated. "In a way. It might explain his death. People sometimes commit suicide, if they have inoperable cancers. Or AIDS."

Teddy's braced attitude collapsed and he swayed forward. He stared at the detective. "AIDS!"

"He had . . . I gather . . . extensive sexual contact. He was in failing health. Why not AIDS? Something to check for." Anderson shrugged.

Then, before the shock of the suggestion had time to fade, Anderson followed with a question. "Mr. Poznan, can you tell me how you know a man named Richard Wolf? Why did he come to see you this morning, and why did he go back to Cotati before doing so?"

Ted Poznan gave out a small noise that expressed self-pity and waved his hands in the air.

Da Mihi Manum

Pádraig's left foot slipped on the mulch and he clung to Long's arm for support. The light of the sun was dimmed and relit again three times in swift succession, as clouds blew north from the sea. Each time Pádraig's face went rosy and Long faded from sight entirely. Except for his eyes.

"She's down there," said the young man. "I could throw a stone to hit her. I know it."

Long shook his head at this preternatural information, but it was not a gesture of denial. Long felt oppressed. In another moment the thin man was shaking all over and he did not know why. He put one well-shod foot in front of the other and began a loose, half-sliding progress down the slope. His bony hands wrapped around the branches of the trees as though they had extra joints. Pádraig slid faster and caught himself up on the redwoods to slow his descent. He bumped Long twice. Hard. He was mumbling as he went. Long heard him: ". . . . defend us in battle. Be our safeguard against the wickedness and snares of the devil . . ."

He caught Long looking at him. "It is a strong protection, my friend. You should say the prayer with me."

The older man did not smile, either in mockery or in agreement. His breath was ragged and his lips pulled back from his teeth. He could feel his heart pound, though not with the effort of climbing. "I have already said a drunken rosary with you today. That's enough." No expression showed in his face at all. In the sunlight filtered through branches, his eyes gleamed yellow.

197

The sun was obscured in another moment, but not
Long's pale eyes. He turned his head on his slender neck
from Pádraig to the house at the bottom of the hill and
back again. Pádraig stumbled back from him.

"Be careful, Mayland! In another moment I will in-
voke my name saint against you, for you're looking as cruel
as a snake." Pádraig giggled, but won no answering smile.
"Mayland, what is wrong with you? You are acting funny."

Long rubbed his hands over his face, like a man
troubled by small insects. Soberly he replied, 'I don't
know what's wrong. I'm no spiritual medium, to be able
to explain this... atmosphere. You are the one with
unexplainable 'feelings,' Ó Súilleabháin. Can't you feel
this?"

Pádraig rolled his eyes. "Frightened is what I feel
now. And I think it's of yourself, my friend. I have this
suspicion you'll bite me in a moment. Maybe you have
walked too far, with the cold on you."

Stepping backward down the hill, still facing Long, he
lost both feet together and fell in a heap. Long sighed,
huskily. It was almost a growl.

He came up beside Pádraig and picked him up by the
shirt collar. Long's face glistened. There was a humming
as of machinery in the air, or perhaps in his head. "That is
as you will, Pádraig Ó Súilleabháin. Be frightened or
brave as a bull. But you have claimed to have knowledge
of things hidden to me. I am waiting for you to stop
playing the fool and find me my *granddaughter.*" All
emotion was damped out of his voice, until he came to the
word "granddaughter," which was hissed in rage.

Pádraig leaned against a tree, and a scared sullenness
spread over his small features. He put the trunk of the
redwood between Long and himself.

He found himself facing an A-frame of unpainted
wood, with a great deal of porch and a front wall of glass
rising to the sharp peak of the gable. This glass reflected
the sky and the black wall of trees, for it was dark within.
The yard around the place was packed earth, forlorn save

for a concrete bird bath standing at the far edge of the trees. Brambles poked from under the porch. A stripe of dark, disturbed earth ran across the bare lot, and there was a pick, and gravel, and white plastic pipe.

The road of dust wound off toward the west, sliced at odd angles by the scars of last winter's rain. It was deadly quiet.

Pádraig shook his head. "We've come to an empty house, I think." He took a step out into the clearing and away from Long. "But if I were a little one and I came rolling down that long hill and found such a place as this, I know what I'd do. I'd have to look in that bowl over there. . . ." He pointed at the bird bath.

There came a rattling squeak. Someone had opened a window. Pádraig leaped straight into the air and came down panting heavily.

Still Long stood at the edge of the woods, frozen and fierce. He moved not his eyes only but his whole head, in sinuous little circles, staring at the blank building and the dusty packed earth around it. "Pádraig," he called sharply, as his angry paralysis was broken. "That hole in the earth. Isn't it a French drain?" Long moved cautiously out of his cover.

The young man giggled, thinking back on his own start of fright. "I couldn't tell you, Mayland. For me it has no accent at all."

Pádraig had not been with Martha on the mall, when someone had been talking about a French drain. For him there was no connection. Perhaps it meant nothing anyway. Long stood undecided, watching the dusty black windows of the house.

"I'd have a look in that bowl over there," Pádraig repeated for his own hearing. He walked across the bare yard, gaining speed as he went. "And wasn't I right, Mayland? Look at the child sitting on the stones as easy as she please. . . ." At the sight of Marty's shirt and rumpled yellow hair he broke into a trot.

But Marty did not smile back, and as he approached closer, there was something about her face that slowed him down. "Máirtín, little pink pig, what a story you're going to have, explaining this to your—"

There was a blast that picked Pádraig up off the ground and smashed him down again. His shirt budded with little black holes that blossomed into red. Twenty feet away, Marty Frisch-Macnamara stood with both hands at her sides, staring at him without interest.

A moment later her daddo struck her in the middle, bowling her over and over until both were hidden from the house by fallen wood and briars. Long found himself hovering over a face he had seen twice before: a face with eyes like boiled eggs and a slack, drooling mouth. Not Marty. Hissing with rage, he flung away from her and went back for Pádraig.

But Pádraig was on his feet again, stumbling toward them. His lips were moving, and as Long reached him Pádraig prayed, "Do thou, O Prince of the heavenly host cast into hell Satan and all his evil spirits, who prowl about the world. . . ." His blue eyes were round and blinking.

Gently Long eased him over a log. "No princes here, my lad," he whispered, while he peered carefully back for further sign of movement from the house. Long yanked up the back of Pádraig's oxford shirt to find the white skin pocked with shallow holes, in which something was embedded. He touched a piece of it and Pádraig cried out like a dog.

"Salt," said Long aloud. "Rock salt in a shotgun. That's a mixed blessing. At least it will dissolve." He dragged Pádraig over to Marty. "Keep her here, if you can. No matter how bad she . . . how bad it seems. No matter the pain. Keep her here until I return. Or until someone comes to help you."

Pádraig turned his head with difficulty, for the back of his neck was lacerated and his scalp laced with blood. "You can't, Mayland. They'll kill you."

Long used a tree to get him to his feet, keeping the trunk between himself and the house. "Shall we crawl away into the woods then, Kerryman? Bleeding and with a child whose mind is—is stolen? Someone or something

must answer to me for all this." Pádraig stole a glance at
Marty, shuddered, and cried with the pain of his movement. When he looked back, Long was gone.

The window of the van was dirty. The gas was down
to less than a quarter of a tank.

". . . we got in fairly early Friday morning," Martha
was telling her daughter. "She hadn't gotten much sleep
the night before and was cranky on the drive down, and a
little carsick, I think. Then when we got in, Elen's friend
Sandy volunteered to baby-sit while we settled in and set
up.

"That was probably a mistake, because Sandy hauled
her around all morning, visiting and doing errands. Showing Marty off, maybe. She hated it."

"Maybe that's where she met this Judy character,"
offered Elizabeth, as she leaned against the window and
watched River Street pass by.

Martha nibbled thoughtfully at her upper lip. Stopped
for a long light.

"Possible. But if so, she sure made an instant impression, for they weren't gone that long. And when she was
asked about her morning, Marty just got testy."

"I wish people would realize that you can't baby-sit
and do other things at the same time," said Elizabeth with
a great deal of spleen. "It isn't fair to the child."

Martha gazed coolly at her daughter and wondered if
Elizabeth would realize the implication of what she had
said. And what she had asked of her mother. But she did
not, and the light finally changed.

"This was the last place he called from," said Martha,
slowing the van beside the kiosk at the corner of Highway
1.

Elizabeth opened the window, as though a better
view of that ordinary telephone on its stand could help her
understand. "Well, they're not here now."

Martha listened to the tension in her daughter's
words. A honk sounded from behind them and a man
driving a Subaru swerved around them, furious at being

trapped in the intersection at change of light. Pushed by
traffic, Martha drove on.

"I can't think she went up here," said Elizabeth, with
her head out the window. "There's almost nothing to see.
No sidewalk, no houses, and—phew—a tannery right by
the road."

Martha pulled over beside it. The old van rocked to a
stop on its loose suspension. "Nothing to attract an adult,
perhaps. Most adults, that is. I was here once before, and
I found the tannery very attractive. Not just the furs and
suedes, but they have a garden." She jumped the high
step down from the driver's seat, leaving the door unlocked,
and walked down a series of steps. Elizabeth had to follow.

The tannery was quite neat and the garden pretty, but
neither of the clerks at the outlet store had seen a little
girl. They had been asked that question already that day.

This was not news of the highest, best kind, but it
meant that they were on Long's tracks, anyway. Martha
and Elizabeth returned to the van and continued along the
way they had come.

"This is terrible, Mother. This is out-and-out wilderness! Not a house anywhere. Surely Marty wouldn't go in
here, even if she could walk this far."

Martha smiled tightly. No matter how nature-affirming
a person might be, she reflected, times of danger would
spark a desire to be surrounded by walls. Even in a
Californian. "Well, I can't turn around here. Bear with
me."

Highway 9 wound like a string dropped by chance. It
was very narrow and at times without shoulders. Cars
swept by them at frightening speed. Elizabeth cursed as
every bend opened before them, revealing more deep
forest and no place to turn the bulky van.

They were beside a trestle and the road was more
narrow than ever. Martha squeezed through, almost touching the outer guardrail. They bumped over tracks.

"There's a railroad here?"

"Tourist train, I seem to remember," replied Martha.
"Little one: a remnant of the days when these hills were

stripped to rebuild San Francisco. I always have meant to ride it some summer."

A mile into the park, they found a turnaround, and were almost hit broadside by a Mercury Cougar coming in the other direction. They left the park more shaken than they had been at entering it.

"Turn here." Elizabeth pointed left away from the road. Martha did so, not asking why. Hoping no one would hit them from around the blind corner.

It looked like a driveway, surrounded by mounds of spirea that almost met over the dry dirt surface, but the sign called it a private road.

"At least it doesn't say 'Keep Out,'" said Elizabeth to her mother. "And I think this is the sort of thing Marty would want to explore. A drive between banks of flowers."

There was silence. "Don't you, Mother?"

Martha was occupied with holding the steering under control through a fearsome set of ruts. She considered her daughter's statement, and her mind filled with a memory of Marty's bright, overly precocious voice, saying, "I'm not having any fun today: in case anyone wants to know." Marty who had run away from her. Twice. Whose face went gray and blank. Who was looking for Judy. "I don't really know what Marty would want to explore," she said, very sadly.

There was dry grass to the left. Dry grass and thistles to the right. Away to the right, to the south, the ground fell away and the town of Santa Cruz could be seen, all brown roofs and stucco against the blue water. Then the redwoods closed in on both sides.

A drive opened to the left, going up toward the park where the trees were thicker. FLAGER read the hand-painted wooden plaque. It also said PRIVATE. The holes in that drive were much worse.

"What was that?" Elizabeth, not content with leaning out the window, opened the door and leaned out that.

"A backfire?" Martha hazarded. Elizabeth slammed the door again and her face was sweaty. "Up there, Maw. Go!"

Elizabeth had never in her entire life called her mother "Maw." Martha stared sidelong at her, but turned the van's stubby nose. It gave three lurches, slid into a rut, and emitted a whine painful to hear. The air smelled of burning rubber and they went nowhere at all.

Mayland Long stood as still as the trees, half-hidden by them. He looked and listened for anything that might come.

The window through which Pádraig had been shot was still open, but he could see into the darkness well enough to know no one was behind it. The wind was down and there were no birds calling, except a solitary, dull-sounding jay. After two minutes, he stepped forward into sunshine which brought him no warmth.

There was something in that trim little chalet that was horrible. Long could see it, and smell it and feel it through his skin. I am not psychic, he said, under his breath. I am not a thing of sorcery but a natural beast, bound only by the honest rules of nature. He shook all over, like the beast he had named himself, and took another step. The unhappiness increased.

Not bagpipes, not gulls: it was a voiceless, angry lamenting. It was not sound at all but a cloud of misery that washed over Long. His knees weakened and his stomach went into a knot. He stumbled and hit the earth with knees and hands, gaping in surprise at his own weakness. Propped on one hand with his white-trousered knee on the grass, he felt his balance failing in an awful vertigo. Had he had food in his stomach, he would have vomited.

Was he getting sick, he asked himself: suddenly and violently sick with any of these thousand ills to which men were liable? Of course he was sick, came the answer. With a cold.

People with no claim to personal power got colds, and they did not fall to the ground because of it. Ordinary people did not stay home from their labors because they had a cold. Ordinary people, who lived for a handful of years and then died without protest: they took such discomfort in their stride.

What made them ordinary, then?

"I am not sick!" said Long aloud, and he stood up again.

Now the sun was bright, with all clouds rolled away, and his balance had improved. Ignoring the disorders of his body, Long took two more steps, and then he heard crying.

He looked over his shoulder, but it wasn't Marty he was hearing. Marty was sitting on a log, her head sullenly down, and Pádraig had her hand. The poor fellow sat beside her, hunched with pain, and he watched Long intently.

Was Pádraig an ordinary man? Long signaled to him with a wave of the hand which was, unintentionally, gallant.

The weeping was coming from the house, along with the waves of sick nastiness. Though his legs felt rubbery, Mr. Long increased his pace. Then, up on the second-floor balcony of the house, a door opened.

"Go away! I'll shoot you!"

A woman. Long recognized the voice, or thought he did, through its hysteria. There was something prodding through the blackness of that doorway. A gun barrel.

Long darted to the right, so the door itself blocked her aim. His knees felt stiff and he was cold all over. Fear was running over him like water, but it was not fear of the gun. He stepped into the shadow of the house and shivered, his mind filled with wailing. Perhaps it was his own.

What was the prayer Pádraig had uttered, coming down the hill, and which Long had so casually rejected? That had been a very bad act, and it was only justice that the prayer would not come to him now when he was willing to welcome it, nor any other words of aid. Instead a voice within his head said to him that he might die here now, never knowing what this violence had been about.

Or what anything was about. Life had been such a long night, and the meeting with Martha only the beginning of awakening. Five years. Five good years: almost no time, to his standards, but time enough to gain understanding, if he were going to.

The nausea returned, and tears leaked out of the corners of his eyes. No one can teach a person what he does not already know, Martha had said. What Long recognized inside himself at this moment was a huge emptiness.

Mayland Long came to the door and he put his hand on it. He could smell the reek of sickness from within. Here was confusion. Error. Vacancy.

He felt a shameful identity with it and he pleaded—with what he did not know—that he might not have to go in.

But cold and sick as he was, he was still Mr. Long. He had an old habit of finishing things. And under the wailing and beyond all the foul winds in his mind he was still curious. He wanted to know what was going on here. He opened the door onto blankness. Not blackness but blankness. Perhaps he had gone blind. Long heard his own voice, crying shrilly like a cat. He tried again for Pádraig's prayer.

Form does not differ from emptiness. Emptiness does not differ from form.

The words came by themselves to him. He heard them in a surprise that tightened his face.

It was the Prajna Paramita Sutra. Uncomfortable scripture. Nihilist, he had always thought. It had never particularly attracted him.

That which is form is emptiness.

It was all he could think of, so he whispered it to the blank, empty air: Mr. Long's own dry, uncomforting prayer of protection.

There. He could see again. Perhaps his eyes had merely needed time. The light resolved into pattern: a floor and a ceiling. Lines drawn from top to bottom became the juncture of walls.

A hallway. It was fairly empty, as the sutra claimed, and it certainly had form, for the sun reflected off Mexican tile. And not quite empty after all, for there was a terra-cotta tub with a jade plant. Blinking at the little green thing (neither as thick or as healthy as such a plant might have been) Mr. Long began to weep, not knowing why. He touched it and was faintly surprised that it did not die at his touch.

No death said the Sutra, and also the jade plant in the tub in the hallway.

The stench was stronger in here, and it was not a thing of the mind alone. Long put his arm up to his face and tried to breath through the fabric of his shirt sleeve. He found himself staring down the blue-black barrel of a shotgun.

And also no extinction of death . . . said the Sutra, lest he be overconfident.

"Put down the gun, Sandy," said Long quietly. "I'm only Martha's road manager. You can't want to kill me."

The young woman's arm holding the shotgun was shaking so hard that the barrel swept in wide circles. Her hand on the trigger was trembling. She peered up at Long from honey-colored, frizzy hair.

"Oh, Jeezus! It's you," she said, and the tip of the barrel broke a piece of the floor tile as it fell. She dropped the gun entirely. "Oh, Jeezus. Oh, crap! I'm so glad you've come.

"I . . . tried, but I'm no good at this!" Sandy sat down on the cold tiles and put her head in her hands. Her brightly colored dress bore large stains and wet spots, and it rode up to the middle of her thighs.

Long's mouth twitched. "I don't know if I'd agree. You scored a solid hit on poor Pádraig."

She stared, uncomprehending. A wave of nausea crossed her face, and Long's as well. Once again the wailing began. He raised his head and stared at the wall beside him, for it was from that direction it came. Not a thing of the mind alone.

"Pádraig? Pat? No, it wasn't Pat. It was . . . coming at me." She made a despairing gesture toward Long's

outstretched hand. Her face was screwed up like an
infant's.

"I was told not to let anyone in. They'll be looking
everywhere. I'm so scared. So scared. Let her down again
and again. Now it's all turned bad!"

*All dharmas are marked with emptiness. They do not
appear nor disappear. They are neither tainted nor pure.*

Long sat down beside the woman. He wanted to
repeat that to her: all dharmas are marked with emptiness.
Neither tainted nor pure. He watched her rock back and
forth on the hard tiles, and he touched her head. "Things
do not turn bad" is what he said to her. "Neither events
nor apples, nor lives."

"Lives, especially, do not go bad, Miss Flager."

Two meager fists balled and Sandy shook her head.
"Look at the kid and tell me that again! Oh, Jesus, I'm no
good at this."

Long frowned. "The kid? Marty?" Sandy glared up at
him, and her eyes were gray and perfectly round. "No
Marty. The kid. You know."

She pointed beyond the wall of the passage, to the
room beyond.

Mr. Long stood and regarded that wall, while the sun
slanting through the doorframe warmed the back of his
head. On sudden impulse Long pulled the door all the
way in, so that light and wind filled the passageway. "Go
out now," he said again to Sandy, and he drew her to her
feet. Blinking against the light, she obeyed him, leaving
the black shotgun on the tiles. Long himself walked down
the hall and into the house alone.

The living room was lighted like a church, for all the
blinds were drawn on the windows, and the only light
came in through the Gothic arch of the glass wall, eighteen feet tall. The central room had very fine paneling, a
pale shag rug, and a stereo and VCR in an oak stand in the
corner. There was little furniture and that was of wood and
pillows, carefully finished by hand. It smelled like a
shambles.

In the corner opposite the oak stand, wrapped in filthy blankets and propped with hand-embroidered pillows, was the demon source of all the misery and confusion that had been hurting Mayland Long.

It was white and it had a bulging forehead. Its eyes were almost as milky as its skin and its mouth had a shade of blue to it. Its hands were large and it held them like paddles, with the fingers at odd angles. It rocked back and forth, hitting its frightening head against the wall. It was a child, perhaps eight years old, and its face was smeared with shit. Feeling Long's presence before it, it howled.

Long stood above the child, buffeted by the winds of its misery. The smell choked him; he coughed into a tissue.

And it wrinkled its nose in sympathy, and it rubbed a dung-covered forearm over its nostrils, which made things worse. It retched, as Long had done in the yard outside, and like Long it lost its balance and fell against the stained cushions. Its breath made noises.

Mr. Long was fastidious. He abhorred smells. He disliked ugliness as much as he did philosophical error. Perhaps more.

No eyes, no ears, no nose, no tongue . . .

It sounded like the child was choking, there on the floor. He pushed his sleeves up and took hold under its armpits, straightening it in place. It wrapped him round the elbows with its paddle hands. He got away with difficulty.

No cognition . . .

This thing was error itself: without hope of remedy. Long's mouth pulled to a fine line.

No woman with eyes the color of sky could wake this child from its nightmare. It was hopeless. It was the substance of hell itself, and it called to Mayland Long.

Here, the emptiness and confusion he would never, never excise from his imperfect soul. Here, locked in self, was self-loathing. So it had been before Mr. Long was born, and would certainly be after both he and this poor damaged, dangerous thing died. It was pain and it could not be exorcised for once and all.

But perhaps it could be mastered.

Long rose again and considered things. Fear and anguish seeped up from the floor; he snubbed them. The waves of confusion could not obscure the fact that there was simple work to do here. The dharma of action. He regarded the heap of suffering wrapped in blankets and turned aside all pity.

Mr. Long took off his jacket, and his shirt. Looking at the creature again, he took off his raw-silk trousers also, and then he bent down and touched it.

"Give me your hand," he said.

It struck at him with terror, and sickness, and with its smeary hands. He turned his face away.

"None of that," he told it, not too gently. Reaching under, he picked up the small body. Fearfully thin, it was. Frail. He peeled back the blankets. "Well, my boy," Long said, giving the ugly thing the same bounce he had given his shining granddaughter. "We must begin somewhere."

The boy prodded with his blind head, burrowing under Long's chin. He gave a child's sigh and began to sniffle. By suggestion, that brought back Mr. Long's cough.

And with that cough, all the sick delusion, the emptiness and the error vanished from the room as though they had never been.

Gone, gone, utterly gone gone without recall. O freedom.

For a moment Long thought the boy was dead, but he was only asleep. He went out with the child on his shoulder, looking for Sandy and a bathtub.

Martha's patience was worn after twenty minutes of gunning the engine (but not too hard) and rocking back and forth in the ever-so-damned rut. She had let her voice get shrill: almost as shrill as Elizabeth's. Now, by the grace of Something, they were out and continuing down the dirt track, knitting together the shreds of their manners.

Where they had passed, an opaque beige cloud rose,

bscuring rear vision completely, and though Martha had ong since given up hope that anything useful lay at the end of this drive, she had to go on, for the van was too wide to be turned around. (They would have to pass the same ruts coming back too.) Meanwhile Elizabeth was mumbling to herself and biting little holes in an old airport parking receipt she had found on the dash.

Martha caught a glimpse of figures on the road ahead and began to feather the brakes. The van fishtailed a bit on dust as slippery as mud. "What's that?" she asked her daughter.

"A man with a couple of kids," answered Elizabeth without interest. "And . . ."

She didn't want to say that the other figure looked like an ape, but no other image occurred to her. It was hunched and it moved with a halting, sideways stride. She leaned forward.

Martha recognized the silhouette of Long, walking like a king and like a dancer down the road, carrying something on each arm. "That's *him*." There was a kind of pride and triumph to Martha's words that she herself did not understand.

"Marty? He's got Marty?" Elizabeth flung open the door and leaned out, though the van was still moving.

"He has. And she's drubbing his ribs with her heels, as per usual. But there's another kid too." She braked to a stop ten feet from the little procession and hopped out.

There he was: her friend, student, paramour, road manager. Smiling at her as calm and as solid as a rock. There was Marty, very tired. And the other—there was the face of Marty's illness: blank, blind, and without understanding. She saw the boy and nodded, as though something had been explained to her.

And she saw poor bloody Pádraig.

There was a clinic on Ocean Street, not far from the highway. Martha drove there first and stayed with the injured man, while Elizabeth nursed the temperamental van back to the motel. Mr. Long was more experienced at the driving of this vehicle, but he did not dare release the sleeping child's hold around his neck. Marty, too, slept, curled in a ball on the bucket seat next to that of her mother. The seat belt twisted, biting into her middle, but she didn't notice.

"I wonder what we should feed him," murmured Long to Elizabeth.

"Hasn't he told you?" asked Elizabeth in reply. She glanced in the mirror at him, and there was immense respect in her glance.

"He hasn't . . . told . . . me anything, exactly. I'm not a psychic, you know, Elizabeth."

She gave a little snort. Not a contemptuous snort.

"Believe me. It is because I am not overly sensitive to things that I can help him. Strong back instead of a ready mind, you know. . . ." He chuckled at his wan joke, but then went sober again. "When he . . . communicates he can be terribly convincing, Elizabeth."

She spared a worried glance from the road. "That I am ready to believe.

"We'll have to call the police," she added.

Long waited a while before answering. "There is no hurry."

Each of them carried a burden in from the parking lot. Elizabeth Macnamara was happier in hers, and less thoughtful, for Marty's face was pretty as she slept. Her mother pushed open the unlatched door with her hip.

Elen was inside, alone. "Hallelujah!" she whispered, and clapped her hands softly in front of the sleeping girl. "I've done nothing but make promises to Jesus for you all since you left, and I was almost ready to give up chocolate! Did you find her yourself? Or was it another example of our road manager's general usefulness?" She spied Long's head through the crack in the door.

"By the by—the Grand Inquisitor came back and he took away Teddy. I haven't heard anything—"

Long stepped in after Elizabeth, with the handicapped boy. He shut the door carefully with his foot and he looked at Elen.

Her flying hands fell limp and her bright dark face went the color of putty. Elen made no sound.

"Pádraig was shot," Long told her. "He might well have been killed, by all this." He turned to Elizabeth, who had lain her baby down on the bed. "Gather pillows and blankets to prop him up, please. He can't breath when laid flat."

Elizabeth, without demur, went from bed to bed and pulled off all the pillows in both Long's room and the other. It seemed odd to her that Elen Evans did not lift a finger to help, but she was too concerned to feel resentful. Together she and Long stuffed the little shape with the bulging head and blank eyes upright. She ventured to pat his hand, but felt a shock of fright when he grabbed it fiercely and would not let go. She sat down beside him, willing calmness. Waiting.

Elen was talking to Long behind her. It was hard to hear from down on the floor. Elizabeth had to wrap herself up in her own arm in order to raise her head to see them.

What she did see astonished her, for the drawling, self-possessed harp-player had both hands raised like claws, and she was shaking her head violently. "Oh no, not Sandy. Not Sandy," she was saying. "With her stupid shotgun full of salt! And not Pat!"

"It struck his back and the back of his neck. There was great pain and bleeding, but by good fortune, his spine and head were not damaged." He might have been discussing the event with a stranger, for there was no warmth in his words.

Still Elen shook her head. "Sandy did it?"

"Confusion did it," stated Long. "Fear and confusion. She could not endure Jude."

Jude? Elizabeth jerked against the hand that held her.

Elen cried like a bird. "Endure him? No one can endure him, least of all me!" Her voice broke. "I couldn't stand it the day I gave birth to him, and I swear it's worse now!"

Elizabeth's mouth fell open. "Gave . . . birth . . . ?" She glanced repeatedly from the ill-shaped head of the boy to Elen's face: dark-eyed, smooth, delicate as a baby's. As a baby's ought to be.

"This is yours? Your son?"

Elen flinched from the word. She hit the lamp on the breakfast table and it fell crashing. "Mine. And George's, goddamn him. He was born this way." She stared hard at Elizabeth and added, "His name is Jude."

"Judy, you mean?" Elizabeth rocked back.

"Judy," Long stated. "After the patron of hopeless cases."

Elen took a breath and started again, more calmly. "I didn't call him that; the nurses at the home did. I didn't call him anything. I ran away." She braced herself against the table edge and closed her eyes.

Elizabeth gazed from Elen to Long, stupidly. Finally she fixed on the woman. "Why don't you come here now, Elen. Don't you want to touch him? He's been terribly unhappy."

Elen turned her head out the window. "Can't touch him. When I do, he screams. Always has."

Quite abruptly, Jude fell asleep. It was as sudden as quick death, and his hand fell from Elizabeth's arm. At first she was alarmed, but she made sure of his breathing and stood up.

Elizabeth was not an inquisitive person, and she was well aware this was not her business. But she was a mother with one child, and she could not let the issue be. "Let me get this straight. This is the child that my mother talked about—that was stolen from the orphanage a couple of days ago?" Elen nodded, not meeting Elizabeth's eyes.

"And he's also 'Judy,' the one who's had Marty distracted for the last few days?" She glanced involuntarily to the door to the next room: Marty's room.

It was Long who replied. "I can think of no other explanation, Elizabeth."

But Elizabeth did not look at him. "Did you know it

was him, doing that to my daughter?" Her voice rose as she spoke, angrily.

Elen looked away—to the mirror and then down. "I . . . suspected Sandy had taken her to see him when she babysat, Friday. Not a clever thing to do. What can a little girl make of all that? I was afraid she had seen him as a hobgoblin, out to get her. Because he looks funny. But it was different from that: Marty's such a . . . such a fine kid. And when she started wandering off, I felt—I felt . . . well, what do you think I felt!"

Elizabeth's square shoulders settled as her anger leaked away. She thought of her fine daughter, who might not have been so fine. "Why—why did you take the boy if you don't dare touch him? He'd surely have been happier back—"

Long's deep voice cut in again. "I don't think it was Elen who stole Judy from his home, Elizabeth. I think it was George St. Ives."

The Devil to Pay

Long put out his hands, palm upward, together, in a formal, ancient-seeming gesture. The abnormal fingers made a woven bowl. He said to Elen, "It makes no sense any other way. You had not even arranged a place to keep him. . . ."

"Only with poor Sandy, who . . ."

"Is no good at this sort of thing. I know. I have only wondered why you did not take Judy back to his home as soon as you found that George had him."

"George had him? Had who?" It was Teddy who spoke. He had come in silently and now stood staring at the entire scene. His biscuit-brown forehead was set in wrinkles.

"George St. Ives stole a kid? This kid?" The tall man lowered himself onto the bed next to Elizabeth. In form, expression, and hairstyle, they looked like twins. His shoulder jostled her, but she didn't notice.

Elen sat at the breakfast table, her face lit from beneath by the light of the overturned lamp. Her snub nose bore a close resemblance to that of the sleeping boy, and there was also something about the eyebrows. Thoughtlessly, she ran her harper's fingernail between the lamp base and its protective felt cover. "Yes, and yes." She glanced at them all from half-closed eyes. "You get to hear it all. All about Judy *and* about George. It's quite a tale!"

"Maybe you should wait for Martha and Pádraig," suggested Teddy, who was suddenly afraid of the story.

"Better I should wait for the police," she answered

heavily, and as everyone sat silent in wonder, Elen picked
up the telephone and called the station.

It was a close little motel room, with eight adults and
two children in it, for Martha had shown up with Pádraig
Ó Súilleabháin only just after the arrival of a tired-looking
Detective-Sergeant Anderson and his assistant.

During the twenty minutes of waiting, Elen Evans
had not moved once from her seat at the table. No one sat
across from her, though Pádraig might well have done so,
had he been able to sit in a chair. Conversation had been
confused, and now that the police had arrived, had died
entirely.

The window was open, and the evening land breeze
leaked in under the door and flattened the curtain against
the screen.

"I was sixteen when I got pregnant," Elen began, and
she kept her eyes on the tattered felt she had pulled away
from the lamp base. "In Oakland, my first year of college.
After three days in the company of George St. Ives. Sandy
Frager introduced us, you see. That's where she came into
things. Her . . . karmic debt!

"I was an idiot at the time."

No one spoke, though Teddy Poznan came closest to
it. He made a wordless demurral and grinned at Elen.
Pádraig was entirely hidden behind the bulk of the detec-
tives. Perhaps, after the medication he had been given, he
was not paying attention.

"I don't come from the sort of family where such . . .
originalities . . . pass. When I went back to Atlanta for
Christmas there was a scrumptious, bang-up fight, with
me cast in the role of bangee, and I left home. Never went
back.

"I didn't have an abortion. Can't now remember
which of the many reasons I used to hand out to people
was the one that mattered to me, but whatever. I didn't.
Maybe it was just because that's what my father wanted
me to do. Besides. There were always people crying out
for little white babies. I thought." As she talked the felt

came away in pieces from the lamp. Elen did not look up, nor did anyone else make any noise.

"I didn't have an abortion but I didn't go to an OB, either. I was full of the idea that women had been having babies for a long time before doctors got involved. Funny sort of attitude, wasn't it? Goes with traditional music. And I was embarrassed all to hell. So I didn't find out in time that . . . that *he* had had the clap.

"I never got any symptoms of the disease. Or none I could divorce from the weirdness of pregnancy, which is a really extraterrestrial state of life." Elen said the word again. "Extraterrestrial." Her mouth pulled sideways.

"Sandy delivered the baby for me. My best, most closemouthed friend. The only one who ever knew. She always felt so guilty about it, as though she could have helped what George was. What Jude was. Or what I am. Poor, poor Sandy."

Pádraig groaned, perhaps coincidentally. Detective-Sergeant Anderson gave his bandaged torso an interested glance. He was surprised how white the boy's skin was. No sun at all.

"From the beginning I couldn't stand him. The baby. And he couldn't stand me. If I'd been the violent type. . ."

Anderson glanced back at her.

". . . I'd have thrown him into a wall. He just cried, and gushed shit, and screamed. Wouldn't nurse. We didn't guess that he was blind. And retarded." Her voice broke quietly.

"After a few days or so, it became unbearable. I drove him . . . drove him down to the Adventist Home and left him there. Ringing the bell. It was just like something out of Dickens."

Anderson made a little noise, as though warming up his vocal chords for speech. "You didn't have to do it that way, Ms. Evans. It's a perfectly accepted thing to place a baby, if you can't handle him. Even a problem baby. Especially a problem baby."

Elen looked up and her eyes were bright. "Ah, but it's much easier just to ring and run, Sergeant. Then the whole thing never happened at all. You see? And I had just turned seventeen and disowned my family. Does this all sound like the story of a girl who does things the best and most responsible way?

"Anyway." Elen yanked one more time, vengefully, upon the felt circle, which came away in her hand. She blinked at the little mess on the table. "What do you know? This thing is filled with little dead bugs. In the lamp all this time."

Everyone did look, as it was easier than looking at Elen.

"Then I was just seventeen. Now I'm twenty-four."

"So am I," said Pádraig, much to everyone's surprise.

"I thought you were twenty-one," murmured Anderson over his shoulder.

"Twenty-four," said Pádraig obstinately, looking like a small, hunched bull. He glared at the sergeant. "And I'm not the Pádraig Ó Súilleabháin people think I am. I am my cousin. So now we will have no secrets, here, at all."

Mayland Long caught Pádraig's eye and gestured toward Elen, giving him a chiding glance. Another glance shared with Anderson said very clearly that shock and medication affect people in strange ways.

Elen had not noticed the interruption. "If I'm a fool now, it's a very different sort of fool. Not so easily gulled, I hope. Not so quick to cut and run. I've been paying dues . . ."

"The money that comes to Jude in blue envelopes?" asked Anderson.

She smiled tightly. "That's not what I meant, but yes. I sent it."

He gave a satisfied grunt. "That's why we suspected that the boy had been taken by someone who cared. The money that came every month."

She nodded with a bit more animation than before. "The poor nurses. I'm assuming *they* care for him there. I know he doesn't react to everyone as he does to me. . . ." She shot a covert glance at Mr. Long's concerned face.

"My . . . son doesn't like me, still. I found that out this

week, and in spades." Her eyes drifted past Anderson's legs and Martha's skirt to where Jude lay sleeping, propped with pillows and looking almost at ease. "But then, why on this sweet earth should he?"

There was another rustling, wordless response.

"It was Sandy who got George involved again. Her fate, I guess. In San Francisco. He remembered her and her connection with me. Can you believe that? Considering it had been almost eight years, and the hot and cold running stream of girls and women. . . . And he said something that led her to believe he knew about Jude. Something about starting to take on his responsibilities. She didn't know that was just his male menopause trip, or something.

"So"—Elen took a breath and blew all the tiny dry insect corpses off the table—"she spilled the beans. The next thing that happens is Sandy hears on the radio about a kid like Jude being stolen and she calls to ask if I did it."

"St. Ives had taken the boy?" asked Anderson neutrally.

Elen tried a smile. "Got it in one. It was all part of his quest for identity." She shot a removed, very chilly glance at Ted Poznan, who did not look away. "He went out right after the concert on Friday. We'd just had a very nice, well-aged battle in the basement, over a very smarmy little musical trick he'd played on . . . someone."

Anderson started at this. "Another practical joke? And did he admit to it?"

"Not . . . not exactly. Or rather, he said it had been an accident."

Anderson took a deep breath, while his eyes flashed with thought. "And did he happen to mention setting up another . . . accident with a door and a cable?"

Elen stared blankly, but then her attention and the attention of the whole room was pulled to Pádraig Ó Súilleabháin, who had put his hands to each side of his head and was rocking back and forth, crying, "Oh, my! Oh, my!" in perfect imitation of a distracted old woman.

"What is it, Mr. Ó Súilleabháin?" asked Anderson,

with admirable restraint. "Do you know something about either of these practical jokes or accidents?"

Pádraig was making a series of faces, some amused, some overwhelmed, and some only intelligible to himself. "*Cinnte!* How shouldn't I, when one was played *on* me and the other I played myself?"

"You?" It was Martha who spoke. "*You* set the trap with the door that caught Mayland? And you lied to me about it, straight-faced?"

He wilted in front of her, and his unfocused blue eyes blinked very fast. "Well, I did and I didn't, Martha. Don't bite me too soon.

"You see, I always wanted to try that trick with the pins of the door, ever since I heard about someone doing it to their uncle in Watertown. But you have to have a big window, and a drop, and all in a straight line. When I saw this theater, with the dock and even that big chunk of concrete there . . . it seemed heaven itself had set the thing up."

Long, in his corner, groaned. "Perhaps I owe Don Stoughie an apology."

"No you don't!" snapped Martha, but she didn't explain. She said to Pádraig, "Didn't you know you might have killed someone with that loop under the door?"

Now Pádraig looked completely miserable as well as unfocused. "I'm sorry, Martha. I didn't, really. I was being clever, you see. I did up the cable, trim and neat, and then I stood back and thought, 'You donkey. Anyone looking at this will know it's you was here, for no one else makes a decent knot in the company.' So, piece by piece, I did it again, as badly as I could think how. That big snarl in the middle was the worst, most unseaworthy part of it, and I was proud of the idea. But I never thought the stiff cable would spring itself under the door."

"You got Mayland badly bruised. *And* in a lot of trouble," said Martha.

Pádraig hung his wounded head.

"And you lied to me."

Long put his hand around Martha's ankle and whispered to her. She fell silent.

Anderson scratched his head. "So, Mr. Long. Your wild ride is explained at last. Have you any desire to press charges?"

"None," said Long. "I think this very unimportant digression has worn itself out."

Elen felt the room turn to her again. She shrugged. "I'm guilty too, Martha. I lied when I let you think he hadn't been out of my sight all morning. I only knew about the incident what you told us, but I thought that anything Pat had done to revenge himself upon George needed support, even if it was cockeyed.

"He had just told me—George, I mean—that he knew about Jude. He made it seem as though I'd just borne the baby like a hen lays an egg and walked away from it.

"He, on the other hand, said he was going to apply for custody. Can you imagine any institution handing over this multiply-handicapped child to a dirty old crank like St. Ives? With no better reason that he happened to be the father?

"I guess George realized that would be too much to expect when he calmed down; he didn't bother asking at all but just jimmied a window and took the boy away. I guess he found him by Sandy's description, or by the name on the door, because he'd never even seen him before. Too bad, too, for one visit might have cured him."

Elen swayed forward. Her black eyes, completely without focus, glittered in a white face. (White as Sullivan's back, thought the sergeant.) Then, slowly, she fell back until her head touched against the wall. Her eyes closed and he thought she had gone to sleep, until she lifted her head again and beat it against the wall. Again.

As Long had seen her son do in his pain and confusion, wrapped in blankets smeared with dung. "Elen!" he called roughly, and Elen stopped. Jude whimpered in his sleep.

Anderson's feet moved on the carpet and he included

everyone in the room in his thoughtful glance. "I'm sorry this is so difficult for you, Ms. Evans. Do go on. You were able to find where he had taken the boy?"

She shook her head, to clear it. "He called and told me. Right after the Saturday concert. 'Chickie,' he said. 'Haul your ass down here right now!'

"Turns out he had this idea. . . . He'd hired a Mexican girl to take care of Jude. She didn't speak much English, and he didn't know a word of Spanish. I don't know. Maybe he was sleeping with her too. He thought they'd go back to Ottawa and find a little house, and he'd have a little ready-grown family, to dab into whenever he wanted. When he wasn't on the road.

"What a sweet picture! And how impossible. I don't even know where he was going to get the money to pay the Mexican lady. . . ."

"He was pretty broke," said Martha ruefully. Then she sat bolt upright. "No! Wait! I *do* know where the money came from." She reached up and took Long by the elbow. "Mayland. The disappearing cash."

His face remained impassive and he gazed beyond Martha to the sad slumped shape that was Pádraig. Martha's eyes narrowed as he avoided them.

"You knew all about this, didn't you?" Again, no answer. "What I heard yesterday in the other room, when I was on the phone with Elizabeth . . ."

Long sighed. "I'm sorry, Martha. It is not something I am permitted to talk about."

"Mr. Long . . ." began Anderson, with heavy patience.

"He pledged you to secrecy? No. I heard. You pledged *him* to secrecy. And now he is dead, so there is no release for either of you. Is that it?" Martha stood up, her face strained and thoughtful. "Well, how about if I tell *you* what happened?"

Long looked embarrassed. "Martha, you make too much out of—"

"He admitted taking the money and told you he was going to pay it back. He said he had needed it for . . . for family matters. Right? And you said you'd replace it in the kitty and make the theft into a personal loan to him from yourself, right? Better no one else in the group was to know?"

"Much better," he replied, with a shade of temper. "Much better if no one did. And it was our business, I think."

Martha sat down again, breathing hard. "I'm sorry, but I don't agree."

"Elen, do go on."

Elen Evans glanced from Martha to Long. "That is entirely all we need, now. For you two to start snarling at one another." She passed her hand over her forehead, with all fingers spread. "You know we all depend upon your shining romance as the one perfect thing in this imperfect world." She repeated the last two words to herself as Anderson leaned forward and waved her on.

Elen frowned, thinking. "By the time I got there—"

"Where, please?" asked Anderson.

"Sprays Hotel is where he was keeping the kid. Just around the block from here. Maybe that's why Marty..."

Martha dropped a curse into the air.

"By Saturday night his sweet plan had already gone sour. Judy. He had left his lady alone with the boy most of the day and planned to do so all evening too. Like potted plants on a shelf... When he got back after an afternoon of new-age harmonies, Jude was upset and his caretaker at her temper's end. Sergeant, that boy of mine is brain damaged, all right, but he has a way of making his wants known! He could drive you to suicide, could Judy."

The detective didn't ask what Judy's way was. "And was that it? Did his dissatisfaction with the boy drive George St. Ives in that direction?"

Elen opened her eyes wide. "I didn't mean that, exactly. I don't know. All I do know is that at seven-thirty the Mexican girl up and went, leaving George in full possession of infantile fury, with explosive diarrhea. He kept thinking he'd be able to make it on time for the show, and then that he'd show up late, until it was all over, and the neighbors walking out of the hotel because of the smell, and the landlord pounding on the door. . . . Lawks, what a scene!" Elen rubbed her eyes in a spread-finger gesture that was a ghost of her usual, wry manner.

"When I got there, George had tied Judy up—the rope, of course, which he'd snitched as part of his kidnapping tools—and when that hadn't stopped the noise, George had started to hit him. There was the boy, howling and poking the air, blindly, and George, with his face like a brick, tearing his own hair out: Fine 'home life,' I think.

"I felt so sorry for them both at that moment, that I could not tell you which was worse off."

Elen's words faded in and out. She rested her head on her hand. "Poor pig that he was. Not asking for so much, I don't think. A good tour, making his own kind of music. Someone . . . something of his own." Elen pushed the lamp aside and laid her head down where the dead flies had lain.

Martha stirred. "He chose his life, Elen. Every moment of it. Few people get so much freedom."

Anderson scratched his nose, as though to remind them all the law was present. "And he let you take the child away again?" She nodded forcefully. "He was endlessly grateful. In fact, he ran out of the room and left me alone with Judy."

She laughed bitterly. "Now *that* was not pleasant."

"Leaving the rope behind, Ms. Evans? Or did he take it with him?"

Elen made a huge frown and groaned. 'I have been trying to remember that all day. I can't think why he would take the rope, though."

"And the boy. Why didn't you simply take him back home? To his home."

She lifted her head off the table. "I did call them, but no one answered. So I called Sandy. I felt she owed me something, though now I can't think what. She said she'd take him for the rest of the night, which was just a few hours, by this time.

"Judy never reacted badly for Sandy, or at least never before. She'd always liked him. Gone to see him a number of times. Fancied she had a way with him. But the night turned into a real hell for us both, and next morning— whomp! Here we were in the middle of a murder, with me the last one to see the victim alive. And we're up to our eyebrows in terrible secrets. . . ."

"Are we sure, yet, that this is a murder?" asked Anderson, with no expression. Heads turned toward him. No one answered.

"We will want to see the hotel room where all this happened, of course."

"It's over by Front Street," said Elen.

"That's right by the pier?"

She nodded. "I'll take you there."

Anderson nodded, as though it went without speaking that Elen would be leaving with him. He then pursed his lips and made a note in a little notebook that he pulled from his upper jacket pocket.

"In your own words, Ms. Evans: in what sort of mood was Mr. St. Ives when you left him that night? Depressed, I imagine, if all his domestic . . . uh . . . hopes had let him down?"

"Just ashy," agreed Elen. "Also quite drunk."

"Umm." He closed his notebook with a pop. And stood.

"I think, Ms. Evans, that after we peek in at the motel room, it would be a good idea if we went down to the station and had this story done up in regulation fashion."

"Am I under arrest?" she asked, looking at him from under lowered lashes.

Anderson's trick eyebrows shot up. "Do you want to be, Ms. Evans? Once you can explain to me how you lured a man much larger than yourself to the end of the pier and then convinced him to stick his head in a noose that wasn't likely to hold him anyway, then I will be most happy to oblige. Till then . . ."

His eye fell on Pádraig, who was leaning against Martha. "Before I go, Mr. Ó Súilleabháin, would you care to explain how it is that you are not yourself, but your cousin?"

Martha took a step nearer. Long gave an unmistakable hiss. Pádraig waved them both away. "The passport belongs to my cousin, who has the same name as me. I used it so I would not have to apply for a work permit and probably not get it. There, I have no secrets left, either, and you can boot me out of the country before my sailing class starts!"

Anderson put his hand in front of his mouth and stroked his moustache. Martha stepped past him. "No you don't, Pádraig. There are alternatives. You can always marry an American."

Pádraig flinched and looked at the bed. "Don't make sport of me like that, Martha. I only told the truth."

But Martha's face was determined. "But you can marry an American. Lots of women would have you. Me, for example."

Pádraig looked up with round, drugged blue eyes.

"Martha!" bellowed Long, and he grabbed her by the elbow. His face was perfectly black. "How can you! How dare you!"

"What the hell?" cried Elizabeth, no less outraged.

She shook him off. "A perfectly legal, countertop registry service, eh? Not religious of any kind? And then if it doesn't work out. After six months, say . . ."

"That is not a marriage at all, according to the church," said Pádraig."

Anderson watched all this with no expression on his face and his mouth hidden behind his hand. "I'm in over my head, you know," he said to the room in general. "This is a federal matter. Or perhaps diocesan." He raised his voice, to be heard.

"Mr. Sullivan, I suggest you get your passport updated at your soonest convenience. And don't marry until you're very certain. Perhaps not for another twenty years.

"And, Mrs. Macnamara, don't throw yourself away on callow youth. I'm sure he would disappoint you." He rose, smoothing his jacket and trousers ostentatiously.

"Now, Ms. Evans, let us go prepare a lovely, coherent statement on our new word processors. You'll feel better if you do. We can drop off little Jude on our way."

He turned to the boy, to find Long was standing between them. "I advise you most strongly, Sergeant, to let me do that. Or to call the institution and have some person used to him come for him. Neither Judy nor you would be happy if you were to take him off in a car again."

Anderson stared, with a hint of distrust, at the dark man in front of him. "You sound very sure I can't handle him. Or just very sure of yourself."

"Jude and I have been good for one another. It has nothing to do with any quality of mine or lack of yours, but he and I do get along. And he . . . has a way of spreading his dissatisfactions around him. So do we all, of course."

"What goes around . . ." began Teddy.

Elizabeth shot him a venomous glance.

Anderson missed none of this, but his expression remained private. "Then so be it, Mr. Long. Take the boy home. But do it now, please, for they're expecting him.

"And, by the way, I'm very glad to be able to tell you that Mr. Stoughie has decided to drop charges against you."

Mayland Long opened his sunny eyes in surprise, and he grinned his white teeth. "That is good news. Why?"

"I have no idea."

Martha smiled quietly.

Elen Evans rose now from her chair, brushing lint and insect parts from her skirt. She picked her way to the door. She looked at no faces in the crowded room. As she passed, Pádraig came next to her, bent and earnest as Quasimodo. "Lots of girls have babies," he whispered a bit too loudly into her ear. "It doesn't mean anything anymore."

She glanced back at him, astonished, as she closed the door behind her.

*   *   *

Don Scherer thought about changing out of his uniform. He looked at the clock again. He compromised, taking a shower and putting on a clean regulation shirt.

In the five minutes he'd been in the shower, Anderson had come in again. Scherer hurried after and caught him closing the door.

"Can I sit in?" he asked, and was embarrassed by the sound of his own words. The sergeant expanded his forehead upward.

"I thought you'd gone home an hour ago, Don," he said. "There's really no reason you should wait."

Scherer stood silent, unable to think of an excuse that would get him in and unwilling to turn away. At last he asked, "You have her with you?" The sergeant nodded. "We have both Evans and Frager."

"Then you . . . it'll all be over by tomorrow when I get on, won't it?"

Now Anderson's mobile forehead descended. "After this coroner's report . . . Yes, I don't think there'll be much more to do." His nostrils twitched and he sighed.

"Okay, Don. Come in. Be quiet."

Long returned to find Pádraig flat on his stomach, lying on Long's bed. The young man's eyes were open, but they displayed a complete lack of interest. He found Martha in what had been Marty's room, yanking at her battered old suitcases.

"Are you so sure they're going to let us go tonight?" he asked her.

"*We* can go right now, my dear. That's what the officer said on the phone. Now it depends on Pádraig."

For a moment he stood there, and then went over and lay down on the bed with his hands behind his head. Evening's last light came through the blind in slices.

Had it only been twenty-four hours since he sat behind his little keyboard, playing with Macnamara's Band for the first and only time? And had it been only at nine this morning that that storm petrel, Anderson, entered this room to tell them St. Ives was dead?

Often his days had gone by with nothing at all to mark their passage. Days and weeks. Not since he had kept company with Martha, though.

"I feel much better," he said at last, adding, "Who are the 'we' that are permitted to leave, Martha?"

She glanced up. "Who can leave? Everyone but Elen, I guess. Maybe Elen too; he didn't say."

"We will have to find that out." Long rubbed his eyes and cleared his throat experimentally. No cough.

"You bet we will!" Martha slammed a suitcase with energy. "All dirty clothes," she murmured. "They seem to swell, when dirty." She felt Long staring at her, but ignored the feeling, until he said, "Would you have married Pádraig, Martha? Merely to keep him in the country?"

She giggled. "Of course, my dear. This sailing thing means so much to him. More than the tour ever could. And it would be strictly pro forma: even the church would not object. Not too much."

"I would," he said, smiling grimly. "Very much."

Now she looked at him. With his clean shirt and ebony skin, he stood out against the blue-green bedspread in sharp black and white. His expression was languid, except for the startling pale eyes.

Like a box of black iron, with fire inside.

"You look a bit different tonight," said Martha, coming to sit beside him. "Happier, oddly enough. And a little daunting too. Did you finally split your skin?"

He caused her hand to disappear in his. "Maybe. Or maybe I'm just through with apologizing for my every inadequacy. Something that happened between Jude and me."

Martha gave a short, almost coarse laugh. "Praise all ye winds and rains!" Her inspection of his face continued.

"What did you do to Judy, Mayland? Or for him. What worked?"

He opened his mouth and then paused, as though he didn't know what he ought to say. Then he grinned in a blaze of teeth. "I recited him the Prajna Paramita Sutra." He kissed her hand.

Martha looked away, into the mirror on the far wall,

and then back again. "Such a cold sort of scripture. 'No eyes, no ears, no tongue . . .' Surely it fits him, but it's still a heavy lesson for a brain-damaged child."

"Or for an elderly man in a business suit."

Now she put their joined hands up to her face. "It would bother you so much if I married someone, even just a paper marriage?"

"Yes, it would, because my heart is set on marrying you myself. And not merely on paper. Come, Martha. I'm wealthy, and you know every beautiful woman is bound by tradition to marry a wealthy old man. It's in half a dozen of your songs."

She snickered and kissed his fingers.

"And I call heaven to witness that I am faithful by nature, and biddable beyond the norm of mankind. You know I have been biddable! My health is improving hourly and I have a certain skill dealing with waiters. Don't you think I have a great deal to offer?"

Pádraig, shuffling through the connecting door, found them with linked hands. He tried to retreat.

"A *bhúacaill!*" called Long. "Pádraig, come back here," said Martha. "We're not doing anything the priest couldn't see."

The young man returned, leaning on the door and squinting fiercely. "I wasn't sure. I was wanting to tell you, Martha, that I can travel tonight, if that was what you had in mind."

Martha gave Long's hand a series of unconscious squeezes. "You don't want to wait for Elen, after all?" She turned her head and explained, "I'm driving Pádraig to the airport in San Jose, either for the night flight to Boston or the one tomorrow morning. It depends how he feels."

"Ah . . ." Pádraig's powers seemed to fail him. Long sprang up like a whip and had a chair under him. He put a steadying hand against the young man's undamaged shoulder. "I don't think so, Martha," said Pádraig. "She'd be better off if I didn't."

"How's that? I think she's fond of you, Pádraig," Martha said hesitantly.

He made a face painful to see. "Call me Pat, won't you? Pat Sullivan. That's what they'll call me at the marina. This other was my mother's idea. And my sister Órla. It's all been so silly!"

"What has?" It was Long who asked, standing in the shadow beside Pádraig's chair. "The name? The tour? Or do you mean twisting the rope with Elen?"

"We never did any more than that!" Pádraig's voice was too loud. "Twisted an effing rope in the car park!"

Very softly Martha replied, "We didn't think you did and wouldn't care anyway. I just . . . I would like to feel there was something—some aspect of this tour—that didn't leave you feeling bad."

Pádraig straightened as far as he was able and glanced up at Martha. She was surprised to see his blue eyes sparkling with tears. "Martha, I'm sorry. That isn't what I meant. You've been grand to me. All of you except George, who was such a swine that it shouldn't matter."

"Then is it knowing that Elen had an illegitimate baby?" Martha kept expression out of her voice.

"Now I *said* that was nothing, didn't I? Poor creature too." The tears disappeared, to be replaced by the pulled face of worry. "No, it's something else, and I don't know . . ." Once more he let his head hang forward. "If I tell you, will you keep it to yourselves? I'd like to tell someone."

"I will," said Long readily. Martha looked unhappy, but at last she nodded.

"Well, then." With an effort, Pádraig sat himself up. "I saw Elen out on the pier last night. Late. After the bars closed. I'm sure it was her. She had a car with her, and that friend with the perm."

Martha and Long exchanged a glance over Pádraig's head.

"I had left my guernsey, you see, because it was so warm in the bar, and after I went out on foot I started to feel the cold. I thought maybe the barman would have left it on the door. That's what they do in Ballyferriter. So I went back."

Long said, "But you didn't talk to her?"

The young man shook his head and winced from the wound on his neck. "Didn't. No. I don't like to talk to a girl if I've been drinking. Never does any good for them to know."

"So you didn't see what they were doing?"

He gave a grunt and another half shake. "No, but I do know that the tale she twisted for the police was a lie. And how am I to meet her again and pretend I don't know?" He looked into Martha's face and then Long's, as though they could tell him.

Martha sighed. Her hands drummed on her knees. "But we already know that, Pádraig. That Elen was lying."

"It is very uncomfortable for all of us," added Long.

There was a shove against the door behind Pádraig, and Elen Evans came in. The people who had been talking about her all looked up.

Her eyes were red and her face a terrible color. Her hair stood at odd angles from her head. She was half-asleep, and glanced dully at them all.

"I didn't hear you come in," said Martha.

Elen yawned. "That's because for once I'm not dragging along my piano wrench." As though to prove it, she flung her macrame bag onto the bed beside Martha. "No 'bang, thump bang.'" She shoved between Pádraig and the wall, and sat down on the far corner of the bed. Then she glanced around the room. "Where is everybody?"

"Elizabeth has taken Marty home," answered Martha. "Teddy's next door, napping."

It seemed to take Elen a long time to make sense out of these words. At last she bounced her weary head upward in affirmation. "Ah, well. I had hoped to tell everyone the good news at once.

"I'm not arrested for murder." She didn't seem to notice the strained silence.

"No one's arrested for murder."

Martha straightened her skirt over her thighs. "They decided he killed himself, then?"

"Something like..." Elen let herself fall back on the

bed. Her head rested only inches away from Martha's knees. "Oh, sweet Sacred Harp, I don't think I'll ever sleep again." In complete contradiction to these words, she closed her eyes and seemed to doze off.

"Elen!" It was Pádraig, who got out of his chair and stumbled over to her. "Elen, wake up." He looked left and right: "I think we should tell her. We have to tell her."

Elen's dark eyes came open, warily. "What are you going to tell me, Pat? Is it awful? Should I run away again?"

"It's bad enough, I think."

Long stepped over to Pádraig's side. Martha remained where she was, by Elen.

"I saw you last night, on the pier," said Pádraig.

The dark eyes blinked once. "Did you? Just *what* did you see? On the pier? Are you saying that you saw me murder George?"

Pádraig balled his hands in his lap. "I'm saying I saw you there. With Sandy. And to the *gardaí* you said nothing about that."

Elen looked as much confused as anything. "What time was that?"

He shrugged and gave an involuntary yip of pain. "Late. After the bars closed. I didn't have a watch on me."

"But you didn't say this to the police?" Her eyes sought his out.

"Of course I didn't. I like you, Elen. I . . . didn't like George a bit."

Elen laughed, short and harshly, and she glanced over at Long. "What do you think of this, Mayland? Do you think I'm the hidden murderer after all?"

Long didn't bend to her. "I also know that you lied."

Elen made a face and looked away.

"You see, Elen, I listen to language," the dark man explained. "The language of individuals as well as of nations. You said to the detective that St. Ives called you 'chickie' when he called you yesterday evening."

"So he did," replied Elen, roused out of her exhaustion. "Called me that many times. And 'baby' and worse."

Long nodded. "I'm sure. But not last night. Not in the course of this tour. Not sober and not drunk and not under the influence of narcotics. George had given up calling women such things."

Now Elen was clearly angry. "If you think that hog had changed in any real way since—"

Long cut her off. "I don't know how real you would call it, but it was a change in vocabulary at least. For we do change, Elen. Those who cannot in large ways, at least change in small."

Martha scratched through her unruly hair. "I agree with him. But I think it was more because it made no sense for an old lech to go about offending three out of four 'girls' that he met. I certainly didn't hear him calling anyone by politically incorrect terms—not even the teeny's he sopped up."

"He did it to me to offend," Elen mumbled.

"But he didn't want to offend you. At that moment," said Martha. "He wanted your cooperation with the baby.

"But my reason for doubting your story is different," she continued. "It's the knots. The lark's head, in particular."

"Sailor's knot," Pádraig interjected. "But I didn't do it."

"Yes, that's what you said to the sergeant. But it's not *just* a sailor's knot. Even I knew how to make it, though I never knew it had a name. It's a thing you find in hammocks, and hangings and..." Martha poked a pink finger at Elen's bag.

"Who made that, Elen? Didn't you yourself?"

Elen pulled the bag away. "You know I did."

"And aren't those lark's heads attaching the strings to the wooden dowels?"

Elen stared. "For the life of me, I don't know the names of all those things. I did it from a book."

That phrase rang through Mr. Long's head. "For the life of me."

"Is it only that that convicts me in your eyes, Martha? That I can tie a knot?"

Martha took a difficult breath. "And that George couldn't."

"What?" said Long and Pádraig together.

She shook her grizzled head. "Nope. If George St. Ives had wanted to hang himself, he would have had to have done it with two grannys. And likely they would have slipped open."

Pádraig's features clouded. "But he was out of Cape Breton, where the tradition . . ."

"Where the tradition is all fishing boats. I know. But I knew his aunt, remember." Martha glanced from one to another. "Actually, George was brought up in Ottawa. In a flat with his aunt and grandmother. And like most pipers, he was so obsessed with his music he never did much of anything else. Never learned things for fun: not about people, nor how things worked, nor any sports or games. . . . I knew his aunt, and as far as his being a sailor: I happen to know he couldn't take the motion of a ferryboat, let alone a dinghy. Not from childhood.

"It was all just too bad for him." Martha's face was bleak.

There were thirty seconds of quiet, while everyone gazed at nothing, except for Elen Evans, who glanced from one face to the next. She looked longest at Pádraig.

"And none of you . . . Not one of you who knew these damning things said a word of it to the police when you were asked?" She started to giggle, but Pádraig's hurt glance cut her off. Martha looked out the black window. "I told Sergeant Anderson I would find out what happened to George. My word means a lot to me. But Elen, my dear Elen . . ."

Elen Evans glanced wearily at her. "All right, duckies." She sighed. "I had thought I might spare you all, but as it is, I'll tell the truth."

Long, who had been standing all this time, sank down onto his heels on the carpet. Pádraig braced himself against the chair. Martha's jaw tightened, but she remained fixed on the window.

"George called all right, after the concert and just

before I was about to go out looking. And he gave me that bit about responsibility and how the Mexican nanny had let him down. I don't remember his exact words; maybe they weren't quite so ugly. But his tone was. Not placating at all. And he said he needed help with Jude. Right away. And it was entirely my responsibility. George seemed to think it was more natural for a woman to wash up shit.

"I, for my part"—and Elen wiped her hair from her face with her long-nailed hand—"told him to go fuck himself. I hung up on him. I thought the whole thing would serve him perfectly. Remember, I knew Jude!

"But then I started thinking about the kid, and though it served George right, it wasn't fair. I considered calling the Adventist Home, but . . . but there was still Los Angeles tomorrow, you see?"

Martha let out a little moan.

"I know. I know. But at the time it seemed important. So I went out to get Jude and take him back myself.

"I found the room with no problem; only had to follow the smell. But by the time I got there it was empty, except for the mess."

She reached into the pocket of her army fatigues and drew out a tissue with which she wiped her nose.

"I started wondering what an old drunk would do, in the middle of the night, with a sick retarded boy that screamed inside people's minds and had chronic runs. Hell, I thought; he was only a few doors from the beach. He'd dunk the kid in the ocean, of course.

"I ran out and found George crossing empty Front Street with that poor sick spastic child tied up like a caterpillar in Pádraig's rope. My guess was faultless: he was going to clean Jude off in the surf. What is it in June: maybe sixty degrees?

"I was doing femme yesterday—remember? I wobbled after them in my four-inch spike heels, tripping and twisting left and right, and he heard me and started running. He didn't head for the beach at all, but for the pier. Maybe he thought I had the police with me and panicked, or maybe he had already decided . . . Oh, I don't know.

"Believe it or not, I chased him the length of the pier, past all the closed shops and stinking fish vendors and dark bars, and there wasn't a single soul out there but us and the moon.

"And Jude was *howling*.

"I didn't know at this point what he had in mind, but when we got to the end of the pier he lifted Judy onto the rail, and I knew he was going to throw him in the water. Drown him.

" 'It's better,' he kept yelling, as I pulled against him. " 'It's better and cleaner, this way.' And: 'A lifetime of cowardice,' Again and again: 'A lifetime of cowardice.' " Elen took a deep breath and held her head between her hands. Suddenly she looked straight at Martha.

"You know, without Teddy's magic pill, I don't think this would have happened. George was a crank, and a sick crank, but he wasn't a nut! Ted's another guy who has a right to feel lucky he's not in jail."

Martha waved this aside. "How did you get Jude away from him?"

Elen's head drooped again. "I hit him. George. I hit him one good one on the back of his head with my piano wrench." She snorted. "Not femme at all, that. And then he fell against the rail, and the kid too. Jude nearly went over in spite of it all. Into the drink. And the poor boy was practically in convulsions of terror." She shuddered.

"It was then that George lay there, looking so like Jude, and both of them so full of hopelessness. . . . I started getting sick myself about then. Miserable sick, and with my heart pounding—that was Jude, doing that. I might have just shoved them both over and followed them into the cold water. Then you'd all *really* have had a puzzle on your hands in the morning."

She looked earnestly at Martha. "I got really, really frightened. Just like Jude. Can you understand how that was?"

"I can," said Long.

"I sat out there on the bare wood in the cold and I didn't want to die. And I also didn't want George, with all his craziness, to wake up and come at me again. I was terribly afraid of George, as he lay there. As afraid as Judy was. Of course. And he would know that I hit him!

"I thought things would be so much better if he just didn't open his eyes again. . . ." Elen opened hers and found Long very close to her.

"Why didn't you just push him off?" he asked, with simple curiosity. "That would have been much easier."

Elen nodded bleakly. "I almost did. But I was crazy scared. What if the cold water woke him? What if he swam after me? I imagined him waiting at the foot of the pier as I came off, like some material ghost, dripping seaweed, and enveloping me in that heavy ragg sweater of his, smelling of salt and human shit. . . . I couldn't bear the thought. So I took the rope and made a knot at one end and a noose at the other and slowly lowered him down it. I wrapped my skirt around my hands, to spare them."

"Slowly?" Long knit his brows. "But his neck was broken. There must have been an abrupt drop."

With certainty Elen shook her head. "No. I should have tossed him over, all at once, I know, but I couldn't bear the thought. Besides, I wasn't sure about the rope." She glanced imploringly around and said again, "I was crazy scared. I kept seeing him rising out of the tide, coming back for me.

"So. I did it.

"There's a phone at the end of the pier. I called Sandy. Poor Sandy, again. She drove out and picked us up. Didn't see you at all, Pádraig, and that was just as well that we had Jude in the car with the windows closed by then, or we'd have had a drunken, accordion-playing sailor on our hands too.

"I couldn't think, and Sandy got hysterical as soon as she touched Jude. A mess. We piled him into the car and drove out to her house." Elen ground her jaw.

"It has been a thoroughly unfortunate few days for all concerned!"

Pádraig made a funny, old-maidish sound with his tongue. "You poor creature," he said to Elen. His face looked almost grown up.

Long stared at the steeple of his own fingers with narrowed eyes. "And the detective caught none of this? None?"

Martha let her back slump into a half circle and her hands were balled in her lap.

"Hah!" Everyone glanced up at Elen's brittle cry. "Anderson caught *all* of it!"

Long's eyes flashed. Pádraig frowned. Martha straightened, looking very stupid.

"He caught all but the bit about being called 'chickie. He found out about George's not being a sailor all right He glommed onto my bag. Easiest of all, he had already grabbed Sandy, who had had more than she could stand People heard the shot, you know.

"Poor Sandy." Elen's lips tightened compassionately and then she glanced again at Pádraig. "Sandy wants to come and throw herself before you in gratitude and peni tence. If it wouldn't bother you too much. She's awfully sorry she shot you with rock salt."

Pádraig squirmed sheepishly. "Aw, there's nothing to that!"

Martha burst out: "I don't understand! How is it tha Anderson knows and yet he let you out?"

Elen's tight smile grew tighter. "Because it wasn' murder after all. But it also wasn't suicide."

Long growled. "This becomes a Chinese puzzle."

"It was manslaughter. I killed him in the course of struggle, trying to keep him from committing murder."

"But he was unconscious already when you kille him," said Long stubbornly.

"Not at all. What I did was to hang the body of a dea man over the Santa Cruz pier."

Martha stood up suddenly, rocking the bed. He mouth was a large O and her eyes were smaller ones "With the piano wrench. When you hit him with the pian wrench. That's how his neck came to be broken."

"Got it in one." Elen tried to smile, but it ended in a shudder. She gazed up at Martha with a spark of her old animation.

Long was still struggling with the information. "But . . . but you *meant* to kill him, when you lowered him on the rope. You thought he was alive."

"Yes." The animation faded. "But meaning to is not the same thing as murder. Anderson said they will balance that against the fact that I hit him to prevent *his* committing murder against a child.

"I may very well be charged with manslaughter. Or something else. But . . ." She stood up.

"Not murder. So—la!" She started back toward the door. "I must tell Teddy how lucky he is, because I think Anderson knew that his friend Wolfie came up here with drugs for him."

"But Teddy says he doesn't *use* drugs," protested Martha. "And I believe him."

Elen nodded. "But George used drugs. I think—and I think Anderson thinks—that George was somehow forcing Teddy to supply him. But Anderson is not a narc, thank God. And Teddy is a very lucky boy."

She turned again at the door. "Kiss, kiss," she whispered, and went out.

Pádraig turned ponderously. "*Ná* . . . Elen . . . Don't bolt off like that. . . ." And he knocked his chair rattling into the wall heater as he blundered by.

"Yes, you do," said Martha to Long.

They were alone now, in the dark and unhomey room, and he fixed his yellow eyes on her in puzzlement. "I do what?"

"Don't you remember what you were saying? Just before Pádraig came in. You were listing your points for me, my dear. Some of them are quite valuable.

"Your wealth can be useful, I grant you. It can also get in the way. . . . If I were a younger woman, I think it would mean more to me.

"Your faithfulness is quite an asset, of course, and by

that I don't mean the fact that you don't go nosing under all the ladies' skirts, like a dog. I mean your intellectual integrity. And consistency." She ticked off these matters on her fingers.

"As for your vaunted biddability . . . well, I think that always had its limits, for you can be as unbending as a wall, Mayland. Almost as stubborn as I am. And I further think that I'm going to see less and less of your yielding nature, after today." Her eyes were sky blue under the fading light as she measured him. "You don't seem to need your 'spiritual teacher' anymore."

He sat in front of her in his accustomed chair. "I'm sorry. I mean, I'm sorry I was such a bother to you for so long. I can see now how difficult it must have made things, having me dump everything in your lap. I wonder you didn't just swat me away."

Now her glance was startled. "I'm not such a fool as that. Besides, you'd be a hard fly to swat! Ah, wait till you have rapturous acolytes treading *your* heels. As you will, my darling. I predict you will." She gave an incisive nod and crossed her legs neatly at the ankle.

"But I think the reason I will marry you is partly because of the waiters (how I hate to cook) and partly because of your amazing virility. . . ." Mayland Long rose with a gasp, coughed, and knocked the table lamp over once again, reaching for Martha. This time it broke.

In the subsequent darkness Martha struggled to finish her sentence. "But . . . umph. Mostly I think I will marry you because of the wonderful way you wear your clothes."

THE UNFORGETTABLE FANTASY NOVELS OF
R. A. MacAvoy

Special Offer
Buy a Bantam Book
for only 50¢.

Now you can have an up-to-date listing of Bantam's hundreds of titles plus take advantage of our unique and exciting bonus book offer. A special offer which gives you the opportunity to purchase a Bantam book for only 50¢. Here's how!

By ordering any five books at the regular price per order, you can also choose any other single book listed (up to a $4.95 value) for just 50¢. Some restrictions do apply, but for further details why not send for Bantam's listing of titles today!

Just send us your name and address and we will send you a catalog!